# A CALL AWAY

# What Reviewers Say About
# KC Richardson's Work

**New Beginnings**

"Pure and simple, this is a sweet slow-burn romance. It's cozy and warm. At its heart, *New Beginnings* by KC Richardson is a story about soul mates that fall in love. …If you're looking for a sweet romance, the kind of romance that you can curl-up with as a fire crackles in your fireplace, then this could be your book. It's a simple love story that leaves you feeling good."—*The Lesbian Review*

**Courageous Love**

"Richardson aptly captures the myriad emotions and sometimes irrational thought processes of a young woman with a possibly fatal disease, as well as the torment inherent in the idea of losing another loved one to the same illness. This sensitively told and realistically plotted story will grab readers by the heartstrings and not let them go."—*Publishers Weekly*

"Take one happy and well centered ER nurse add one handsome Cop and the scene is set for a happy ever after. But throw in a life threatening disease and KC Richardson ramps up the angst. …This is a great storyline and felt very well done. While there is a heavy dose of angst, it's justified and well handled."—*Lesbian Reading Room*

# By the Author

New Beginnings

Courageous Love

A Call Away

# A CALL AWAY

*by*

## KC Richardson

2018

**A CALL AWAY**
© 2018 By KC Richardson. All Rights Reserved.

ISBN 13: 978-1-63555-025-2

This Trade Paperback Original Is Published By
Bold Strokes Books, Inc.
P.O. Box 249
Valley Falls, NY 12185

First Edition: April 2018

**CREDITS**
Editor: Cindy Cresap
Production Design: Susan Ramundo
Cover Design By Jeanine Henning

# Acknowledgments

First, and always, I'd like to thank Radclyffe, Sandy Lowe, and everyone at Bold Strokes Books involved in helping produce outstanding books. Special thanks to my editor, Cindy Cresap, who always teaches me something new. I love being a part of the BSB family.

Thank you to my beta readers, Penelope, Dawn, and Inger for helping me write a decent first draft. And thank you to Tina for cleaning up my rewrites.

I want to thank my family and friends for your unwavering support in my writing journey. A special thank you to my niece, Sophie, for teaching me about horses, and just for being a super human being. If more people were like you, this world would be a much better place. Now close the book, Sophie. You're too young to read this story.

Last, but certainly not least, thank you to the readers for your messages on Facebook, Twitter, and email. Your kind words inspire me to keep writing.

## Dedication

To my parents for accepting me, supporting me,
and loving me. You two are the best, and I love you.
Now close the book. This is as far as you're allowed to get.

## CHAPTER ONE

Sydney Carter took in the smells, sights, and sounds of Chicago as she walked down the cracked sidewalk. It was early enough in the morning that the air wasn't filled with bus and car exhaust, and only one or two cars were honking their horns. Spring had just begun so there was a chill in the morning, and the afternoon wouldn't have the oppressive heat they'd get in just a few short months. As she did every morning, Syd made her way to the Englewood Youth Center and couldn't help but smile as she thought about today's activities. She and a volunteer, Lana, were taking six of the kids to the natural history museum for a tour and lunch. Frequenting the different museums in the city was a favorite activity for Syd, and she looked forward to sharing the experience with her kids.

Two years earlier, Syd had made a life-changing decision to quit her job as an investment banker for one of the largest firms in town and took a position working at Englewood Youth Center, an inner city recreation center for underprivileged children. The salary she earned working for the center was a small fraction of what she earned in her previous career, so she chose to do things and go places that were little to no cost. But that didn't matter because working with the kids and exposing them to activities they might not have otherwise was what was important to her.

As she opened the glass door that was protected by black iron bars, her phone rang. She looked at the screen and guessed it was probably a telemarketer since she didn't know anyone from Iowa.

She considered answering it, but she decided that if it was important, they would leave a voice mail. She had better things to do with her time than listen to someone try to sell her something she didn't even need.

She stepped into the bland room that was in serious need of updating. The once-white paint was chipping off the walls, and the beige carpet was now mostly brown from various stains. There was a bit of a smell—something along the lines of stale sweat and mold, but once she'd been in the building for five minutes, she could no longer smell it. She heard the footfalls before the child making them was even visible.

"Ms. Syd! I'm ready to go to the museum." Alisa stopped just short of running into Syd, and she sported a huge smile on her face. Alisa was always ecstatic when the center had field trips. Her mother worked long hours to keep a roof over their heads, so she didn't have a lot of time to spend with Alisa. That's where Syd and the other workers at the center came in. It was mostly an after-school program where tutoring and socializing occurred. It was also a safe place for the kids to gather so they wouldn't have to spend their afternoons and evenings in an empty apartment or hanging out on the streets. On the weekends, it was all fun and games.

"I see that, Alisa. Are you ready to see the dinosaurs?"

"Yes. I've been ready all week."

"Good. Let's round up the others and we'll get going." The chime coming from Syd's pocket notified her she had a voice mail. "Let me check this message and I'll be right there." She smiled as she watched Alisa run to get the others ready. Syd pushed the voice mail icon and held the phone to her ear.

"Hello, Ms. Carter. I'm an attorney in Charville, Iowa, and I need to speak to you about your grandmother. Please call me back as soon as you can."

Syd looked at the phone like it had sprouted legs. Why would an attorney in Iowa be contacting her about her grandmother? She was just about to call him back when Alisa returned with the other kids, saying they were ready to go. She'd have to call the attorney back later. Alisa grabbed Syd's hand and walked with her to the van.

Alisa was mature for her ten years, and she seemed to pride herself on being Syd's helper. Syd had a soft spot in her heart for Alisa since the first day she came to the center. Maybe it was because she reminded Syd of herself when she was that age. Alisa was respectful and friendly with the other children and staff. She was also a hard worker, whether it was studying for class or helping out around the center. The difference was that Syd had two parents who worked in education, and they were always home at night to help her with her homework or go to her sporting events.

Syd and Lana loaded the children into the van and drove through the streets of Chicago. Syd listened to the chatter coming from the back seats. If the high and loud pitches of the kids were any indication, they were excited to see the dinosaurs, mummies, and the 3D movie. They pulled into the parking lot and Syd turned off the engine before turning in her seat.

"Okay, young ladies and gentlemen, listen up. The people from the museum were nice enough to let us come here for free today. A very nice lady is going to take us on a tour of the different exhibits, then we'll have lunch, then we'll walk around for a little while before we leave. Most important rule is we stay together. I don't want to have to deal with any of your mamas if we lose you and don't bring you home." That last comment, along with a mock glare, made her captive audience laugh.

"Keep your hands to yourselves. This means don't touch *anything*, including each other. If you have a question, raise your hand and wait to be called on. If you have to go to the bathroom, let me or Ms. Lana know. Does anyone have any questions?"

A chorus of "no" signaled they were ready for their adventure. They made their way up the three steps and through the grand front doors. Their tour guide met them at the information desk and started their tour. The first exhibit the guide showed them made the children, and Syd and Lana for that matter, gasp in amazement.

"This is Sue." The kids laughed at the name, but they quickly regained their composure and listened raptly to the guide. "This fossil is the largest and best-preserved T. Rex ever found. Can you guess how big she is?"

Everybody took a guess, and while they were all pretty close, the guide had to give them the correct answer. Every exhibit they visited, the guide gave them information that made it interesting for the adolescents and adults. By the end of the visit, they had learned about DNA, how Earth had evolved, and they saw inside ancient Egypt. On the way back to the center, the kids excitedly talked about what they liked best, and they were still talking when they arrived. There was still enough daylight for the children to walk home with the older ones looking out for them. Syd hugged them all good-bye and retreated to the office to fill out some paperwork.

Syd recalled the events of the day, the look of wonderment that was evident on all their little faces, especially when they saw the life-sized replica of a dinosaur on display. Her heart felt full as she absent-mindedly played with the collar on her shirt, a habit that had formed when she was no older than most of the children she worked with. The old habit had a way of soothing her, and she often did that when she felt overwhelmed. However, today, the overwhelming feeling was in a good way.

Syd's career in investment banking never fed her heart the way working at the center did. It was by happenstance that her former firm had sponsored the Englewood Youth Center in an all-city sports competition. That was Syd's first exposure to the center, and how she met her current boss, Christina. Christina had told Syd that she had been skeptical at first to hiring her, knowing that she'd had no experience working with children and that she would be taking a severe pay cut. However, Syd was able to convince her that she felt this was her calling, and that she'd be willing to do anything to help the center, and the kids, grow and thrive. Two years and counting, and she still didn't have a single regret.

She checked to make sure there weren't any lingerers left behind before she locked the doors as she made her way out of the building. She pulled the sunglasses over her eyes and walked to the train with a spring in her step, having all but forgotten about that mysterious voice mail she'd gotten earlier in the day.

Syd greeted the doorman as she walked to the elevator. The squeaking of her rubber soled tennis shoes on the marble floor was the only sound in the lobby in the early evening hours. She shut her eyes as the elevator ascended to her thirtieth-floor condo, her home that she had purchased when she was still making a six-figure salary.

She placed her backpack on the dining table before pouring two fingers of her favorite Scotch in a crystal glass. It was one of the few luxuries she continued to indulge in that carried over from her days as an investment banker. She didn't bother turning on the lights; the muted light from the city view was more than enough for her to navigate her way to the balcony. She looked out on the Chicago skyline as she sipped her drink and felt the burn in the back of her throat before it warmed its way to her stomach. In the daylight, she had views of Lake Michigan and Millennium Park, but it was this view at night she savored the most. She often ended her workday sitting outside listening to the muffled sounds of honking horns and the distant rumble of the train. She loved working with the kids, but it was a constant stream of noise at work, and she relished the quiet time her balcony afforded her.

Syd went back inside and poured another finger of Scotch then headed to her en suite bathroom. She filled her Jacuzzi tub, poured in some lavender essential oil, and turned on the jets. She stripped down and slid into the warm water. She let the hard stream of water pound on her tight muscles as she finished her nightcap. She inhaled the lavender fragrance and slowly finished her nightcap. It wasn't long until her body and mind felt more relaxed. She emptied the tub, dried herself off, and slipped between her Egyptian cotton sheets, hoping she would be able to grab a few restful hours of sleep.

It felt like she had just closed her eyes when her cell phone rang and the Iowa number came up on her screen. She was sorely tempted to let it go to voice mail again and try to fall back to sleep for another hour, but she figured if someone was calling her at eight a.m., it might be important. Her one day of the week when she didn't have to get up early to go to work, and her sleep was interrupted by the phone. She cleared her throat to dislodge her fatigue.

"Hello."

"Hello. May I speak with Sydney Carter, please?"

"Speaking."

"Ms. Carter, my name is William Kramer and I'm an attorney in Charville, Iowa."

Syd sat up in bed, wondering why he was calling her. She remembered the strange voice mail from the day before and cleared her throat once more. "How can I help you, Mr. Kramer?"

"I'm sorry to break this to you over the phone, but your grandmother passed away recently, and she left her property in Iowa to you."

"Mr. Kramer, I think you have the wrong number. My Grandmom Carter passed away ten years ago."

"I'm sorry, Ms. Carter. I should have clarified. Your grandmother, Virginia Adams, your maternal grandmother is who I'm speaking of."

Syd felt light-headed and her vision dimmed as she recalled the woman she hadn't seen or talked about in over thirty years.

*Four-year-old Sydney sat in the backseat of her parents' car. The booster seat she was strapped into allowed her to look at the flat land outside the windows. There were cows and horses like she had seen in her picture books. "Mama, what are those tall things sticking out of the ground?"*

*"Those are corn stalks, baby girl. That's where corn on the cob comes from."*

*Sydney kicked her legs excitedly and exclaimed, "I love corn on the cob, Mama!"*

*"I know you do, baby."*

*"Mama, where are we going again?"*

*"We're going to see my parents, baby girl, your grandparents."*

*"Like Grandad and Grandmom Carter?"*

*"Yes. Grandad and Grandmom Carter are Daddy's parents. We're going to see Grandad and Grandmom Adams, my parents."*

*"Yay!" This was the first time Syd and her parents went on such a long trip in a car. Usually, they just went to the zoo or a park. Grandad and Grandmom Carter lived so close, they usually just walked to their house. "Mama, are we there yet? What is there to do? Are there any other kids to play with? When can I give Grandad and Grandmom a hug?"*

*"We'll be there soon, baby. Just try and settle down, okay?"*

Sydney's attention was diverted back out the window by all the different colored cows in the fields. She made herself and her parents laugh when she mooed at the cows, offering them a greeting. When the car slowed and turned into a long driveway, she got more excited the closer the house ahead of her got. She couldn't wait to meet her grandparents and play in the big yard. She spotted a tree that she definitely wanted to climb, but frowned when she realized she wasn't wearing tree-climbing clothes. Her mama dressed her in her best dress, tights, and her shiny black shoes.

The car came to a stop and her parents got out, then unstrapped Sydney from her booster seat. She grabbed her mama's hand and walked to the front door. She couldn't remember ever being so happy. Her cheeks hurt from smiling so much, but she didn't care. She was just thrilled to be in a new place. An older man opened the door and he looked mad. Rather than going to hug him, Sydney hid behind her mama and gripped the fabric of her skirt.

*"Hi, Daddy."*

*"What the hell are you doing here? I thought I told you not to come back if you married this—"*

*"Daddy, I wanted you and Mom to meet your granddaughter. This is Sydney."*

Syd felt her mama try to get her to come out from behind her, and she almost did when she saw the nice-looking older lady standing behind the mean old man, but he raised his voice and she stayed put behind her mama where she felt safe.

*"You can get back in your car and get off my property. You made your choice and now you have to live with it."*

*"Can't we talk about it? Mom?"*

Syd saw that her mama was crying and she started to cry too, but she didn't know why. All she knew was her mama was upset and Syd was afraid.

*"Leave now or I'll throw you off my property myself."*

Her daddy finally spoke as they turned to leave. *"It didn't have to be this way, Mr. and Mrs. Adams. We just wanted you to meet your granddaughter."*

*The next thing Sydney knew, she was being strapped back into her booster seat. She looked at the front door where she saw the old lady crying and hugging herself. Sydney didn't understand why they had to leave or why that old man was so mean. After her mama stopped crying, she asked, "Mama, why didn't they want us there? Don't they love us?"*

*Syd's mama turned around in her seat and reached back to hold her hand.*

*"Baby girl, I promise it had nothing to do with you. You're the best daughter and granddaughter anyone could hope for. My daddy just doesn't like people who have different colored skin than he does. It's how he was raised by his parents and he never learned any better. He believes white people should be with white people and black people should be with black people."*

*"But you're white and Daddy is black. Does that mean you shouldn't be together?"*

*"No, baby. Not everybody believes that. Your daddy and I love each other so much that the color of our skin doesn't even matter to us."*

*"Well, it doesn't matter to me either, Mama."*

Syd shook her head to clear the memories and focused again on her call.

"Mr. Kramer, may I get your number and call you later?"

"Certainly."

Syd jotted down the attorney's number and promised to call. She had to clear her mind and gather her thoughts before she called her parents. She had no idea what was going on, yet she had every intention of finding out. As she headed to the kitchen to make her coffee, she wondered if her mama knew that her mother had died.

## CHAPTER TWO

Syd called her parents as her stomach flipped over. Her parents worked in education—her mother as a teacher and her father as a principal. She knew they would be home since it was Sunday. Her mother answered the phone the same way every time Syd called.

"Hey, favorite daughter of mine."

"Mama, I'm your only daughter. In fact, I'm your only child."

"That you are," Jillian Carter replied. "How are you doing, honey? How's work going?"

"Work is good, but I have something else I want to talk to you about."

"Sounds serious. What is it?"

"Have you received a call from an attorney named William Kramer?"

"No, who is he?"

"Apparently, he's the attorney for your mother. I'm sorry to tell you this, Mama, but she passed away recently. He informed me that she left me her property in Iowa."

"Oh."

There was silence on the line, and Syd wished she had been able to tell her mama the sad news face-to-face. This wasn't something that should have been discussed over the phone. If she had been thinking clearly, she would have showered and gone to her parents' house to tell her in person. She wanted nothing more than to hug her and comfort her. Her parents were the most important people in her life, and she never wanted to do or say anything that would upset them. "I'm so sorry, Mama. I know you never talk about her and that you were estranged from your parents, but then again, I think I remember going to see them when I was a child. Did that actually happen?"

"Yes, and my father didn't allow us to stay. That was the last time I saw them."

"What happened between you and your parents? I vaguely remember you explaining to me when I was a child that your father didn't like people with different colored skin. Is that correct? When I tried to ask you about it when I was older, you said you didn't want to talk about it and that it didn't matter anymore."

"Yes. I grew up in a small town in Iowa, and when I went away to college, I met your father. I didn't know my parents were racists when I brought him home to meet them. Granted, there weren't any black people living in our town, but I never heard my parents say anything bad about anyone. The moment they opened the door and saw Isaiah standing there, they said some pretty awful things and told him to get off their property and never come back."

Syd gasped when her mother talked about her own parents' racism. What would they have thought of their biracial granddaughter? She began to cry when she heard her mother sniffle. She tried to remember what her grandparents looked like so she could picture them as she silently cursed their names for hurting her mama.

"I told them I loved Isaiah and that we were engaged to be married. My father told me that if I left with him, to not bother coming back. They would prefer to see me miserable than to be happily married to a black man. I left my family and home behind that day to be with your father."

Syd's head pounded to the beat of her heart. What an impossible decision her mother had to make. She wondered if it was rational to feel so much anger toward people she'd met only once. "Mama, do you ever regret leaving with Daddy?"

"No." There was no hesitation in her answer. "I've been happily married to your father for almost forty years, and we have the best daughter we could have ever hoped for. My only regret is that my parents were bigots. They missed out on having you as their granddaughter because they couldn't see past the color of Isaiah's skin."

Syd nodded even though her mother couldn't see her. She wiped away the remnants of her tears, and she was suddenly so tired she considered going back to bed and pulling the covers over her head. "Oh, Mama. I'm sorry you had to go through that."

"I am too, sweetheart. I was so disappointed in them, for behaving so coldly to your daddy and not loving me enough to overlook the color of your father's skin. If they had just given him a chance, gotten to know him, they wouldn't have been able to hate him. Your daddy is the best man I have ever known, and I'm proud to be his wife and your mama."

"I don't know what to do, Mama. After what you told me, I really don't want to have anything to do with her or her property. How did she know about me anyway? Or where I lived?"

"I'm not sure, baby, but I'm sure her attorney can tell you."

Syd didn't know what else to say, and when she looked at the clock, she noticed it was getting late. "I better call him back. I'm not sure how long he'll be in his office on a Sunday. I'll call you after I talk to him. I love you, and Daddy."

"We love you too, baby girl."

Syd's mind reeled as she replayed in her mind what her mama had told her. Syd felt sorry for her for having to decide between her family and the man she loved. She didn't know if she could make a choice like that. She also knew that her parents loved her and would never give her an ultimatum to choose love or her parents. Of course, she'd never met anyone she'd been crazy about enough to bring them home to meet her parents. She'd always been focused, whether it'd been in school or work. While in college, she concentrated solely on her academics when she got her bachelor's degree then her MBA. Syd fooled around a little while she was in school, but she didn't allow herself to get caught up in anyone.

When she was hired by her company straight out of college, she was fixated on her work and climbing the corporate ladder.

She'd always worked around eighty hours a week, which didn't leave her much time for a relationship. Now, she put all her time and attention into the children who needed her, so having a relationship was low on her list of priorities. She respected the few women she would occasionally sleep with, but falling for any of them? No. At this point in her life, she didn't know if she would even recognize the feeling of falling in love.

Syd called back the attorney and asked the question that had been nagging her since she talked to her mama. "Could you please tell me how you found me? According to my mother, she was estranged from her family. And I assume my grandfather is no longer living since she left me her property."

"Yes, he passed away many years ago. Mrs. Adams had hired a private investigator who gave her your information. That's all she told me when she wrote her will."

Her grandmother hired a private investigator? Why would she go through the trouble to find out about her yet not contact her? And if Virginia Adams was a racist like her mama indicated, why would she leave her property, or anything for that matter, to Syd? As angry as Syd was with her grandmother, she wished she was still alive to answer her questions. "So, what do I have to do?"

"I just need you to sign some papers, and you'll receive the keys. What you do with the property afterward is up to you. I can overnight the papers to you if you'd like."

"Mr. Kramer, I'm sorry, but would you mind if I called you back a little later? As you can imagine, this information has come as a complete shock to me and I need to collect my thoughts." Syd's mind felt like it was in a spin cycle and wasn't slowing down enough for her to think clearly.

"Of course. I look forward to hearing from you."

Syd made a small pot of coffee and poured herself a cup. She sat out on the balcony, sipping her morning drug, and gazing out to the deep blue water of Lake Michigan. She had a lot to think about before she called back Mr. Kramer. Did she want to accept her maternal grandmother's property? If so, would she sell it or keep it? What would she do with property in Iowa of all places? She could take the money from the sale and put it down on her own youth center, one that would be geared more toward LGBTQ teens but all-inclusive. She had to see what property values were in Iowa. She couldn't imagine they'd be very high, so her profit wouldn't be all that much. She would also need to talk to Christina about taking some time off work to pack up the house and get it ready for sale.

She refilled her coffee cup and called Christina. Christina was very understanding about Syd needing to miss work for a couple of weeks, and she promised to tell the youngsters that she would be back to work soon. Syd then called her mama to tell her she'd be going to Iowa to get the property ready to sell. Just as Syd had guessed, her mama declined going to Iowa with her but she told Syd to call her with any questions or concerns regarding the property.

She then called her best friend and left a message on her voice mail. "Hey, Vanessa. I have to leave town tomorrow for a couple of weeks. Come over tonight, I'll fix you dinner, and explain everything." Her final call was to William Kramer, letting him know she'd be arriving the next afternoon, and she'd meet him at his office.

Vanessa texted her response saying that she'd be there, and she was intrigued.

Syd went to the store to pick up the ingredients to make a spinach-artichoke deep-dish pizza since Vanessa was a vegetarian and it would be easy to make. She was chopping the vegetables when there was a knock on the door. She greeted Vanessa with a heartfelt hug and they returned to the kitchen. Vanessa opened the bottle of wine she brought and poured them each a glass.

"So, you're leaving town? What happened?"

Syd wanted to laugh since Vanessa probably knew it would take something big for Syd to take that much time off work, but the death of her presumably racist grandmother and the inheritance of her property was no laughing matter.

"You won't believe the day I had. Let me just finish prepping the pizza and get it in the oven, and I'll tell you the whole story."

Once the pizza was baking, they took a seat on the couch, and Syd began her story. Vanessa sat there wide-eyed, taking in everything Syd told her about the call from her grandmother's attorney to why she never had a relationship with them. Vanessa finished off her glass of wine and went to retrieve the bottle to refill their glasses. She kicked off her heels and sat with her legs curled under her, never taking her eyes off Syd as she continued with her story.

"Wow. That's a hell of a day, Syd. So, you're leaving for Iowa tomorrow, and what? Get the house ready to sell?"

Syd shrugged. "I guess. There's a part of me who wants to try to figure out how my grandmother could disown her own daughter for falling in love with a black man. I can't imagine what she must have thought of me. A biracial lesbian." Syd laughed. "She probably would've had a field day with that one." Syd looked at Vanessa. "The look on your face right now is the same one you used to wear when we were in school and the kids were making fun of the color of my skin."

"Well, hell, it pissed me off that the black kids didn't like you because your skin was too light and the white kids didn't like you because your skin was too dark. They were so lame," Vanessa said, sounding like she was back in junior high school. Vanessa always had Syd's back, and Syd always had Vanessa's.

"Do you want me to go with you? I could work remotely and be there for you, for moral support."

"What about helping me pack up her house?"

Vanessa studied her nails and showed them to Syd. "I just got a manicure. I'm not doing anything to mess up this paint job."

Syd laughed and playfully shoved Vanessa. "You're such a girly-girl." And she was. Vanessa was tall and slender, but not too thin, with wavy strawberry blond hair that fell to her mid back. Her eyes were so blue that they often reminded Syd of the lake during the middle of summer. Syd reached over and squeezed Vanessa's hand. "I appreciate the offer, but I think I want to do this on my own. I'll call you if I need you there."

After dinner, they went to Syd's bedroom so she could pack. She opened her closet doors and looked at the array of jeans and polo shirts. She supposed they would do to clean out the house. She threw some shorts and T-shirts into her suitcase, along with the jeans and polo shirts, and zipped it up. She'd pack up her toiletries in the morning, and if she forgot anything, she'd just have to get it in Iowa.

"I better get going so you can get to sleep. You have a long drive ahead of you."

"Okay, let me wrap up the pizza for you to take home. In fact, let me give you everything in the fridge that will go bad while I'm gone."

Syd packed up the fruits and vegetables, as well as dairy products, and put them in a canvas bag for Vanessa. They hugged each other again at the door.

"Don't forget, I'll come out there if you need me. All you have to do is ask."

"I know, sweetie. Thank you. I'll text you when I get there so you know I arrived safely."

Syd cleaned the kitchen, turned off the lights, and took a bath before getting into bed. She was all packed and ready to go. All she needed to do was fall asleep. She had a feeling that that would be easier said than done.

## Chapter Three

Syd woke early, and after placing her suitcase and some snacks in her black BMW sedan, she was on the interstate headed west. She made a couple of stops along the way for bathroom breaks and to stretch her legs, and after three hundred and fifty miles and almost six hours, she arrived in Charville, Iowa. She felt she had traveled back in time about sixty years to a sleepy little town. She certainly wasn't in Chicago anymore. To be honest, she hadn't traveled much in her life. She grew up in Chicago, went to college there, but other than a few family vacations to nearby destinations, she didn't know much about any other place.

As she approached the courthouse in the center of town, she had to pull over and just admire the red brick building that resembled a smaller version of a castle. She marveled at the architecture of the building, but it was the clock tower that made her actually get out of her car. She walked the perimeter of the courthouse, unable to tear her eyes away from the clock for too long until she bumped into an older gentleman who was exiting the courthouse carrying a briefcase.

"Oh, excuse me."

He looked up then back at Syd. "Beautiful, isn't it? Can I help you find something?"

"I'm looking for a Mr. William Kramer's office."

"Oh, yes. Bill's office is around the corner on Main Street. It's right next to the candy store." He pointed in the direction she needed to go.

"Is it safe to leave my car here?" She indicated her vehicle parked at the curb.

"Uh, yeah." He chuckled as he walked away with a relaxed gait.

She grabbed her backpack out of the front seat and slung it over her shoulders. Syd began strolling down the sidewalk because wasn't strolling something people did in the 1950s? That was what this felt like. People *strolled* past her and said hello. Who did that anymore? The sidewalks in Chicago were full of business people talking on their cell phones or texting, in a hurry to get to where they were going. Their eyes were down, not up looking at people. And the people certainly weren't engaging with strangers. The people in this quaint little town looked like they weren't in a hurry to get anywhere and were just enjoying their time in the sun.

She looked up to the street sign that actually read Main Street. She chuckled and shook her head. Where the hell was she? Mayberry? The suites in the two-story red brick building had red-and-white-striped awnings extended over the sidewalk, and sure enough, right past a quilt shop and before the candy shop was the Law Office of William Kramer. She knew that because it was written in gold lettering on the storefront window. The bell on the front door rang when she opened it, and she walked into an inviting waiting room. There were four comfortable looking wingback chairs, two on each side of the room divided by two end tables with older copies of *Reader's Digest* sitting on top. There was a small oak desk that had the minimal necessities—a phone, a pen holder, and a desk calendar. There were old framed prints adorning the walls, including one she recognized as the courthouse she just left. She went to get a closer look and the date read 1893.

A clearing of a throat made Syd turn around to find an older gentleman with thick, silver hair looking at her. He was an imposing man, tall, and looked to be in good shape considering he was probably close to retirement age. He had a grandfatherly look to him that made Syd trust him immediately.

"Good afternoon, young lady. May I help you?"

"Yes, sir. My name is Sydney Carter."

"Ah, yes, Virginia's granddaughter. So very nice to meet you." He walked over to shake Syd's hand. "I'm William Kramer."

"Nice to meet you as well, Mr. Kramer."

"Why don't you come back to my office and we'll discuss your grandmother's last wishes."

Syd followed him down the hall that was lined with wood paneling on the walls and dark green carpeting. It was definitely 1970s décor. They entered a room spacious enough to hold a larger version of the oak desk she saw in the waiting room, a black leather couch, and two more wingback chairs in front of his desk. He held his hand out, indicating the chair Syd should sit in. He sat behind his desk and opened a manila folder.

"So, as I told you over the phone, your grandmother left you her property, which includes everything on it and in the house. She didn't have much money, but she left that to her neighbor and the neighbor's granddaughter who helped Virginia with her farm."

*Farm?* Syd didn't know anything about farms. What the hell had she gotten herself into?

As if he was reading Syd's mind, he said, "It's up to you if you want to sell it, rent it out, or keep it for yourself." He removed his wire-framed glasses and smiled at Syd. "If you want to sell it or rent it out, I can give you some referrals for real estate agents. I just need you to sign these papers, and I'll give you the keys."

Syd felt oddly detached, a little numb, as she read through the will of a woman she knew practically nothing about. But that was why she was here, right? To try to learn more about the woman who was her maternal grandmother. She signed the papers and slid them back across the desk to Mr. Kramer, and he handed her a key ring with three keys on it.

"What do these other two unlock?"

"My guess is one goes to the barn and the other to the back door. Her neighbor, Bernice Price, has another set to the house. I called her this morning to let her know you were arriving this afternoon so she could plug in the refrigerator and other appliances for you. I would advise you to do some grocery shopping while you're here in town today. Her farm is about a forty-minute drive from here, and there's not much in the way of a grocer close to her place."

"Okay. Anything else I need to know?"

"No, I think that's it." He handed her his business card and shook her hand. "Call me if you have any questions."

Syd turned around to leave then turned back to Mr. Kramer. "I do have one question. Where's the store?"

Mr. Kramer let out a hearty laugh that made Syd smile. "Just turn right at the corner and go up four blocks. You won't miss it."

Syd placed the copy of the will and keys in her backpack and walked back to retrieve her car from the courthouse. She followed Mr. Kramer's directions and easily found the grocery/farm supply store. It was like a farmer's version of Walmart. Foodstuffs on one side, farm stuffs on the other. Syd decided to wander the farm side first. They had everything from tools to feed to clothing to machines. It was a farmer's dream come true. She looked at the brown sandals on her feet and decided she should buy a pair of work boots, two pairs of work pants, and some T-shirts to add to the clothes she'd packed. She also added three sleeveless button-down shirts. She wasn't sure how much work needed to be done to get the house ready for sale or what the farm consisted of, but she figured this would get her by. She took her cart to the food section and bought enough food to last her at least a week. She would just have to return later if she needed more.

Syd loaded her purchases into the backseat, punched in the address to her grandmother's farm into her GPS, and drove away, leaving civilization as she knew it behind. With every mile she drove, the less she saw until there were just long two-lane roads with a house here and there, and an occasional horse or cow. Again, she asked herself what in the hell had she gotten herself into. It seemed like she drove for hours until the voice on her GPS told her the destination was one hundred feet ahead on her right. She slowed and signaled even though she hadn't seen another car for ten minutes.

Syd drove up a long paved drive that was lined with mature trees that looked like some sort of oak, until she came around the bend and stopped the car. She wasn't exactly sure what she was expecting when Mr. Kramer told her she was the new owner of a farm, but this certainly exceeded her expectations. The two-story house that sat in front of her was gorgeous. A large expanse of green, luscious grass lay in front of the house and was divided by a brick walkway. Her childhood memory of this house was nothing like what was in front of her. She got out of her car, leaving her suitcase and food, bringing only her backpack.

The smell of freshly cut grass and warm dirt assaulted her senses. These were foreign to Syd, as she had grown up in a concrete jungle. And it was so quiet, also something she was unfamiliar with. She retrieved the keys to the house and approached the front door. She slid the key into the lock and was almost surprised it actually turned. She entered and was flooded with a rush of emotions. She could almost envision herself as a little girl, excited to visit Grandmom and Granddad. Even though this was the first time stepping into this house, there was almost a familiarity to it.

Syd flashed back to her four-year-old self hiding behind her mama and being frightened of the scary old man. She felt a shudder flash through her, however she was able to quickly shake it off.

Syd stepped farther into the house that was flanked by two living rooms. She kept moving toward the back of the house, past the staircase and into the kitchen that looked like it had been updated recently. She ran her fingers along the granite-topped island as she made her way into the family room where she set down her backpack. She looked out the French doors to the backyard that seemed to go on for miles. What surprised her the most was a large pond with a small dock. If circumstances had been different between her mother and grandparents, she would have loved coming here to visit them as a child. Syd unlocked the doors and stepped outside onto a wood deck that had two Adirondack chairs and two chaise lounges, as well as a small square table with four chairs.

Syd looked to the left to see a barn the color of burnt red with white trim. The tall double doors were open. She didn't know if she was being robbed or had been robbed, and her heart hammered in her chest as she got closer to the barn. Not that she would know if she had been robbed. She didn't know what was supposed to be in there. She cautiously turned to step inside the dark building when she heard the rustle of boots shifting through hay and she ran into another person. There were screams, she was sure they were hers, and she started to swing her arms, making contact with the intruder.

"Ouch!"

The woman's voice made Syd stop swinging.

"Who the hell are you?"

"I'm Abigail. Who the hell are you?"

"I'm Syd. I'm the owner of this barn."

"Syd? Virginia's granddaughter?"

Syd looked at Abigail skeptically. "I know your name, but I still don't know who you are or what you're doing here."

They stepped outside into the daylight, and Syd got a better picture of Abigail. She was a few inches taller than her five foot six frame, and she was solidly built from what Syd could tell when she punched her in the arm. She couldn't really tell what the rest of her body looked like since she was wearing a baggy T-shirt and even baggier overalls. Her golden blond hair was pulled back in a messy ponytail, and sunglasses sat atop her head. Her skin was bronzed, evidence of many hours spent outdoors, and it made her ice-blue eyes stand out against her sun-kissed skin. Her high cheekbones, slight cleft in her chin, and oval-shaped face gave her a unique but attractive look. Syd felt the immediate flutter of attraction deep in her belly.

"I'm sorry for scaring you. I'm your neighbor down the road. I live with my grandmother who was best friends with Virginia. Mr. Kramer called to say you'd be coming into town today and asked me to get the house ready. I figured since I was here, I'd do the chores and feed the chickens."

"You did the chores? And wait. There are chickens?"

Abigail laughed and Syd noticed that her front teeth were adorably crooked and she had deep dimples in her cheeks.

"Yep. And a horse, but I moved her down to our barn so she wouldn't be so lonely."

"There's a horse?"

"Of course," Abigail said, which sent her in a fit of laughter.

Syd looked around the property and smelled the freshly cut grass and the smell of hay coming from the barn. She definitely was in a different world than the one she was used to.

"Come with me to the chicken coop. I was just about to feed them before you started beating on me."

Abigail's smile indicated she was teasing, and Syd was relieved that she was being so nice and helpful. She picked up a faded yellow plastic bucket and Syd followed her behind the barn to a small coop.

"I'm really sorry about Virginia," Abigail said. "She was a nice woman and was like a second grandmother to me."

"Thank you." Syd didn't know what to say without delving into her personal family business. "I didn't know her, but I'm hoping to learn more about her while I'm here."

Abigail didn't respond and continued as if she didn't hear what Syd had said. "As she got older and her body started slowing down, I came over to do her chores in the yard and help take care of the animals."

Syd looked sideways to Abigail. "How many animals are there, Abigail?"

That made Abigail laugh again, and Syd was finding she was really enjoying the melodious sound.

"Call me Abby. And to answer your question, only the chickens and the horse. Your grandfather used to stock the pond with fish, but when he died about fifteen years ago, Virginia stopped having it stocked. She wasn't interested in fishing. She said it was too still and boring. The fish take care of themselves, and whatever else is in there. You don't need to worry about that."

Syd heard the chickens clucking as they got closer to the coop that was made of weathered wood and chicken wire. The area where the chickens could mill around was quite large but enclosed to keep them safe from predators. They arrived to the coop and Abby started spreading the seed. There were five chickens, and Abby was talking to them like they were children, telling them to be nice and share their food.

"Have you fed chickens before, Syd?"

Syd shook her head in disbelief and barked out a harsh sound. "Uh, no. No, I've never fed chickens. I've never even seen a live chicken before that I can remember."

"Well, tomorrow will be your first lesson."

Syd wasn't sure what she thought of having to learn how to feed chickens, but the idea of seeing Abby again tomorrow appealed to her.

"Oh, shit. I forgot I have groceries in the car."

"Come on. Let me take this feed to the barn and lock up, then I'll help you bring everything in. After we get the food put away, I'll give you a tour of the house. Oh, and my grandmother sent some beef stew with me that I put in the fridge so you'd have some food to eat tonight."

Syd was surprised how thoughtful Abby and her grandmother were being to a perfect stranger. "Thank you, Abby. And please thank your grandmother for me."

When they arrived to Syd's car, Abby whistled and slowly circled it. "This is a nice ride."

For the first time since splurging on her car, Syd felt a little embarrassed and self-conscious. She had made a lot of money as an investment banker, but she was never one to exploit that. Besides her condo, her car was her greatest luxury. She had worn nice clothes to work, but other than that, her life hadn't been that extravagant.

Maybe it was the banker in her that made her invest a lot of her money into savings and retirement accounts rather than spend it on frivolous things. She grabbed the suitcase out of her trunk and the bags with her new clothes while Abby grabbed the groceries. Syd left her clothes at the foot of the stairs and followed Abby into the kitchen.

She didn't get a good look at it as she was passing through the house initially, but she loved what she saw. This was a cook's dream kitchen with a five-burner gas stove and double convection ovens in stainless steel, tons of counter space, and cherry wood cabinets. The rack hanging from the ceiling held various pots and pans that were easily accessible. She couldn't wait to use it tomorrow. Syd loved to cook but only had time for elaborate meals on the weekends. She would make simple meals during the week that she could take the leftovers for lunch the following day. She had already decided she was going to return the favor and have Abby and her grandmother over for a nice dinner.

"This is a great kitchen," Syd said as she opened the cupboards and found white plates with floral print around the rim and matching bowls. "Did my grandmother like to cook?"

"Oh, she loved it. She and my grandmother would trade off on cooking meals. The three of us would have dinner together almost every night and Sunday breakfasts." Abby closed the refrigerator door and frowned. "We both really miss Virginia, but my gran is having a very hard time dealing with this."

"I didn't think to ask her attorney, but how did she die?"

Abby placed her right hand over her own heart. "The coroner said it was probably a heart attack. Gran came over last Monday night to check on her and found Virginia in her recliner. At first, she thought Virginia was sleeping. She skipped dinner that night with us, saying she wasn't feeling well. When Gran tried to shake her awake, Virginia slumped over."

Abby's eyes filled with tears, and Syd moved to hug her but stopped herself. She didn't know this woman, so why did she have an overwhelming need to comfort her? Instead, she placed her hand on Abby's arm in an act of comfort.

Abby looked away and wiped her eyes. "I'm sorry. I didn't mean to do that."

"Do what? Cry over the loss of a woman you described as your second grandmother?" Syd was normally a private woman when it came to personal things, especially with someone she didn't know, so it shocked her when she asked Abby to stay for dinner. "I'd like to ask you some questions about her if that would be all right."

"I'd like that. Let me call my gran. We'll eat and I'll give you a tour of the house."

## CHAPTER FOUR

A bby dialed her home number and waited for the line to be picked up. "Hey, Gran. Are you doing okay?"

"Yes, dear. Where are you?"

"I'm down at Virginia's place. Her granddaughter, Syd, arrived and we've been talking. She asked me to stay for dinner, and she wants to ask some questions about her grandmother. I won't be home until later."

"Okay, dear. You be careful."

"Love you, Gran."

Abby hung up and returned to the kitchen to find Syd stirring the stew and humming. She had her back to Abby, so she used that opportunity to take a nice long look at Virginia's granddaughter. Sydney was a very attractive woman with light brown skin. When they were outside earlier, Abby noticed Syd's heavy-lidded bedroom eyes that were the color of warm milk chocolate. She had high cheekbones, hollow cheeks, and a soft jawline. Her hair was straightened, parted just left of center, and neatly combed. It fell just to her shoulders and was the color of brown sugar. She was lean but looked athletic, and she was possibly the most beautifully exotic looking woman she'd ever seen.

"Do you do that often?" Abby asked.

She laughed when Syd jumped and nearly dropped the wooden spoon.

"Jesus, you scared me. Do what often?"

"Sorry. Hum while you cook."

"Yes. Cooking relaxes me, and when I'm relaxed, I hum. Why do you ask?"

"Virginia would do the same thing."

A look passed on Syd's face, and Abby couldn't tell what it was. She watched as Syd dished the stew into the bowls and admired how comfortable Syd looked in the kitchen.

"Food's ready. Let's have a seat. Would you like some wine?"

"Yes, that would be nice."

Abby took the food to the table while Syd poured the wine. They ate silently for a few minutes after Syd raved how delicious the stew was. Abby would look up every once in a while, to glance at Syd and was struck by how attractive she was. Her skin was flawless, her pink lips were full and lush, and her eyes had a shape to them as if she were constantly questioning something in disbelief. Or maybe it was the arch of her eyebrows. Her observations were interrupted by Syd clearing her throat.

"Can I ask you some questions about my grandmother now?"

"Of course. What would you like to know?"

"Did she ever tell you why we never came around?"

Abby looked down at her hands. "Yes and no. She never told me directly, but I overheard her telling my grandmother one day."

*Abby had entered the kitchen to grab some water after working in the barn. She heard crying coming from the next room and feared something had happened to her grandmother. She and Virginia were sitting on the couch with their backs to Abby, and her grandmother had her arm around Virginia's shoulders, comforting her. Abby turned to leave so they could have some privacy but stopped when Virginia said, "Why won't she even open my letters? I'm trying to apologize to her, Bernice. I want my daughter back and I want to get to know my granddaughter."*

*When Virginia began to cry harder, Abby quietly slipped out the back door. She sat on the porch and pondered the little information she had heard. Virginia had a daughter. And a granddaughter. Abby wondered where they were and why they never visited. When she*

*asked her grandmother about them later that night, she told Abby
that was a private conversation and it wasn't any of her business.
Abby got the message loud and clear and never asked again. But
that didn't stop her from wondering.*

"That's all I know, Syd. Gran never told me and I never asked
Virginia."

"How long ago was that?"

Abby thought for a moment. "Probably about ten years ago.
Your grandfather had passed away just about a year prior to that."

Abby watched the different expressions pass over Syd's face,
and could almost imagine the wheels turning in her brain. She was
curious as to what Syd was thinking but didn't feel comfortable
delving into her personal business.

"I must have been about twenty-six then," Syd said.

"I'm not sure what exactly happened, but your grandmother
seemed pretty broken up about it."

The harsh bark of laughter that came from Syd, and the even
harsher, "Yeah, right," startled Abby.

"Why do you say that?"

Syd waved her hand as if to say never mind, and Abby had
a feeling that was the end of that conversation. She couldn't help
notice the fire in Syd's eyes, like she was angry, and she could see
her jaw muscles contract and relax, and her lips were pursed. She
wanted to ask Syd why her family hadn't come around, what had
happened between her grandparents and her mother, but she felt
that if Syd wanted to talk about it, she would. Abby was curious by
nature, and for some unexplained reason, she felt a connection with
Syd and she had a need to help her. If she knew what had happened
to keep Syd from her grandparents, maybe she could offer some
comfort or answers. For now, she would mind her own business and
move on to less personal conversation.

"Would you like me to show you around the house?"

"Sure."

Abby felt the best place to start would be the informal living
room. She led Syd into the room that Virginia spent much of her

time in. This was the room she entertained her friends in, where she would often knit, where she would look out the window overlooking the pond and watch the sun set.

"So, this is the living room Virginia spent most of her time in." Abby indicated to Syd. Abby watched Syd as she moved throughout the room, looking at the books, photos, and knick-knacks on the built-in shelves. Syd spent a good amount of time studying each photo as if she were trying to memorize them. She picked up one and showed it to Abby.

"This is my mama. She looks like she's about ten years old in this picture. They looked so happy then."

Abby looked at the picture of Syd's mother standing between Virginia and Harold, Virginia's husband, with their arms around each other. The smiles on their faces were beaming, but the look on Syd's face was wistful.

"You know, if you ever want to talk about it, I'm a good listener."

Syd looked up at Abby. "Talk about what?"

Abby placed her hand on Syd's shoulder and squeezed gently. "Why you look so sad."

Syd placed the photo back on the shelf. "Thanks. I'll keep that in mind. Okay, what's next?"

Abby showed Syd the other living room and the half bath on the first floor before leading Syd upstairs. She opened the first door on the left of the hallway at the top of the stairs. "This is Virginia's sewing room. She was an expert seamstress and made most of her own clothes." The room had a sewing machine in front of the window and a female mannequin in the corner. There were more shelves with fabrics and patterns stacked neatly. Syd touched just about everything in the room as if she could tactilely receive the answers she was searching for.

Abby pointed out the linen closet across the hall, and farther down on the left was the guest room. Abby had spent the night here occasionally if they had been up late playing cards or talking. She and her grandmother would share the queen-sized bed, and they would have breakfast together in the morning before Abby would help Virginia with her chores. Whereas Syd appeared to be angry and sad to be in this house, it held nothing but happy memories for Abby. She hoped she would eventually be able to help Syd have happy memories here too.

"This is the guest room. You can sleep in here or in Virginia's room, whichever you feel more comfortable in."

Syd walked in and sat on the bed. She looked around the room at the simple but tasteful décor. "No, this room will be fine. I think it would feel like I was intruding to sleep in her room."

"Well, I've slept here and this bed is really comfortable so you should sleep well."

Syd looked down and nodded, and Abby wondered again what was going through Syd's mind. She had an overwhelming urge to walk across the room, sit next to Syd on the bed, and take her in her arms. Instead, she shoved her hands in her pockets and rocked back on her heels, waiting for Syd to say or do something. Moments passed with Syd continuing to look down and fidget with her hands.

"The only other room I have to show you is Virginia's room. Would you like to go see it?"

"Actually, would you mind if we didn't? I'm feeling a little overwhelmed right now and I think I need to be alone. I'm sorry, Abby."

"No, please. I completely understand. Is there anything I can do for you before I go?"

Syd surprised Abby by hugging her and holding on like she was a lifeline. Abby relaxed into the hug and reciprocated, enjoying the feeling of having Syd in her arms. She smelled like cocoa butter and lavender, and Abby slowly inhaled the scent, hoping to memorize it. "No. I really appreciate all you've done around here and for me. So, you'll help me with the chickens tomorrow?"

Abby laughed, mostly at the apprehensive look on Syd's face. "Of course. I'll be by around seven if that's not too early."

"That's fine. I'll make us breakfast, so come hungry."

Abby handed Syd a slip of paper with her phone number on it. "If you need me, I'm only a call away. Good night, Syd."

❖

Abby sat in her office and opened up her email that she used specifically for her publisher, editor, and publicist. The first email she opened was from her editor acknowledging she received the page proofs and her newest release would go to print in just a few weeks. Abby still considered herself a fairly new author, even though her sixth book was about to be published, but with each book, her readership grew, as did the number of positive reviews. Her sixth book, *Open to Love*, was already getting advanced praise, and her editor told her it was her best story yet.

She loved writing stories, starting at an early age. After her parents were killed in a car accident, she would write letters to them, telling them about school, about living with Grandma and Grandpa on the farm, and telling them how much she missed them and loved them. When she got a little older, she began writing stories of what life would've been like if her parents were still alive. Of course, it was fiction, but it made her be more creative, and it made them seem to her like they were just on a long trip.

She had entered short story contests in high school, and she actually won three of them. It was a no-brainer what she would study in college, and she got her undergraduate degree in creative writing. She read books, attended seminars, and took classes that would hone her craft. When her first submitted manuscript wasn't accepted, she paid a professional editor to take a look and give her advice. She reworked the story, submitted it again, and it was accepted. That was the beginning of her professional writing career. To her grandma and her friends, she was Abigail Price, Iowa farm girl. But to her many fans, she was Leah Griffin, published author of romance novels. Her pen name was very meaningful to her. Her parents' names were Leah and Griffin, and this was a small way Abby felt she could honor them.

Abby logged out of that email address and logged into Leah's. She scanned through the list and deleted the spam. Companies offering to move her books to the top of best-seller lists for a price. Why would she pay someone to do that when her publisher did it for her as part of her contract? She took her time reading through her fan mail, appreciating how readers took the time to write to her to tell her how much they loved her books. The least she could do was answer their emails herself. Once she was finished with her responses, she pulled up her manuscript and reread the last page to see where she left off. She tried to think of what to write next, but her thoughts kept drifting back to Sydney.

Abby noticed more than once that Syd looked sad, maybe a little overwhelmed, but she wasn't open yet to telling Abby why. All Abby could do was let Syd know that she could talk to her if she felt comfortable. Abby started to wonder what Syd's story was. As a writer, whenever she came across interesting looking people, she loved to try to figure out who they were. What kind of background did they come from? What was their family life like? What did they do for a living? There were times when Abby would go into town, grab lunch from her favorite deli, and go sit in a park and people-watch. She sometimes got ideas for characters by doing just that. She tended to write stories that were character-driven, and once she had her character profiles complete, they would tell their story. She'd never admit to hearing the characters' voices in her head though. She didn't want people thinking she was crazy or anything. Abby chuckled to herself and looked to her white board hanging above her desk.

The board contained her story arc, the characters' physical and emotional traits, some interesting tidbits about them, and pictures of what she imagined they looked like. If ideas popped into her head about things she could work into the story, she'd write those down too so she wouldn't forget. This was as close to an outline that she'd do. She was never any good at outlining, and as long as she knew the beginning, middle, end, and the "black moment"—the part of the story where the couple was torn apart—the rest of the story she wrote by the seat of her pants.

It seemed tonight, though, her characters didn't feel like talking to her. She knew better than to try to force the words that weren't there. She exited the program and powered down her laptop before taking a long, hot shower that always helped her relax before bedtime. Once she was in bed, she drifted off to sleep in no time at all.

## CHAPTER FIVE

Syd woke as the sun was starting to shine in the window. She wasn't used to being up this early since she usually didn't start work until late morning. She was exhausted from the traveling and she was emotionally drained after talking with Abby about her grandmother, and she had gone to sleep earlier than her normal bedtime. It took most of her energy to carry up her clothes and fall into bed after Abby left.

Syd thought about Abby, and she could feel the tug of a grin. She liked Abby and felt an attraction to her, and she had a feeling she would like her a lot, especially when she got to know her better. Abby didn't look like the women Syd usually hooked up with or found attractive, but there was something about her that drew Syd to her. Maybe it was her hospitality. Maybe it was her adorable smile and dimples. Maybe it was the solidly built body she imagined to be under her baggy overalls. Whatever it was, Syd was looking forward to getting to know Abby better, even if she planned on leaving in a couple of weeks.

Syd stretched out in bed and took in the guest room's décor. It was what she expected a farmhouse bedroom to look like. Most of the room was white with a few splashes of color here and there. And while it wasn't a style she preferred for her downtown Chicago condo, it was cute in a farmhouse-in-Iowa way. She turned on her side to face the window that had a bench seat beneath it. The leaves on the trees just outside the window were still, and she could hear the birds chirping away. Her suitcase and bags of new clothes sat on the floor in front of the closet.

After she showered, she pulled out a pair of jeans and T-shirt and put them on, as well as her new boots she bought yesterday. She decided that she would put away her clothes later after Abby left. She would be arriving soon, and Syd needed to get started on breakfast. She wanted it to satisfy Abby. For some reason, satisfying Abby was high on Syd's list of priorities. Going through her grandmother's room would have to wait, but that was fine by Syd.

She felt trepidation at what she might find out about Virginia, how she really felt about Syd's parents. The biggest question she wanted answered was why. Why did Virginia disown her own daughter because of who she fell in love with? Syd wasn't sure if that question would ever be answered by going through Virginia's personal effects. Perhaps Abby's grandmother would be a better source of information. Abby did say they were best friends, after all. But would she give Syd what she was looking for without feeling like she was betraying her friend?

Syd rummaged through the cabinets looking for the items she needed. She was amused to find the kitchen organized as she would have done it, which made everything easy to find. She knew kitchen organization wasn't a genetic trait, but she couldn't help but think some of her maternal grandmother's traits trickled their way down the family tree to reach Syd. Her parents' kitchen wasn't organized this way or like Syd's, and she speculated if that was on purpose, that her mama didn't want anything that reminded her of her mama. She was just pulling the bacon out of the warmer when Abby appeared at the back door holding a basket.

"I stopped by the coop and picked up some eggs in case you wanted them."

Syd was amazed and relieved at the thought of just having to walk out back to get eggs. She realized as she was looking in the refrigerator before she started cooking that she forgot to buy eggs and she wouldn't have time to drive forty-five minutes into town. She had mentally kicked herself while she had been cooking the rest of breakfast that she could have forgotten something that she used in so many recipes. But now, at least for the next couple of weeks, running out of eggs wasn't something she would have to worry about.

"Thanks, Abby. I'll cook those right up. How do you like them?"

"Over easy, please. It smells great in here."

"Thanks. I just made some bacon and oatmeal. I don't think there's a better smell than fried bacon. Well, maybe freshly brewed coffee, but bacon is definitely in the top two. Go ahead and pour us some juice and I'll have everything ready in a few minutes." Syd shut her eyes and mentally chastised herself for rambling.

Syd flipped the eggs over for just a moment before she put them on their plates along with the bacon. Abby brought over the bowls of oatmeal and they sat down to eat.

"So, how did you sleep last night?" Abby asked around a bite of eggs.

"Like a baby. I don't remember closing my eyes."

"Must be the fresh farm air."

Yes, the fresh farm air that smelled like musty barns, dirt, straw, and chicken poop. Who wouldn't be able to sleep soundly after inhaling those scents? Syd laughed when Abby smiled and winked. "Yes, that must be it. What's on the agenda today besides feeding the chickens?"

"Well, I thought I'd give you a tour of the land. How do you feel about ATVs?"

Syd looked up mid-bite of her oatmeal. "ATVs? I'm not sure I know what that means."

"It stands for all-terrain vehicle. I rode mine over this morning, and I thought you could ride with me to look at Virginia's land."

Syd felt her eyebrows scrunch together, and she rubbed her forehead. She had the faint throbbing of a headache coming on. "Um, Abby? Exactly how much land are we talking?"

"Oh, about thirteen acres."

"Thirteen acres? Jesus! I had no idea how big this was."

Abby laughed. "That's not big at all. Some of the folks around here have over a hundred acres."

Syd looked down and dragged her spoon through her oatmeal. For what seemed like the thousandth time, she wondered what she had gotten herself into. She also pondered what else could be on this land. Would she find livestock? Corn stalks? Small wild animals roaming around? The possibilities were endless and a little frightening. After the dishes were rinsed, Syd and Abby went to the barn to get the feed.

"What exactly do chickens eat?"

Abby scooped some feed into the bucket and motioned for Syd to follow her to the coop. "They eat poultry pellets mostly. I ground some dried eggshell into a powder and add that to the feed. Sometimes they'll eat fresh fruit and vegetables, rolled oats, cooked pasta, bread. That's basically it." Abby tossed the feed into some bins. "We'll stand here to make sure there's no dominance when the chickens eat. The chickens should have clean water readily available, but I took care of that when I got the eggs this morning."

Syd watched Abby out of the corner of her eye as she fed the chickens. The smell of the feed, the pinging sound of the pellets hitting the bins, the clucking coming from the chickens, the fluid motion of Abby moving about the coop made Syd yearn for a simpler life. Yearn? Is that what she'd call it? This feeling was still foreign to her. When she worked as an investment banker, she rarely had time to relax, take in the sounds, smells, and motions that occurred in her everyday life.

It was just something she took for granted that was always there. She was always focused on her clients and sealing the deal. Syd couldn't remember any other way of life. She started to slow down when she started working at the center because she wanted to be present with the children and not rush through her time with them. Slowing down had been a hard habit to learn.

Yet how was she able to imagine living this kind of life after just one day? A slower, quieter, simpler kind of life. One where she'd feed chickens and ride a John Deere mower to cut the expansive lawn and have the pond stocked again so she could learn how to fish and sit at the dinner table with Abby every night.

Wait. What? Where and how did Abby pop into that picture?

Sure, Syd found Abby adorable and sweet and attractive. Extremely attractive, to be honest. But having dinner together every night? Like a couple? Syd lived in a high-rise condo in downtown Chicago, the city she'd spent her entire life in. She was used to noise, lights, people, tall buildings, concrete. What could she possibly have in common with a white farm girl who lived with her grandmother? She didn't even know what Abby did for work, where her parents were, where she went to college. Did she even go to college? She knew nothing about Abby, and yet she envisioned having dinner with her every night? What the hell was happening to her? And the farm? Sure, it would be a nice place to get away for a few days from the noisy city. But actually live there? On a farm? Maybe all that fresh air was getting to her and causing a mini hallucination. What other explanation could there be?

"You ready?"

Syd shook her head as she was interrupted from her musings. "Sorry, what?"

Abby grinned at her, clearly amused. "Are you ready to go look at the rest of the property?"

"Oh, sure. I guess." Syd followed Abby back to the barn to drop off the supplies. She accepted the helmet Abby handed her and got on the back of the ATV.

Abby turned her head to talk to Syd. "You need to scoot closer and wrap your arms around my waist. I don't want you falling off the back."

Syd did as Abby instructed, and if she were being honest, she didn't hate it. Her arms wrapped around Abby's solid midsection, and she had a strong yearning to run her fingers up and down the muscular abdomen she felt under Abby's T-shirt. Syd believed Abby shuddered as she pressed into Abby's backside. Maybe Abby would be up for a little fooling around while Syd was in town. It wasn't like it would, or could, develop into a relationship. Once Syd was finished with the house and it was up for sale, she'd go back to her life in Chicago.

❖

Abby was sure Syd couldn't hear her pounding heart over the motor of the ATV, but feeling Syd's hot center pressed up against her wasn't making it easy for her to concentrate on navigating the terrain. Abby was attracted to Syd, there was no denying it. Her seductive smile and bedroom eyes had Abby wrapped up all in knots and Syd probably had no idea that just a simple raised eyebrow said so much. Or maybe she did. Abby didn't know Syd hardly at all, but she wanted to. She had been pretty secluded from female companionship on the farm but certainly sought it when she went on trips, which unfortunately wasn't often enough, especially recently as Virginia's health seemed to be failing.

Over the past few months, Abby observed Virginia moving a bit slower, taking more naps, being a little more lethargic. Abby insisted on taking her to see her doctor, but Virginia just said she had "a little bug." Ever since Virginia died, Abby cried in the privacy of her own bedroom at night and blamed herself. If she had just forced Virginia to go see the doctor, she might be alive today. She blinked back her tears and was grateful that Syd was behind her so she couldn't see her face. She took a deep, shuddering breath and shifted in her seat, ashamed that she felt such a sexual attraction to Virginia's granddaughter while she was still mourning her death.

They drove around the property, occasionally stopping for Abby to point out certain areas to Syd, such as property lines. There wasn't much to see overall. Most of the scenery was near the house, especially the mature trees that lined the outer edges of the pond and a walking path around the small body of water that led to a small picnic area. Abby and Virginia would occasionally walk back there with a basket full of sandwiches, chips, and drinks and enjoy the fresh air in between chores. She felt the thickness in her throat and found it difficult to swallow as she recalled the happier times she spent with Virginia. Abby would have to take Syd there for a picnic, to show her that place that was so special to her grandmother. She hoped that Syd would find it as peaceful as her grandmother had. They arrived back to the house, and Syd invited Abby in for lunch. As Abby heated up the leftover stew, Syd threw together a salad. Abby realized Syd hadn't said much since they got back.

"What do you think of the property?"

"It's amazing. And humongous."

Abby laughed. "It's a pretty decent size. Virginia always complained that they didn't need that much property, but when your grandparents were younger, they had a small herd of cows and some other livestock. Virginia sold them after your grandfather passed away. She didn't have much interest in keeping them around because it would have been too much work for her, but she said the chickens were easy."

Syd nodded as Abby spoke. "I imagine it would have been difficult for her to manage the cows and other animals by herself."

Abby cleared her throat to try to dislodge the lump that seemed to be a constant reminder of all that she had lost when Virginia died. She had offered her help to Virginia to take care of the cows for her, but she declined the offer. Abby would have done anything for the woman who showed her just as much love as her own grandmother. "Have you had a chance to look around the house yet?"

Syd shook her head. "I was planning on starting that today. I was too exhausted last night to do anything."

"Do you want any help?"

"I might at some point. Can I let you know?"

"Of course." Abby took their dishes into the kitchen and rinsed the food off. "Would you like me to come back later to feed the chickens again?"

Syd smiled. "No, I think I can manage. Thanks for all your help today, Abby. I really appreciate it."

"Anytime. Remember, if you need anything, I'm only a call away."

Feeling disappointed in being dismissed and ending her day with Syd, Abby put on her helmet and rode back to her farm, hoping Syd would take her up on her offer to help. She really didn't have any idea of what Syd would find, but she sincerely hoped she would get the answers to her questions and also discover how loving her grandmother was.

❖

Syd didn't know where to begin. Once Abby left, she walked into the living room and slowly turned in a circle. What was she supposed to do with all the framed pictures on the shelves? She wasn't too concerned about the books or knick-knacks; she could just donate those. She pulled her cell phone out of her pocket and called the one person who she felt could help.

"Hi, Mama."

"Hi, baby. Are you in Iowa?"

"Yes. I'm standing in the living room and I have no idea where to start. There are a ton of framed photos of you and your parents. Should I keep them? Throw them away? Give them to you?"

"Oh, Syd. I wish I could answer that for you, but it's your house now and it's up to you what to do with everything there. I don't want the pictures so you can either keep them or throw them away."

Syd shook her head at her mother's attitude. "Gee, Mama. Thanks for your help," she said sarcastically.

"I'm sorry, baby, but you have to realize how I felt about my parents. We were always so close and I loved them so much, but they broke my heart when they gave me that ultimatum. I was already so madly in love with your daddy that I couldn't, or didn't, want to live my life without him. Isaiah even suggested breaking up in order to make my parents happy, that he didn't want to be the reason I lost my family. That showed me he truly loved me and cared about my happiness, so it was him that I chose. I tried calling my parents a couple of years later when I found out I was pregnant with you, and my daddy hung up on me. They never even knew I was pregnant with you. I was terribly hurt that they turned their backs on me. So, no, I don't want anything of theirs."

Syd took a moment to think about what her mother said and how she felt, and she became more sympathetic. Her chest tightened as she tried to imagine her parents turning her away for who she loved. They would never do anything like that. Of course, her mama probably thought the same thing about her own parents. "I'm sorry they treated you and Daddy that way, but I just don't know what to do." The stress of the situation hit Syd, and she felt the tears well up in her eyes. It was as if she had reverted back to being a child and needed her mama to make everything all right. She wept and her throat tightened, making it difficult to speak. She pounded her fist into her thigh, upset that she felt so impotent. She had always been in control of her feelings and situations she had been in, and she was completely out of her element at that moment being so out of control.

"Oh, baby girl, I wish I was there to hug you. Do you want me to come out there and help you? I can leave first thing in the morning and be there by early afternoon."

Syd wanted to scream "yes" into the phone. She wanted her mama here with her, going through all of the pictures and personal items that should be for her and that would eventually be passed on to Syd. It was like her mama was the middle-woman that had been completely cut out of the picture and Syd had been thrust to the front of the line. But she couldn't do that to her mama. That house held sad memories for her, and Syd wanted to protect her mama from feeling sad if she could help it. She would just have to put on her big girl panties, buck up, and take care of that once and for all. "Thanks, Mama, but it's okay. I'll take care of it. I've never had to do this before and I was just feeling a bit swamped. I can do this if I can just figure out where to start and take care of one thing at a time." She wiped her eyes and held her head high, proud of regaining her control.

"How about this? Leave the pictures for now. Start with less significant things. Does she still have her sewing room?"

"Yes," Syd said as she wiped the last of her tears.

"Okay. Start there. You can throw away the patterns, pack up the useable materials to donate. That kind of thing."

"Yeah, that sounds like a good place to start. Thanks, Mama. I'm going to get started so I'll talk to you later. Love you."

"I love you too, baby. Promise me you'll call me if you need me to come out there."

"I promise." Syd placed her phone in her pocket and went in search of trash bags. She would have to make a trip into town tomorrow to get some boxes. She let out a huge breath and felt ready to conquer the list of things she needed to do over the next two weeks. Maybe Abby knew of a place that would take donations. Syd made a mental note to ask her about it tomorrow. She had made good progress on the sewing room when she realized it was getting late. She still had to feed the chickens and prepare dinner for herself.

She put her boots on and went to the barn to get the feed. She made quick work of it, made sure the chickens behaved themselves, then went back inside to fix dinner. She pulled out the ingredients then realized how tired she was. She put the food away and fixed a tuna sandwich instead.

After dinner, she went back upstairs, but rather than going back into the sewing room, she went to her grandmother's room. She stood in the hallway looking at the closed door, uncertain of what she would find beyond it. She grabbed the doorknob, then just as quickly pulled her hand away as if it had scalded her skin. She reached out and skimmed the door with her fingertips, then leaned her forehead against the white barrier. She stood there for minutes or hours, trying to gather the courage to perform the one simple task of opening a damn door. Syd felt as if she were intruding and snooping around. This wasn't her house. Well, technically, it was, but it didn't feel like it. *Stop being silly.* She shook out her arms and hands like she was getting ready to run a race, then let out a deep breath before taking the plunge.

Syd opened the door and felt along the wall for the light switch. Once the lights turned on, Syd took in the room. The furniture was all white and the walls were painted a light taupe. Syd imagined the three large awning windows behind the headboard would let in lots of light during the day. The bed was covered with a white quilt with brown square patterns, as well as a few throw pillows, and flanked by two nightstands. Syd was stunned to find the eight-by-ten framed picture on the chest of drawers was of her dressed in a business suit. It looked like downtown Chicago in the backdrop. Syd had a phone to her ear and she was smiling.

She wondered who she was talking to at the time, and even more so, who took that picture. "The private investigator," she said to herself. The fact that Virginia had this picture in a frame made Syd feel a sadness so deep, she had no idea where it came from. She briskly rubbed her chest over her heart as if that would help it heal. She was hurt that the woman who cared enough for her to hire a private eye to keep tabs on her didn't care enough to try and see Syd when she was a child. She sat on the edge of the bed, picture in her hands, and fantasized of what could have been. Syd imagined what it would have been like to take road trips to see Grandmom Adams, and she bit the inside of her cheek to try and prevent herself from crying.

She was used to being alone most nights back in Chicago, where she knew she could see her parents or Vanessa within thirty minutes, so she never felt lonely. But she felt lonely here in this strange house. She didn't want to worry them, as she knew they would be once they heard her crying. Hearing their voices would make her feel even lonelier because she wouldn't be able to be physically wrapped up in their love. She supposed she could call Abby to come back over, but that's not what Syd needed. With her tight string of emotions, it would be dangerous to have Abby back in the house, and she might look for a physical comfort that would have no bearing on making her less lonely. She needed time alone to think up a game plan. It had been a whirlwind since she got the call from William Kramer. She needed to just slow down and come up with a plan.

She placed the frame on the dresser and closed the door on her daydreams of what could've been. She was too tired to dig through her grandmother's bedroom items. She was feeling raw and emotional, and she was hanging on by a very thin thread. She just wanted to try to finish packing up the sewing room. She carried a couple of trash bags out to the garage and was surprised to see how many boxes that were still on the shelves. She ran her fingers through her hair as she squeezed her eyes shut and yelled. Jesus! It was going to take her forever to go through all that. She shook her head and muttered a few expletives while she climbed back up the stairs. Maybe she would ask for Abby's help after all.

# Chapter Six

A bby rose with the sun and listened to the birds chirping out the window. Last night, her grandmother had asked her to invite Syd to dinner, but she realized she gave Syd her number but didn't get Syd's. She'd go over after breakfast and invite her personally. Abby had enjoyed showing Syd around the property and sharing meals with her. She'd be lying if she said she wasn't a little disappointed to leave her yesterday afternoon. She could tell Syd was overwhelmed with the size of the property, and Abby hoped she would ask for her help. There was something about her that intrigued Abby, but she couldn't quite put her finger on it. Yes, she was attractive. That was probably an understatement.

Abby didn't know much about her except she lived in Chicago and she used to be some sort of banker, but now she worked with kids. Before Syd went back home, Abby hoped she would get to know her better. Maybe they could even remain friends. Abby sometimes went to Chicago for book signings, and there wasn't any reason why they couldn't have dinner together when she was in the city. She didn't have much time to get to know Syd though. Syd mentioned that she would be there for two weeks and it was already day three.

Her phone buzzed on her nightstand, interrupting her musings. A number she didn't recognize popped up on the screen and she answered.

"Hi, Abby. It's Syd. I hope I didn't wake you."

"No, you didn't, and I was just thinking about you."

"Oh, yeah? What were you thinking about?"

Syd's voice was low and sexy, and it sent a delicious shiver throughout Abby's body. She wondered if Syd might be up for a little fun while she was there. It wasn't the first time that thought ran through her mind, but the more she thought about it, the more she realized it probably wouldn't be a good idea. Why start something that they couldn't finish. Abby had a strong feeling that she would want more than just a night in bed with Syd, and having more just wasn't geographically possible. She quickly wiped out the strong wish to volley back the flirtation.

"Well, I was thinking a few things, actually. Like that I hardly know anything about you except where you live. I thought about how overwhelmed you looked when I left yesterday, and I wondered if you wanted some help today. And last, but not least, my gran wanted me to invite you to dinner tonight at our place."

Syd chuckled, and Abby felt warm inside.

"First off, I'll tell you anything you want to know. All you have to do is ask."

Abby thought she heard an innuendo in that statement, and it made her stomach do a little flip.

"Second, you were correct that I'm overwhelmed and I was calling to ask for your help if you weren't too busy today."

The only thing Abby had planned on doing was writing in between chores. She could skip a day though. She was ahead of schedule of her weekly word count goal, so not writing for one day wouldn't disrupt her getting her manuscript in on time.

"I'm not busy, and I can be there after my morning chores, probably in a couple of hours."

"That would be great. Thank you so much. Now, most importantly, please tell your grandmother I'd love to have dinner with you both tonight. What can I bring?"

"Oh, not a thing. Just yourself." Abby couldn't help but do a mental happy dance that Syd would be joining them for dinner. That would be a great opportunity to get to know her better. *Get real, Abby. It would be a great opportunity to gaze into her warm brown eyes and fantasize about kissing her full, pink lips. You're not fooling anyone.*

"Abby, my mama told me never to show up at someone's house empty-handed. How about I make a dessert?"

Abby laughed. "Okay, you can bring dessert."

"Great. I'll see you in a couple of hours."

Abby held her phone to her chest as if it were Syd she was holding. Before she forgot, she saved Syd's name and number to her contact list then got dressed to start her chores. She arrived to Virginia's—Syd's—two hours later and entered the house when Syd yelled for her to come in. The smell of apples, cinnamon, and sugar assaulted her senses, and her mouth watered. Abby found Syd in the kitchen with her back to Abby bending over to pull something out of the oven. Abby found her mouth watering again, but for an entirely different reason. Syd's shapely backside filled in her dark blue jeans quite nicely. A whole list of ideas of what to do to that backside started flipping through Abby's mind, and she quickly and conveniently forgot her vow to keep things with her on a platonic level. Syd turned around holding a pie, and she must have caught Abby staring because she smirked as she brushed past Abby to place a perfectly golden-brown apple pie on a hot pad.

Abby bent over to smell the pie and thought she might have died and gone to heaven.

"Syd, this smells delicious. Is this for tonight? Please, please say this is for tonight."

Syd bent close to Abby and inhaled with her eyes closed, and the sexiest moan Abby had ever heard came from Syd, making Abby's knees go weak. Syd opened her eyes and turned her head. Just another inch and she would be close enough for Abby to kiss.

"I hope you like it," Syd murmured.

Abby's mouth that was just watering was now bone dry. All the moisture that had been in her mouth had escaped to a destination much lower as the wetness pooled in her panties. Abby slowly blinked and broke the spell. Damn it! Syd pulled back and untied the strings to Virginia's apron. Abby had bought that apron for Virginia for her birthday a few years ago, including some baking sheets, muffin tins, and cake pans. Virginia thanked Abby by baking her chocolate chip cookies on her new baking sheets while wearing her new apron. How could Abby be fueled with need and desire one second, then crushed by sadness the next? Her eyes welled with tears at the memory and she turned away from Syd. She clapped her hands together trying to give herself just a few more seconds to recover from that memory.

"So, what do you need me to help with?"

"I was hoping you could help me go through the boxes in the garage and help me identify anything that would have value— sentimental or monetary. And if you see anything you want to keep, I want you to have it. I know how much she meant to you so it would only be right."

Abby felt her throat tighten again. She hadn't expected that offer to come from Syd. She wasn't sure what Syd had planned to do with Virginia's things, but Abby appreciated her willingness to accept how close Abby was to Virginia. She tried hard to imagine if the roles were reversed, but she just couldn't. Her grandparents took her in after her parents died, and they always encouraged, supported, and loved her.

Abby missed her parents every minute of every day, but she was grateful she was raised by such loving grandparents. Her heart ached for Syd that she didn't have the same relationship with Virginia and Harold. Abby didn't have much of a relationship with Harold because he always seemed to keep to himself, but after he passed away, she and her gran spent more time with Virginia. She supposed it was to keep Virginia from being so lonely, but the more time they spent together, the closer they became until Abby began to think of Virginia as another grandmother.

"Are you sure about that?"

"Absolutely. You probably knew her better than anyone, except maybe your grandmother. You deserve to have some of her things."

"Thank you. I can't tell you what that means to me. I have an idea. Let's go through the boxes together instead of individually. I think we'll get through them faster. We'll make piles for things to donate, things to keep, and things to throw away." Abby took a box off the top of one of the shelving units that lined the two side walls of the garage.

By the time they took a break for a quick lunch, they had gone through about a quarter of the boxes. A few of them contained papers that Syd would go through, but most had contained some of Harold's clothes that they put in the donation pile. They spoke easily about what it was like for Abby to grow up on a farm. Other than missing her parents, Abby loved farm life. She enjoyed being outside and working with her hands, feeling the sun shine down and warm her as she helped her grandmother in the garden. The smells of the dirt as they turned the earth, the freshly mowed grass, she loved everything about it. When she was older and stronger, she would help her grandfather chop wood, burn leaves, and build things in the garage. She could almost smell the leaves burning in the chilly fall air and the faint smell of gasoline and exhaust in the steamy heat of the garage in the middle of summer.

They resumed going through more boxes after they ate. By the time they had gone through all the boxes from one side of the wall, it was late afternoon.

"I think this is a good place to stop for today. Gran said dinner would be at six, and I need to get home to clean up."

Syd looked down at her own hands and clothes, and she couldn't believe how dirty she'd gotten. They'd had the garage door open while they'd been working, but it had still been extremely warm. It wasn't the humid heat she was used to in Chicago, but it was still hot, and she had sent up a silent prayer that it was still early spring. The smell of motor oil, concrete, and cardboard took over as the temperature rose. Now she felt grimy and she smelled bad. She was a little embarrassed to have Abby see her this way, although living on a farm, Abby was probably used to getting dirty.

Syd stood and stretched her arms over her head to try to loosen up her stiff body, and she let out a deep groan of relief. When she opened her eyes, she caught Abby staring at her midsection where her shirt lifted up over her lower abdomen. Syd's pulse raced when Abby looked up and her eyes had darkened. Syd recognized Abby's look of arousal, and she took a step forward with every intention of taking Abby in her arms and kissing her senseless. Abby's eyes widened, like she had come out of a trance, and she cleared her throat, stopping Syd in her tracks.

"Um, I'll see you at six. Just turn left on the road and we're the next house on the left side of the street." Abby's shoulder brushed Syd's as she hurried by and left. Something obviously spooked Abby, but Syd had no idea what it was. Was it possible Syd was getting the wrong signals from Abby and that she wasn't a lesbian? No, the way she was looking at her ass in the kitchen was a dead giveaway, as was the blush of her skin when Syd caught her looking at her just then. Or did she have an issue with Syd's skin color? It wouldn't be the first time Syd experienced racism, but up until then, Abby had been friendly with her and never hinted that Syd's race was an issue.

Syd had half a mind to call Abby and tell her she'd changed her mind about dinner, but that wouldn't be fair to her grandmother. Syd sighed as she closed the garage door before going inside to get cleaned up. She was being way too judgmental toward a woman who had just spent the day helping her clean out half the garage and who had done nothing but help her since the second she arrived. Obviously, there was something that kept Abby from being swept away by the kiss Syd so desperately wanted to give her. She'd wait it out and see how Abby reacted to her at dinner later, and maybe she'd get a chance to talk to her about it before the night was over.

## Chapter Seven

A bby ran the half mile home hoping to simmer down the arousal she still felt. When Syd's shirt hem rose and exposed her light brown skin and smooth abdomen, Abby wanted nothing more than to caress the skin to see if it was as soft as it looked. But when she saw the smirk on Syd's mouth, she knew she'd been caught. Again. Then the step Syd took toward her betrayed her intention and Abby freaked out. Why? Was she embarrassed for getting caught leering at Syd, or was she embarrassed about what she would've done had Syd come any closer? If she had let Syd kiss her, they'd still be in that garage working up a different kind of sweat, and they would have probably missed dinner. God. She was going to see her in less than two hours. How was she going to explain herself?

Abby was out of breath by the time she reached her front door, and she knew the run was only part of the reason. She called out to her gran that she was home and she was going to take a shower. She took the stairs two at a time in hopes of avoiding her gran for now. She debated whether her shower should be cold or hot, and she settled for warm.

Abby considered what she was going to wear to dinner more than she should have, but then again this was an opportunity to show Syd she owned more than Carhartt overalls and baggy T-shirts. She didn't know why it mattered what Syd thought of her, but it did. She probably thought Abby was just some poor, uneducated farm girl, but that was far from the truth. Abby thought somehow that if she dressed in nice clothes, wore her hair down instead of in her messy ponytail, and maybe wore a little cologne, it would maybe change Syd's perception of her. She chose a royal blue button-down blouse that would enhance her blue eyes, slate gray slacks, and black loafers. She had worn this outfit before when she had done a reading at a big chain bookstore, and she had noticed more than a few admiring glances from some of the women in the audience.

When she felt she looked and smelled as good as she could, she found her gran in the kitchen putting the final preparations on dinner. Abby recognized the smells of her favorite dinner—pot roast, gravy, mashed potatoes, and cooked carrots. This meal is what her gran cooked whenever Abby was feeling down and needed comfort food.

Abby placed a kiss on her grandmother's cheek. "It smells fantastic, Gran. Is there anything I can do to help?"

"No, dear. It's almost ready." She looked Abby up and down, and Abby slid her hands down her thighs nervously.

"Well, don't you look lovely. Is there a special occasion I'm unaware of?" her grandmother teased her.

"No, Gran. I just felt like dressing up since we're having company."

Abby recognized the look her gran was giving her. Abby secretly called it the "bullshit face." It was the same look she gave Abby anytime she gave a lame explanation, but she was too kind to call her on any of it.

"Did you and Sydney get a lot done today?"

"Quite a lot, actually. You know the shelving units Virginia has—had—against the garage walls? We went through half and made a big donation pile."

"That's wonderful, dear. I never could understand how she could keep all of that stuff neatly organized in her garage. I kept telling her she needed to get rid of it, but she insisted she needed it all."

"We found a lot of Harold's clothes that Syd will donate and some papers she needs to go through, but that's pretty much it so far."

The knock on the door interrupted their discussion, and Abby again ran her hands down her thighs. She stared in the direction of the door, unable to take a step forward.

"Abby, dear, you look nice. Now go answer the door."

Abby's heart thudded with each step she took. She needed to apologize to Syd for her behavior earlier, but when she opened the door and saw Syd standing there looking even more striking in a simple pair of blue jeans and a polo shirt than Abby could've even thought possible, everything she wanted to say flew from her mind. Even if she could've remembered, Syd looked closed off and unreceptive to what Abby would say.

"Abigail, are you going to just stand there or are you going to let her in?"

Abby mentally shook her head and stood aside. "Right. Sorry. Please, come in, Syd. This is my grandmother, Bernice Price."

Syd extended her hand. "It's a pleasure to meet you, Mrs. Price. Thank you for the beef stew you sent over the day I arrived. It was very thoughtful of you."

"You're very welcome, Sydney. Oh, you baked a pie. It looks delicious."

"Yes, ma'am," Syd said as she handed it over.

"Let me just put this in the kitchen and we can go into the living room to talk. Dinner will be ready in ten minutes."

Abby led Syd to the living room and was a little disappointed that Syd chose to sit in a wingback chair rather than on the couch, not giving Abby an opportunity to sit next to her. She felt the wanting to be near Syd, even if it might be three feet away on the other end of the sofa. Abby's grandmother walked in and sat next to her.

"Tell me how things are going, Sydney. What do you think of Virginia's property?"

"It's amazing, Mrs. Price. I didn't know what to expect when her attorney called me, but the house is beautiful and the land is, well, huge." Syd laughed.

"Did you know about your grandmother?"

"Yes, well, not really. I never really met her, and truthfully, I forgot about her and my grandfather until the attorney called me.

My mother filled in some of the blanks, but I'm hoping I can find some answers while I go through her things."

"What kind of answers are you looking for, dear? Maybe I can help."

Syd took a deep breath and clasped her hands together. Abby had an inexplicable urge to go stand next to Syd and hold her hand or place her hand on her shoulder, but she remained still.

"I want to know how they could disown their own daughter because of who she fell in love with. I want to know what made my grandmother hire a private investigator to find me and spy on me. I want to know why, when she found me, why didn't she reach out to me."

Abby's heart broke at what Syd had said. She had no idea that had happened, and she had a hard time believing Virginia could ever do that. It certainly wasn't consistent behavior for the woman she had known. No wonder she never met Syd or her parents, or why they never came to visit.

"Do you know why, Mrs. Price?"

"No, Sydney, I don't know. I asked her about it, but she wouldn't tell me the whole story. She said she was too ashamed and that it never should have happened. I'm sorry I can't answer your questions." Her grandmother stood. "Dinner is just about ready. Abigail, take Sydney into the dining room, please, then help me with the food."

Abby approached her and placed her hand on Syd's forearm. "I'm so sorry. I had no idea."

"It's okay. How could you know?"

"I…"

"Come on. We don't want to keep your grandmother waiting."

Abby understood Syd didn't want to talk about it, at least not yet, and she led her to the dining room. There was so much she wanted to say, to ask, but now was not the time. "Have a seat and we'll be right back." Abby and her grandmother returned with the food and a bottle of wine, and took their places at the table.

"Everything looks delicious, Mrs. Price. Thank you again for inviting me."

"It's my pleasure, Sydney. And please, call me Bernice. It's my understanding you're from Chicago. Have you lived there long?"

"Yes, ma'am. Born and raised. This is so different from Chicago. It's so quiet here and, well, spacious. I live and used to work in downtown so being here has been quite an experience."

"I could see how that would be. I've never been to Chicago myself, but from pictures, movies, and television shows, it looks quite crowded and busy."

"Yes, ma'am, but I love it. There are so many great restaurants and museums. So much to see and do. I could do without the freezing winters, but it's the price you pay to live there."

Abby sat quietly, intent on letting her gran ask the questions. She was having difficulty pulling her gaze away from Syd's full lips as she answered, lips that she had the opportunity to kiss just mere hours ago, but she'd squandered it. It wasn't that Abby wasn't attracted to Syd, because she most certainly was. And it's not like she hadn't had flings before, because she most certainly had. But Syd was going to leave in less than two weeks to go back to Chicago. What was the point in starting something she wouldn't get to finish? And she knew that a time or two with Syd would be like a drug that she would get hooked on and would look to constantly satisfy that craving. Abby had all but resigned herself to the fact that unless she moved to a big city, she would most likely spend the rest of her life alone and be subject to the occasional dalliance when she traveled. Charville wasn't exactly a hotbed for lesbians. Abby refocused to the present and realized that nobody was talking and Syd and her gran were staring at her.

"I'm sorry. What did you say?"

Her grandmother looked at Abby quizzically. "I asked if you were feeling all right. You haven't touched anything on your plate."

"I'm okay, Gran. Sorry." Abby cut a piece of meat covered with gravy and closed her eyes when the deliciousness of her gran's pot roast hit her tongue. "It's wonderful." Abby started paying more attention to her dinner while continuing to listen to their conversation.

"Do you go to museums a lot, Sydney?" her grandmother asked.

"Occasionally. I work for a youth center, and we sometimes take them on fieldtrips to museums or other similar activities to expose them to the arts. We've been to some concerts and musicals. The kids really seem to enjoy it, and it gives me joy to be able to do that for them."

"It's so important to do the things that we love or have always wanted to do. We don't know how much time we have in this life."

Abby noticed the melancholy on her gran's face with that last statement. She knew firsthand that life was too short. Some people had the privilege of living long, fulfilling lives. Others left too soon. Once her grandmother was gone, Abby would have no one special left in her life. She cleared her throat and stood to clear the table. The thought of losing her gran was too much to bear so soon after losing Virginia. It wasn't anything she wanted to think about, especially in the presence of Syd. "I'll put a pot of coffee on to have with dessert and clean the kitchen."

Syd noticed the sad look on Abby's face as she cleared the table and her gaze followed Abby into the kitchen. "I think I'll help Abby with the dishes if you don't mind, ma'am."

Bernice nodded and Syd came up behind Abby and heard her sniff. When Syd arrived earlier she was still feeling irked with the way Abby left, but she forgot her ill feelings when Abby reached up and looked like she was wiping away a tear.

"Abby," Syd said quietly, not wanting to startle her. Abby turned and Syd saw the fresh tracks of tears on her cheeks.

"Syd, I…" Abby turned away and wiped her face.

Syd stepped toward her and placed her hand on the small of Abby's back. "What's wrong? Why are you crying?"

Abby turned to face Syd after she turned off the water that was filling the sink. "I was just thinking about what Gran said, that we never know how much time we have." Abby wiped her hands on the dish towel and hung it back up.

"Do you want to talk about it?"

Abby gave her a watery smile. "Not tonight. I want us to enjoy the rest of our evening. I'm sorry about earlier, for leaving so quickly."

Syd tilted her head in question. She wanted to talk about earlier, but she wasn't expecting Abby to bring it up. "Why did you?"

"I thought you might kiss me and I freaked out."

"I see. I'm sorry if I overstepped, and I did intend to kiss you, but I won't again. I thought you might be attracted to me like I am to you."

"Oh, Syd. That's not the issue. You're going back home in less than two weeks, so why don't we just stay friends and work on cleaning out Virginia's?"

Syd took a tentative step forward and wiped an errant tear off Abby's cheek with the pad of her thumb. "Is that what we are? Friends?"

Abby barely nodded and licked her lips. Syd wanted badly to lean a little closer and claim Abby's mouth, but she kissed her cheek instead, lingering a little longer than she probably should've. "Okay," Syd said huskily. "Friends it is."

Syd pulled her shoulders back and stood taller. Now that she knew it wasn't because of Syd's race that stopped Abby from kissing her earlier, her heart felt a lot lighter than it did just a few minutes ago, but still, it was a shame that Abby wasn't looking for a little fun over the next couple of weeks. Syd certainly could have used the distraction and release from all the stress she'd been feeling over the past few days. "Where's the silverware? I'll dish out the pie while you get the coffee." Syd took out Bernice's piece of pie and coffee to her in the living room and returned with her own followed by Abby.

"Sydney, this pie is delicious. Do you get a chance to cook or bake often?"

"I do now that I work more regular hours. When I worked as an investment banker, I worked really long hours and I didn't have much time for anything else. I would cook on the weekends and pack those meals up for lunch and dinner during the week."

"You took your dinner to work?" Abby asked after she sipped her coffee.

"Yes. It wasn't uncommon for me to leave the office around midnight. Working at the center, I still work late, but I get home at a more reasonable time."

"What made you leave investment banking? You must have had to go to school for a long time to get in that field. Not that working with children isn't important, but to go through all that college for nothing."

"Grandma!" Abby exclaimed. "What's with the third degree?"

Syd laughed and held up her hand. "It's fine, Abby. I have my bachelor's in finance and an MBA, all from the University of Illinois at Chicago. I did an internship at the firm I worked with up until a couple of years ago, and they were impressed enough to hire me after graduation. I worked very hard to get where I was," she said proudly.

"My former firm had sponsored the youth center I'm with now in a city-wide athletics competition, and that was my first exposure to working with the kids. I began to volunteer on Saturdays, and I started to feel much happier when I was there. It wasn't that I was unhappy where I was, but working at the center gave me a fulfillment that working in investments didn't. I wanted to make more of a difference in the world, and I feel like I finally am. Although I'm no longer using my college degrees, they are something nobody can ever take away from me. Besides, they'll come in handy again one day because I plan to open my own center."

"That's wonderful. I think it's very important that we can do something we love, and we can make a difference in people's lives. Abigail got her degree in creative writing from Iowa State. I'm very proud of my granddaughter."

"I can see that, ma'am, as you should be. Abby has really helped me out this week, and I hope we remain friends," Syd said as she smiled at Abby. The blush creeping up Abby's face was adorable, and Syd fought hard to stay seated rather than kissing Abby senseless. It wasn't too difficult of a fight though since Abby already told Syd her wishes. And what would Bernice think if she knew of Syd's lascivious thoughts about her granddaughter? Time to make a break for it.

"Bernice, it was a pleasure to meet you and I'd like to invite you and Abby for dinner in a few days after I've gotten things a little more cleaned up around the house."

Bernice surprised Syd by giving her a warm hug. "We'd love that, dear."

Syd looked to Abby, who had her hands full with dessert plates. "Would you like help with those?"

"No, but thank you. Would you like my help again tomorrow?"

"I'd love it if you don't have other plans."

"No plans. I'll be over after I'm done with my chores."

"Great. I'll see you then. Good night, and thank you again for tonight."

Syd thought about her evening as she got into bed. Already she adored Bernice and looked forward to spending more time with her. More importantly, she looked forward to spending more time with Abby. It was going to be a long ten days trying to keep her libido tamped down around Abby, but she would respect her wishes and try to concentrate on getting this house ready to sell.

## Chapter Eight

S yd was in the kitchen the next morning pulling a pan of banana nut muffins out of the oven when she heard a loud noise outside. She opened the back door to see a guy unloading a large dumpster next to the garage.

"Excuse me, I didn't order this," Syd said, although she had been meaning to.

"Abigail Price ordered it, ma'am," the guy yelled over the whining of the motor.

"I thought I'd get this out here today since we're making a lot of headway going through Virginia's things," Abby said as she walked up the driveway.

Syd turned around to find Abby smiling and walking toward her. When she stopped within a foot of Syd, she wanted to hug Abby for her thoughtfulness—and to feel Abby's body up against her. Syd wasn't normally so tactile with people she hardly knew, but she had a constant wanting to touch Abby anywhere and everywhere. She shoved her hands in her pockets to avoid making a fool of herself by making an unwanted advance.

"How much do I owe you?"

"Nothing. I'm taking care of it since you gifted us with the best apple pie we've ever tasted."

Syd wanted to argue, but she couldn't when Abby was so close to her that it made her want to do anything but argue. It made her want to take Abby into her arms and kiss her like she'd never been kissed then take her upstairs and have sex with her all day and all night. But not argue. "Thank you. And in that case, wait until you taste the banana nut muffins I just pulled out of the oven."

Abby made herself at home in the kitchen by pulling out a coffee mug, placing it on the counter next to Syd's empty cup, and filling them both. Syd appreciated how comfortable Abby seemed to be in the house.

They sat at the table, and the moan that came from Abby when she bit into the steaming muffin made Syd's stomach flip over a few times. She watched Abby chewing slowly with her eyes closed. Syd wouldn't mind sitting here all day staring at her. Hell, she'd bake a kitchen full of muffins if it meant bringing as much pleasure to Abby as she'd seemed to have at that moment. Syd cleared her throat and took a sip of the scalding coffee, hot enough to clear the images of her taking Abby in her arms and kissing her until they were both gasping for breath.

"I really appreciate your help, Abby. I'm sure you have other things you could be doing with your time."

"Nothing pressing," Abby replied as she smiled. "We can finish up in the garage, and if we have time, we can work on another room in the house."

Somehow, with Abby's help, Syd didn't feel as overwhelmed with all of the stuff she needed to go through. Abby would know what to donate, what to throw away, and what to keep. They resumed where they left off the day before after putting the trash in the dumpster. Box by box, they had added to the donation pile and to the trash, but the pile of items to keep hadn't grown much. Syd opened a plastic bin and found many framed photos of her mother and grandparents. She pulled each one out and studied the photos carefully.

"What is it?"

Syd held up a photo of her mother when she appeared to be in her late teens. She had her arm around her father and both of them were laughing. "I just don't understand, Abby. Look at them." Syd showed Abby the picture. "I can't believe this came to an end all because my grandparents didn't want my mama marrying my daddy."

"Are you sure that's the reason?"

Syd looked up at Abby. "What do you mean?"

Abby shrugged. "Maybe your mother said or did something that upset your grandparents. I didn't know your grandfather well, but I never heard your grandmother say a racist thing, and I spent a lot of time with her."

Syd stood up so fast that it made Abby stumble back a few steps. Syd moved closer to Abby and pointed at her, her internal body temperature rising. "The only thing my mama did was fall in love with a black man. It's not her fault that her parents couldn't accept that fact, and I don't appreciate you insinuating otherwise. You weren't there. I was, and I saw how Harold spoke to my parents. He had no interest in meeting me or getting to know me because I was the product of an interracial marriage." Syd wiped the tears off her face and ran into the house. She filled a glass of water and took sips in between the deep breaths to calm herself. How dare Abby blame her mama. She didn't know her parents and how loving and accepting they are. Her mama would never say a hateful thing about anyone.

"Syd?"

She hadn't heard the back door open or Abby's footsteps, and she didn't turn around when she heard Abby's voice. "Go away, Abby." She felt her tears return to her eyes and wiped them away. She was hurt but also embarrassed that she had lost control of her anger so quickly. The tears came faster when she felt Abby place her hands on Syd's shoulders.

"I'm so sorry that Harold behaved that way, and I'm even sorrier that you didn't get to know Virginia. After spending the past few days with you, I'm certain she would've been crazy about you. I wish you didn't experience racism at all, but especially as a little girl, at a time when we're full of innocence and joy."

Syd turned, wrapped her arms around Abby, and cried into her shoulder.

Abby's heart ached for Syd and she tightened her hold. She hadn't experienced racism, but that didn't mean she hadn't experienced cruelty of some kind. Shortly after her parents died, she started school in a new town where she didn't know any of the kids. Two little girls had befriended her, and while they stood by Abby, some of the other kids had somehow found out that she was an orphan and they made fun of her. Kids could be such assholes. Her two friends stuck up for her, and eventually the rest of the kids settled down until something else they could make fun of came along.

Abby did know what it was like to be different. She found herself kissing Syd's temple and cradling the back of her head with her hand. She knew she shouldn't be doing such an intimate act to Syd. Abby was the one who told her she just wanted to be friends, and Abby intended the kiss to be one of comfort, but when Syd lifted her head to look at Abby, and her eyes dropped to Abby's lips, she couldn't help herself from lowering her head and gently kissing Syd's mouth. The kiss was chaste, and Syd made no further move to continue the kiss. Abby wasn't sure if she was relieved or disappointed, but she knew she needed to step back and get some space between them.

"Why don't I fix us lunch, and if you're feeling up to it afterward, we'll finish up the garage."

Abby was grateful when Syd nodded and said she'd be right back. She made some sandwiches and cut up some fruit, and lunch was waiting at the table by the time Syd returned. She watched Syd fiddle with her napkin, anticipating that Syd had something to say, and she waited her out.

"I'm sorry I yelled," Syd said as she continued to look down like a punished child.

Abby placed her hand on Syd's arm and waited for her to make eye contact. "Apology accepted," she said with a small smile. Abby was relieved when Syd picked up her sandwich and took a bite. She followed suit, and they eventually made their way back out to the garage. Abby stood by silently as she watched Syd take the box of pictures and place them to the side. Syd had remained fairly quiet over the next couple of hours with the exception of answering a question every so often. When they finished with the garage, Abby noticed the sun starting to lower and she had an idea.

"I think we've done enough work for today. Come on, I want to show you something."

Syd didn't say anything, but she followed Abby out of the garage and to a path that circled the pond on the property. They stopped at a bench on the east side to watch the sun set in the west. They sat there quietly with no other sound other than their breathing and crickets chirping. Syd sat ramrod straight with her hands on her thighs and Abby could feel the tension vibrating off of Syd. She reached out and placed her hand over Syd's. She felt Syd flinch which only made Abby curl her fingers around Syd's hands.

"Your grandmother used to come out here a lot. She said it was a scenic and peaceful place to reflect, especially when the flowers were in bloom and the sun shone on the water. I once asked her what she thought about when she looked like she was a million miles away, and she said her family. She didn't expand and I didn't press. When I would see her sitting in this spot, all I wanted to do was come sit next to her and be a source of comfort, but I never did. I wasn't sure if I was afraid of intruding on her time or if she would shoo me away. I don't want to make that same mistake with you, Syd. I'm here to listen if you want to talk about it. If you want to cry, I'll be your shoulder. And if you just want to sit here quietly to watch the sunset, I hope you'll allow me to join you and hold your hand."

They sat there quietly as the blue sky turned into vibrant oranges, pinks, and purples. Abby startled when Syd began to speak.

"When I was four, my mama, daddy, and I traveled here from Chicago so I could meet my grandparents. I was so excited, I couldn't sit still in the backseat."

Abby grinned at the visual of a young Syd bouncing in her seat.

"Mama knocked on the door and Harold answered. He did not look happy to see us, and to be honest, he frightened me. He told us we weren't welcome and he'd throw us off his property if he had to. I remember Virginia standing behind him, crying, looking like she wanted to say something. But she didn't. She just stood there and watched us drive away. That was my first encounter with racism and I had no idea why Harold didn't want us."

Syd tilted her head until it rested on Abby's shoulder. She lifted her arm to allow Syd to get closer, and Abby wrapped her arm around Syd's shoulders, holding her tightly against her.

"Mama was so upset and she had to try to explain to her four-year-old child that her daddy didn't want us because my daddy was black. How is a four-year-old supposed to understand that, Abby?"

Abby rested her chin on the top of Syd's head. "I don't know, sweetheart. It's not something anyone should have to understand, and I'm so sorry you had to experience it at all, let alone as a child. I've never been able to understand why some people can't look past the color of skin, or religion, or sexuality. Underneath it all, we all bleed the same color. We're all human and we should treat each other with respect."

As the sky turned darker and the silence ensued, Abby gave Syd one final squeeze and stood. "We better get back before we can't see our hand in front of our face."

Syd stood and reached for Abby's hand, threading their fingers. "Is this all right?"

Abby nodded and she squeezed Syd's hand. As they reached the back door, Syd turned to Abby with their hands still linked. "Would you like to have dinner with me?"

Abby knew she should say no. She felt her affection and attraction for Syd growing the more time they spent together, but the idea of leaving now, when Syd looked so sad and vulnerable, had Abby saying yes. "Only if I get to help."

After dinner, Syd and Abby refilled their wine glasses and sat in the living room. It had been an emotional day for Syd, and she should be exhausted to the point of not being able to keep her eyes open, yet she felt energized while she cooked with Abby. They moved about the kitchen like a well choreographed dance, passing each other while one removed the pots and pans and the other retrieved the food from the refrigerator. They resumed their dance after dinner when they cleaned the kitchen. Syd wasn't used to sharing a kitchen with anyone, but doing it with Abby had given her pleasure. It was nice to have someone to talk to as she prepped the food.

Her home life was one of solitude because of her long work hours at the youth center. When she did have anyone over to her condo, it was usually just Vanessa or her parents. Her home was sacred to her in that it was the one place she could unwind with cooking, having an occasional drink, and reading. She didn't want to disturb her space with people she wasn't particularly close to. Even when she had sex with other women, it was always done at the other's place, and she never spent the night. She usually met her friends for dinner or drinks, and sometimes dancing on Saturday nights, but she never invited them to her home. She wondered what Abby would think of her place. Would she love the views from her living room and bedroom windows? Would she like being in the city amongst the tall, crowded buildings and the throngs of people? Or would she feel caged in, not having the wide-open plains she was used to in Iowa? Syd wondered if Abby would want to come visit her in Chicago, and at that moment, she realized that Abby was becoming an important person in her life. Her thoughts were interrupted when she heard the clink of Abby setting her wine glass on the table.

"How long have you been working with the kids?"

"Hmm. Overall, close to ten years now, I think. I've been working there full-time for about two years."

"How did you get started?"

"There's a competition every year with the different community centers in Chicago and the surrounding areas. Kind of like a smaller version of an Olympics of some sort. The kids compete in games, obstacle courses, sporting events, that sort of thing. The company I worked for is a sponsor, and a lot of us volunteered at the event keeping score, handing out water and snacks. The first year I did it, I loved it so much, seeing the kids laugh, compete, show sportsmanship, that I didn't want to get involved just once a year. I wanted to do it all the time."

"That's very admirable of you."

"I don't think so. I love seeing the kids and doing things with them that they might not otherwise get to do. They think of me as a big sister, someone they can be themselves with, someone they can talk to. I'd love to start a program that the kids can go to every day that will help keep them off the streets and give them the confidence and ability to strive for something better. I want them to learn life skills, like how to write a résumé and interview for jobs. I want them to have tutoring available, not just for studying, but also help with filling out college applications. I was fortunate to have two parents who work in the education system and were home at night to eat as a family and they could help me with my homework. They went to my basketball games and track meets, and kept me too busy to get into any kind of trouble."

Abby joined Syd in laughing, and Syd knew she had been grinning from ear-to-ear talking about the kids. She loved them and appreciated them, and she would do anything to keep them safe and help them succeed.

"But the kids I work with don't have the same luxury I did. A lot of them are being raised in single-parent homes, some of the parents have to work two or three jobs to make ends meet, and they aren't home a lot. Most of them do what they can to take care of their children, but kids need supervision, someone to be in charge, to make rules and stick to them. Otherwise, they flounder. They're not old enough to know better, even though a few would argue they know enough," Syd said wryly. "I just want to help them be responsible, productive members in our society. I want them to know that I care what happens to them."

Syd looked up from the half-full wine glass she'd been staring into to the see the tears in Abby's eyes threatening to spill. "What's wrong?"

Abby wiped her eyes and cleared her throat. "Absolutely nothing. I just really admire your dedication, and I wish I could do something similar, but there really isn't anything like that here. I volunteer at the animal shelter in town twice a month, but I'd like to do more. I want to make a difference."

"What do you do at the animal shelter?"

Abby waved her hand as if she was dismissing her duties. "Whatever needs to be done. Cleaning out the kennels, taking the dogs out to play, that sort of thing." Abby didn't mention that she anonymously donated a lot of money to the shelter because it wasn't something she did so she could be recognized, and nobody except her gran and her attorney knew about Abby's trust fund, and that she was worth millions. The money didn't mean anything to her, and she'd gladly give it away to have her parents back. But since that wasn't an option, she put the money to good use. The royalties she received from writing novels provided enough money to live on, especially since she paid off her gran's farm and they were mortgage-free.

Syd reached out and held Abby's hand. "I'm sure you make a huge difference to the dogs, having someone take them out to play."

Abby squeezed Syd's hand and nodded. She wanted the attention off her because she wanted to know more about Syd's work with the kids. "Do you think you'll ever start that program?"

Syd looked down to her lap, and Abby could see her face color. "Actually, I applied for a grant and I'm waiting to see if I get it. I have the money to put a down payment on a small building that I can use for my center. I invested well when I was working in banking and I was able to cash in on enough money to get started. I just hope I can get the grant so I can keep the place running once it opens.

Abby would love to be involved in helping Syd get her project off the ground, but she'd have to wait and see if Syd got her grant. And should Abby tell Syd, or just donate money anonymously like she did to the shelter? "Well, I'll keep my fingers crossed for you." Abby looked at her watch and couldn't believe how late it was. Did they really talk for two hours? "I better get going. It's getting late."

Syd stood and grabbed her keys off the table. "I'll drive you home."

"You don't have to do that. I can just walk."

"Abby, it's dark and I'd worry about you getting home safely."

Abby agreed and slid into the passenger side of Syd's BMW. She felt like she'd been enveloped in a hug. The leather seats were soft and supple, and Abby fell in love with the car immediately. All too quickly, they had arrived to Abby's and she was surprised when Syd turned off the car and exited. She suppressed her grin when she watched Syd make her way to the passenger side and open the door for Abby, and she walked her to the front door.

"I had a great time with you this evening, and I really appreciate your help."

Abby looked into Syd's eyes, and she felt a shift internally. Something had happened. Maybe the emotions of the day had caught up to her, and Abby felt herself being pulled closer to Syd. She slowly took a step, then another until she was mere inches away from Syd. Just a little farther and Abby's mouth could be on Syd's, exploring, tasting, soaring high. The night was silent except for the faint sound of crickets chirping in the distance. The air felt thick and hot between them. Syd closed the distance, and at the last second, she placed a gentle, sweet, chivalrous kiss on Abby's cheek. Abby stood frozen in time, eyes closed, and Syd's scent wafting through her nose. Syd's warm cheek pressed against hers, and Abby never wanted this moment to end. She despised the internal tug-of-war that was going on. One part of her wanted to step back and reiterate that she and Syd could only be friends. The other part wanted to pull Syd against her so there was no space between them and kiss her breathless. She wanted Syd to take her back to Virginia's—Syd's— and make love to her all night long. God, she finally met a woman she was attracted to and felt a connection with, a woman she'd come to admire, and she lived six hours away.

Syd cupped Abby's cheek and sighed. "Sweet dreams, Abby."

Abby watched Syd turn and walk back to her car. She wanted to yell at Syd to wait. She wanted to run to her, jump in the car, and go with Syd. But all she could do was watch the taillights fade in the distance.

# CHAPTER NINE

Syd was sitting at the kitchen table sipping her coffee and picking at a leftover muffin contemplating what project she was going to tackle next. With the sewing room empty and the garage cleaned out, she was ready to move to the next room. Thanks to Abby and her hard work, Syd felt she was ahead of schedule. She still had the two living rooms and Virginia's room to go through, but she was relieved to be done with the garage. They managed to fill up about two-thirds of the dumpster, but she didn't want to call the company to come get it before it was as full as she could get it. She was guessing by the time she had the house cleaned out, it would be ready for pickup.

Syd looked out the sliding glass door to the pond. There was a little breeze that rippled the water. The sun was still low in the sky, and the last of the orange and pink dawn was dissipating. She thought back to last night of Abby standing on her porch in the moonlight, looking almost angelic. Syd's desire to take Abby in her arms, taste Abby's lips on hers, was overwhelming, but Abby's words took root in Syd's brain. Abby had no wish to fool around with someone who wasn't going to be staying. Syd understood, but she'd be lying if she didn't say she was disappointed. Abby was so different from the other women Syd slept with. They were typically professional women who wore makeup, dressed in business suits or dresses, and drove expensive, fancy cars. They were also women that Syd connected with only superficially. Abby was a far cry from those other women. She had a natural beauty with sun-kissed skin and a sparkle in her eyes, a face that would look good with light makeup, but probably looked better without it. She was adorably goofy, down-to-earth, not afraid to work hard or get dirty, and she had a huge heart. If circumstances and geography were different, Abby would be the type of woman Syd would date, seriously date, to see if it would lead to something more.

She was certain Vanessa would like her and approve of her. Her parents would too. But would Abby leave her grandmother? Her farm? Syd shook her head and chuckled. Wasn't she getting a smidge ahead of herself? Wondering if Abby would like living in Chicago? Syd watched the sun climb higher in the sky as she took a sip of her coffee. She thought more of Abby in Chicago, and the hours Syd worked. It wasn't like she would have a lot of time to spend with Abby because she would be busy getting the after-school program off the ground. And how would Abby make a living in Chicago? It wasn't exactly cheap to live there. What did Abby do for money anyway? Did she even have a job? Syd didn't think so since she'd spent all day helping Syd for the last four days. She realized that she really didn't know much about her, but she wanted to know everything.

Syd checked her watch and was surprised how late it was getting. She'd risen before the sun and fed the chickens as the sky was just turning light before showering and having breakfast. Abby hadn't mentioned anything about coming over to help today, and the last thing Syd wanted to do was assume that Abby would always be available to help her sort through Virginia's things. The text notification made Syd pull her phone out of her pocket and smile when she saw Abby's name.

*I'm volunteering at the shelter today so I can't come over. Sorry I forgot to tell you last night. Talk soon.*

Hmm. There was something strange about that text. Something…short. Unlike Abby. Syd hoped Abby was all right. She typed back her reply.

*No worries. Have fun with the animals.*

Syd sent the text then thought of something else.

*I'd like to have you and your grandmother over for dinner tomorrow night. Please let me know if you're available.*

Abby texted back that she would get back to her and let her know about dinner. Syd decided to take the day off from cleaning out the house since some everyday chores were in order. She would make a trip into town for more groceries, and she needed to wash her clothes. It wouldn't hurt to vacuum and dust the house either. Suddenly, Syd was feeling very domesticated. She was actually looking forward to her chores and errands today.

She took her time driving to town and paid attention to the landscape she didn't notice when she arrived less than a week ago. This really was a picturesque part of the country—mostly flat land with an occasional rolling hill. Green fields of grass and tall stalks of corn occupied some of the land. Farmhouses, barns, and silos were the primary buildings on the properties. Syd had the windows down and felt the warm spring breeze brush across her face. She inhaled deeply and tried to identify the scents—cut grass, hay, earth. Something about the combination of smells, or maybe the deep breaths, was relaxing to Syd.

She decided to park near the courthouse so she would have the opportunity to inspect the historic building more closely. After circling the building, she took a seat on one of the few benches that were shaded by a large white oak tree and protected her from the high-noon sun. There was a smattering of acorns on the ground and a few squirrels that displayed no fear of humans and were too busy collecting the acorns to be bothered.

Syd rose and started walking down the nearest street that seemed to head into town. Gone were the men and women dressed sharply at the courthouse, replaced by more casual dressers. Every person she passed said hello or wished her a nice day. So different from walking the streets in downtown Chicago. She came across an old-fashioned soda shop and diner. Curiosity—and hunger—lured her in the diner. She nearly laughed when she spotted the soda jerk behind the counter dressed all in white with a black belt, black bow tie, and a white paper hat. With every passing day, Syd was becoming more charmed with the town and its residents. He smiled at her as she sat on a stool at the counter.

"Good afternoon, ma'am. What can I get you today?"

Syd quickly perused the menu and asked for a bacon cheeseburger, fries, and an Oreo cookie shake. She usually ate healthier meals, but being in a place like that, she needed to experience the food culture. She looked around and noticed old license plates from different states, framed posters of old Coca-Cola ads, tin signs advertising fifteen-cent hot dogs and five-cent Moon Pies. She saw a vintage jukebox against the wall near the entrance to the bathrooms, and when she listened closely, she could hear an old Elvis tune coming from the speaker. It wasn't so loud that you couldn't have a conversation, but it provided a nice background noise.

Syd was quite sure her eyes bugged out when the soda jerk placed her lunch in front of her. The burger was stacked high with lettuce, tomato, and onion, and she could see the steam rising from the piping hot fries. The shake was poured into an old-fashioned malt glass with a dollop of whipped cream and a cherry on top. The remainder of the shake was in a frosted stainless steel malt cup. She had no idea if she could open her mouth wide enough to take a bite of her burger, but she was certainly going to try. She reached for the red ketchup bottle and squirted some on the bun and next to her fries. She picked up the burger and noted the guy behind the counter watching her, and she smiled at him right before she took a bite. He nodded as if he approved of the bite size, and he resumed wiping down the counter. It took Syd a while to finish her burger, having to stop occasionally to give her jaw a rest from chewing. She used that down time to wash the food down with her shake. By the time her plate was clean and her cup empty, Syd wondered how she was going to finish running her errands when all she wanted to do was go back to the farm and take a nap. She settled her bill, said good-bye to the guy behind the counter, and hoped a stroll through town would help settle her food.

Syd spent the next two hours in and out of shops, looking at anything and everything from books, to candles, to clothing, to candy. There was something to be said about the smaller mom-and-pop shops. The employees and managers were very attentive, asking where she was from, giving her a little history of the town and their store. It was evident to Syd that the town folk were proud of where they lived and the work they did. She was thoroughly enjoying her time in town, but she really did miss Chicago. She missed her parents and Vanessa. But what she really missed, and what she couldn't wait to get back to, were the kids she worked with. She'd been gone less than a week and she already missed them. The only thing that had made this trip worth it was meeting Abby and Bernice.

She thought about them as she drove to the store. She wanted to make them a special dinner to thank them for the help and kindness they'd shown her. What to make? Syd knew they ate meat since Bernice made pot roast the other night. Maybe something Italian? If she were home, she'd have the necessary equipment to make homemade pasta noodles, and she refused to buy store-bought. Besides, spaghetti was kind of boring, she thought as she mentally went through the Italian dishes she knew. She decided on an Italian meatloaf, salad, and garlic bread. As she stood in line, Syd noticed how full her cart was and thought she might have bought too much food. Well, she'd just have to ask Abby if she was interested in eating more meals with her. Syd smiled at the thought of them sitting at the table, eating dinner, drinking wine, and getting to know each other better.

Syd put away the groceries, started a load of laundry, and began cleaning the house. She took her time dusting the shelves and picture frames in the living room, and she studied each photo closely, trying to commit them to memory. The pictures of her grandparents and mama seemed like it was a happy time for Harold, Virginia, and Jillian Adams. Syd couldn't remember ever seeing a picture of her mama when she was young, but looking at those photos, Syd realized how striking she was, even at a young age. Virginia was also very attractive, and Syd now knew where her mama got her delicate bone structure. Their eyes and nose were similarly shaped, and they both had high cheekbones and lighter colored hair. Harold, on the other hand, was a large man, towering over Virginia by a good foot or so, and solidly built. Yes, they were a good-looking family in the earlier photos.

The later photos, though, told a different story. Pictures of Harold and Virginia when they looked to be in their late fifties or early sixties. Harold looked indifferent, yet almost angry. Virginia looked lost, maybe sad. There was a vacant look in her eyes, and anyone looking at those pictures could see the distance between them, physically and emotionally. The earlier pictures showed them with their arms around each other, Virginia snuggling into Harold's side. But the later ones showed them standing apart. Syd felt like Virginia couldn't get far enough away from Harold. Obviously, the latter pictures were taken after Syd's parents were together. Could that be the reason? Was Virginia regretful that they expelled Syd's mama from their family? What was Virginia's role in that whole debacle?

Housecleaning forgotten, Syd put down the rag and opened the cabinet doors under the bookshelves. One cabinet held dishes, but at a closer look, Syd realized it was china. She pulled out a white dinner plate that had a gold rim. Simple yet elegant. She put the plate back and opened the middle door. There she found a wooden box that held silverware and crystal water and wine glasses. For a woman who lived on a farm, Virginia had some pretty pricey place settings, and Syd realized her misconception. Just because someone lived on a farm didn't mean they didn't have good taste in the finer things. The final cabinet revealed photo albums, and Syd pulled one out. She sat on the floor in front of the cabinet turning page after page of photos of her mama and grandparents. Her mama's childhood was chronicled from the time she was born to when she was starting college. The transformation of a young, blond-haired, hazel-eyed child dressed in frilly dresses to an awkward teenager in jeans and flannel shirts working on the farm or fishing with her father at their pond. Prom pictures of her mama wearing a fancy dress, makeup, and hair styled for the times. Syd relished seeing her mama in the different stages of her childhood. She had already decided she was going to bring these home.

Syd looked at her watch when the room started to darken, and she was amazed to realize she'd spent over two hours going through the albums. She placed them back in the cabinet, stood, and stretched, making her back and joints pop and crack in relief. She checked her phone and was disappointed there wasn't a text from Abby. Was she still at the shelter, or was she home having dinner with Bernice? She decided to text Abby, just to say hi. She missed her.

*I hope you had a great day. I spent some time in town, ate an amazing cheeseburger for lunch, and found Virginia's photo albums. Can't wait to show you. Are we on for dinner tomorrow night?*

❖

Abby checked her phone when the text notification came up from Syd. She'd had a great morning at the animal shelter, taking the dogs for walks and playing fetch with them in the fenced yard behind the building. This weekend was an adoption event, and she hoped some, if not all, the dogs would find their forever homes. Abby was hoping to be there Saturday to help with paperwork and other miscellaneous things they might need her to do, although she hadn't made a commitment to be there.

When she got home earlier that afternoon, she ate a quick lunch, then headed to her office to work on her latest manuscript. She'd been neglectful in her writing since Syd had been in town, but she didn't regret the time she'd spent with her. Abby enjoyed getting to know more about her, hearing about the work she did with the kids, eating the delicious food she'd prepared. And if Abby were being completely honest, it didn't hurt that Sydney Carter was very easy on the eyes with a lean body and subtle womanly curves in her hips—hips that Abby could hold to pull her closer into her own body. Abby could feel the heat rising in all her essential areas and thought about taking a cold shower to cool down. Taking a break from being around Syd today enabled Abby to get things back into perspective. Last night, she'd wanted Syd to kiss her. She'd wanted to go back to Syd's and see where the night took them, but she knew she'd want more, and that just wasn't possible since she would be going home to Chicago in a little over a week.

Abby already felt more for Syd than the women whose names she never remembered that she'd slept with in whatever town she was in for her latest book promotion. Every trip was the same. She'd arrive at a bookstore—big chain or independently owned, it didn't matter. She'd do a five- to seven-minute reading, answer some questions from the audience members, then sign some books. She would then have dinner with her publicist, discuss the evening and future events, then go back to her hotel room. She'd change from her slacks and heels to her jeans and boots, and head to the local lesbian bar. Abby would order a vodka tonic and sit at the bar while looking for a woman she could dance with and possibly go back to her hotel room to have a sex-filled night. She would order them breakfast from room service the next morning, say good-bye to the previous night's date, shower, dress, and head to the airport to go back home. Back to the farm and her gran. For a long time, that had been enough. She'd usually have a book event every weekend for the first two months after her latest release, then it would ease up to one weekend a month. But lately, she'd been wanting more than a one-night stand.

Abby was approaching her mid thirties, and she'd started thinking more about settling down, maybe starting a family. She just wasn't sure how that was going to happen since she had no plans to leave her farm or her grandmother. In her perfect world, Syd would stay in Iowa, keep Virginia's farm, and maybe they could live together, sharing everything, including her money. She had enough to live a couple of lifetimes without ever having to work, and she and Syd could spend their days riding horses, maybe restocking the pond so they could fish, have dinner every night with her grandmother, then fall asleep after making love. It sounded nice, but Abby had to bring herself back to reality.

Abby opened the text and wrote back.

*Gran and I will be there. Can't wait to see the pics.*

Abby set her phone down and resumed her typing on the laptop.

## CHAPTER TEN

Abby slept restlessly, thinking about Syd, thinking about her work in progress, thinking about Virginia and her gran. How was a girl supposed to get a good night's sleep when thoughts were pushing and shoving to gain supremacy? She knew what she needed to do today. She needed to sit at her computer and type some words, but she felt clogged, like there were too many thoughts in her head that she couldn't pick just one and run with it. She stood in front of her bedroom window and watched the sunrise. Was Syd awake yet? Was she enjoying the sunrise too? Syd had mentioned finding some photo albums yesterday, and Abby wondered how much progress she had made on the house. She shook her head as if that would dispel Syd from her thoughts. She knew what would though, Abby thought as she looked to the stable. Riding her horse had a calming effect on her, and she always felt she regained clarity after a ride.

She quickly dressed and poured coffee into a travel mug to drink as she got her American quarter horse, Bevin, ready to ride. The seven-year-old brown gelding nickered as Abby approached him, and she offered him an apple. She took some time loving on him and speaking softly. "Are you ready to really stretch your legs today, big guy?" Abby exercised and groomed him every day, but her rides had been shortened since she'd been helping Syd. But today was all hers, and she intended to get Bevin running and clear her thoughts. Abby loved it when she could kill two birds with one stone. She groomed and tacked him before leading him out of the stable. She promised Virginia's horse, Pokey, also a quarter, that she'd be back for her later as she fed her the other apple she brought with her. Pokey was almost twenty years old and didn't require as much exercise as Bevin, just a stroll around their ten-acre property.

She climbed into the saddle and took the reins, leading him along the trail she usually took. Once he was warmed up, she moved him into a trot, then a gallop. Abby could feel her cheeks begin to ache from her smile, and the wind blew through her hair as they made their way across the property. She brought Bevin to a halt on top of a hill near Virginia's property, and she saw in the distance Syd walking across the yard to the barn. Abby should just turn around and go home. She needed to spend the rest of her day writing. Besides, she would see Syd later for dinner. Ah, hell. A short visit wouldn't hurt anything. She and Bevin made their way down the hill, around the pond, and had just made their way to the barn when Syd came walking out. Abby tried to hold back a laugh when Syd jumped once she saw Bevin.

"Jesus Christ! You scared the shit out of me."

"I'm sorry," Abby said while giggling. "Bevin and I went for a ride this morning, and when I saw you come out to the barn, we decided to come say hi."

Abby watched Syd as she slowly stepped back away from the horse. She dismounted and held the reins as she extended her hand toward Syd. "Come here and say hi to my big guy."

"No, that's okay. I'll say hi from right here."

"C'mon, Syd. He's the gentlest animal you could ever see. I promise you'll be okay."

Syd looked at Abby skeptically.

"I promise," Abby said as she extended her hand again.

Syd took a tentative step toward Abby, then another and reached for Abby's hand. Abby gently pulled Syd next to her and put Syd's hand on Bevin's neck.

"Here. He likes his neck rubbed." Abby stepped behind Syd and placed her hand over Syd's to guide her. She felt a shiver then warmth flooded her entire body. Being this close to Syd was a very bad idea, but Abby did nothing to move away. She spoke softly next to Syd's ear. "See? He likes it. Nothing to be afraid of." Abby could've sworn she felt Syd lean back a little, and Abby yearned for contact.

"Do you want to go for a little ride?"

Syd spun around and looked at Abby incredulously. "On that?" she asked as she pointed her thumb over her shoulder.

"Yep. I promise to take it slow. All you have to do is sit in the saddle, hold onto the horn, and I'll lead him with the reins." Abby placed her hand on Syd's shoulder and caressed it down her arm. "You can trust me."

Abby saw something flicker in Syd's eyes. It could have been desire, but maybe that was projection on Abby's part. The slight nod Syd gave Abby thrilled her inside, and she felt a slight buzz. She figured it couldn't have been easy for Syd to agree to that. Just as Syd had told her she'd never seen chickens up close, she probably hadn't seen horses up close either.

"All right," Abby said as she squeezed Syd's hand. "Place your foot in the stirrup, grab onto the horn, and pull yourself up." Abby stood behind with her hand on Syd's hips to aid in the process. Syd settled in the saddle and again looked at Abby like she was questioning her sanity. "All you have to do is sit there and look pretty." Did she just say that out loud? Pretty wasn't the word she'd consider for Syd sitting high in the saddle, her legs straddling the wide girth of Bevin's midsection. Sexy. That was it. Syd looked incredibly sexy, and Abby felt the ratchet of arousal climb higher. Abby cleared her throat and felt her face on fire, along with a few other parts of her body a little lower. "I mean, um, Bevin and I will do all the work."

Abby led Bevin for a leisurely stroll around the pond, frequently looking back at Syd to make sure she was doing well. By the time they were halfway around the pond, Syd looked like she was a little more relaxed, and her body moved in sync with every step Bevin took. Abby smiled to herself as they finished up and arrived back to the barn. Abby looked up at Syd, sitting up high on Bevin, looking like she'd done that a thousand times before and it was where she belonged. Abby cleared the lump that had suddenly formed in her throat.

"So, what did you think?"

"It was actually fun," Syd responded as she leaned forward and stroked Bevin's neck.

"You want to try riding by yourself next time?"

"Now you're pushing it, Ms. Price."

Abby laughed. "I told you I have Virginia's horse in my stable. Her name is Pokey and she called her that for a reason. Think about it and if you change your mind, let me know."

Abby instructed Syd on dismounting, and she stood close to help her down. Syd jumped down and placed her hands on Abby's shoulders with Abby automatically gripping Syd's hips. They stood mere inches apart, breathing each other's air. Time stood still for Abby as she looked into Syd's heavy-lidded eyes, then looked a little farther south when Syd licked her lips. Abby's heart rate sped up as she threw her caution to the wind and ignored the warning bells clanging in her head. The brief, fleeting touch of their lips produced a sigh from Abby and left her wanting more, but Syd was the one to step away. Abby couldn't decide if she wanted to kiss Syd again, harder and deeper, or if she wanted to flee to the safety of her own farm. She was breaking her own promises of staying just friends with Syd. Syd must have sensed Abby's conflict and she took another step back.

"Well," Syd began as she scuffed her shoe in the dirt, "I better get inside and start preparations for dinner. You and Bernice are still coming, right?"

The hopeful look on Syd's face made Abby's stomach clinch, and even if she wanted to, she couldn't turn Syd down. "Of course. What time would you like us and what can we bring?"

"Come over around six and just bring yourselves."

Abby nodded then mounted Bevin in one smooth, swift motion. She tipped the brim of her imaginary cowboy hat which made Syd laugh. "We'll see you soon." Abby turned Bevin around and left the same way they came in, taking off in a full gallop. The entire ride home, all Abby could think about was her hands on Syd's hips, the unmistakable look of craving in Syd's eyes right before Abby kissed her. And despite Abby's reservations of starting something with Syd, it *was* Abby who initiated the kiss. God, Syd's lips were so soft, so plump, so…kissable.

What would it be like to really let go and kiss Syd the way she really wanted? Would Syd's mouth be yielding or demanding? Before she knew it, she was back at the stable. So much for clearing her head. It was even more muddled now than it was earlier that morning. She removed the tack, groomed Bevin, then led him to the paddock to spend the day in the fresh air. She took Pokey out for a stroll, then let her join Bevin before Abby went into the house. She needed to get some words written whether she wanted to or not. Whether the words made any sense remained to be seen.

Abby and her grandmother knocked on the door and waited for Syd to answer. Abby shifted her weight from one foot to the other and felt like a fidgety mess. Abby's grandmother placed her hand on Abby's forearm and looked at her quizzically.

"What on earth is going on with you, child?"

"Nothing, Gran."

Abby's grandmother opened her mouth, but the words were interrupted when Syd opened the door.

"Good evening, ladies. I'm so glad you could have dinner with me tonight."

Abby let her gran go before her and she smiled inwardly when she hugged Syd and kissed her on the cheek. It was obvious to Abby that her gran was warming up to Syd, but then again, it would be hard not to warm up to her. Syd was a genuinely nice and intelligent woman who wasn't afraid to ask for or receive their help.

"My granddaughter has been telling me what a wonderful cook you are, and based on the pie you made us the other night, I'd have to agree. Thank you for going to so much trouble."

"It's no trouble at all, ma'am. I enjoyed your company and I wanted to show you how much I appreciate your hospitality," Syd looked at Abby, "and for all your help."

They were led into the kitchen where the heavenly aroma greeted them and made Abby's stomach growl.

"Dinner's in the oven, but I thought we could enjoy some appetizers and wine on the back deck and watch the sunset. You two go out and have a seat, and I'll be right out."

Abby and her grandmother sat at the glass-topped table adorned with three wine glasses and appetizer plates. Abby knew it must've been breaking her grandmother's heart to be sitting out here without her best friend. It was as if Abby could see the snapshots of memories flickering in her gran's mind. The sound of the door opening transformed the look on her gran's face from melancholy to acceptance and determination as she sat up straight and pulled her shoulders back. If Abby had to guess, it was because she didn't want Syd thinking she didn't appreciate being there. Syd placed a tray of appetizers on the table and held up the wine bottle.

"I hope Chianti is acceptable. If not, I have a Pinot Noir or Chardonnay I can pour."

Her grandmother answered for her and Abby. "Oh, Chianti sounds lovely, Sydney. These appetizers look delicious. What are they?"

Syd replied as she filled each glass. "I made bruschetta, caprese kabobs, and prosciutto and gorgonzola wrapped pear slices."

Abby watched every move Syd made, from pouring the wine, to the way her lips moved as she described the appetizers, to the small, knowing grin she gave Abby as she sat across from her. She filled her and her grandmother's plates with one of each and couldn't wait to dig in, however the presentation and colors were so pleasing, she'd hate to ruin them by eating them. She waited until Syd and her grandmother started before picking up the bruschetta. She moaned appreciatively as the flavors exploded on her tongue. It took all her willpower to take her time and savor it since there were so few of them on the plate. She also didn't want to seem like an uncivilized Neanderthal that had no table manners. Her gran wouldn't hesitate to reach over and smack her hand. She quickly came up with a plan. Take a bite. Set it on the plate. Take a sip of wine. Repeat.

"Sydney, this caprese kabob is wonderful. All of it looks delicious."

Abby saw the pride and pleasure on Syd's face as she sat up a little taller in her chair.

"Thank you, Bernice. I thought I would make an Italian themed meal tonight. If we were back at my place in Chicago, I would've made you a pasta dish with homemade noodles, but I didn't have the necessary tools here. Not that there's anything wrong with store-bought pasta."

Abby swore she saw Syd cringe when she spoke that last statement, but she held in her own laughter.

Syd continued. "I wanted to make you something all homemade, so I decided on an Italian meatloaf, Caesar salad, and bread, but I do have to admit that the bread was store-bought."

"Well, everything tastes terrific so far, dear," Bernice said after she took a bite of the pear.

"It really does," Abby said after she wiped her mouth with a napkin. "Do you need any help in the kitchen?"

Abby was disappointed when Syd said she had everything under control. All Abby could think about was having some alone time with Syd. She wasn't sure what would happen once they were alone, but Abby knew only that she wanted to be near her. She had managed to push thoughts of Syd out of her head long enough to add ten new pages to her manuscript earlier that afternoon, but they were hard-fought pages. She wouldn't know for sure if they were keepers until she was done with the first draft and she went back to layer the story.

There were times during the day when she'd grab her hair in frustration when Syd would pop back into her thoughts. Why was she having such a hard time kicking Syd out of her head? What made Syd so special that Abby wanted to forgo her writing to spend time with her? Abby knew why just by looking at her. She had an air of confidence, yet looked like she was keeping a secret and daring Abby to guess what it was. She was thoughtful, compassionate, and the sexiest woman she'd ever laid eyes on. It was enough to drive a girl crazy. In just a little more than a week, Syd would be going back to Chicago and Abby would get to resume her writing without the distraction of Sydney Carter. She would have a lot of time to make up for, but she would worry about that after Syd left.

"Bernice? Would you mind telling me about my grandparents? I found some old photo albums yesterday. Pictures of them with and without my mother. I have to say I noticed how happy they were in the pictures with Mama, but without her, Harold looked angry and Virginia looked…well…withdrawn."

"We moved here about a year before Abigail came to live with us," Bernice began. "We never met your mother—she was gone by then. My husband, Claude, tried to strike up a friendship with Harold, but they never became true friends. Harold was pretty much shut off from the rest of the world. Once Harold passed away, Virginia started talking to us more and we began socializing. Virginia never said a bad word about Harold to Claude or me because she was respectful, but I had a suspicion that he was the ruler of that household and she did what he said."

"Did he abuse her?"

"Oh, no, nothing like that. But in our generation, it wasn't unheard of for the wife to do as the husband said. Once he was gone, Virginia started coming out of her shell. At first, I think it was because she was lonely. But then we became very good friends and we truly enjoyed spending time together. You probably don't know this, Sydney, but your grandmother was a kind soul and she had a pretty funny sense of humor when she loosened up."

Syd grinned but remained quiet to allow Bernice to continue.

"When my Claude passed away, Virginia was a lifesaver to Abigail and me. She made us meals, cleaned our house, did our laundry. As you can imagine, I was a wreck after my Claude died. We were married for nearly fifty years and he was my best friend. We saw each other through the deaths of our son and daughter-in-law, and worked together in trying to raise Abigail into a respectful young woman."

Syd noted the sadness that swept across Abby's face, and she finally realized that Abby's parents died, which was why Abby lived with Bernice.

"Abby, I'm so sorry for your loss of your parents."

"Thank you."

Syd heard the undertone of Abby's response that she didn't want to talk about it, but later, she would make the same offer in being there for Abby if she did want to talk.

"Dinner should be just about ready so if you'd like to come in, I'll get the food on the table."

Once they started eating, Syd asked more questions.

"What did my grandmother like to do for fun?"

"Oh, so many things. She was a fantastic cook. She'd make us meals that were better than the finest restaurants could offer. And she could bake. It seemed she always had cookies, cakes, or pies to offer us."

Syd looked at Abby and smiled. "Your granddaughter said she used to hum while she cooked. Abby caught me doing the same thing."

Bernice laughed and clapped her hands together. "That she did. She also hummed when she was at her sewing machine. I'm not sure if those activities relaxed her to hum, or she hummed to relax while performing those activities."

"I think I do it because cooking makes me happy."

Bernice placed her hand over Syd's. "That's a very good reason. Now, let's see. She loved being outside and working in the garden, and we enjoyed playing cards."

Syd saw the joy in Bernice as she talked about Virginia. They must've had a great time together, and suddenly she was a little jealous that Abby got to have a relationship with Virginia. The more she got to know of Virginia, the more she wished she could've been in her life personally and not through a private investigator. She would've loved spending time in the kitchen with Virginia, learning all of her recipes. She could have taught Syd how to garden and play cards. So many would haves and could haves that were wasted in her family.

"I appreciate you telling me about her, Bernice, and I'm so grateful she had you and Abby in her life. I wish I'd had the opportunity to know her the way you two did."

"I do too, dear. I have to say, from what I know of you so far, your grandmother would've been crazy for you. You would have been her pride. You mentioned that you were hoping to find the answers to your questions. Have you had any luck with that?"

"Not exactly, but I haven't gone through her bedroom yet. I know it's silly, but I feel like I'm intruding and invading her privacy by going in there to go through everything. I'm also worried that if I do find the answers, I might not like them."

"Yes, I suppose that's a possibility, but you won't know if you don't try. You're not alone in this, Sydney. Abigail and I will be there for you if you need comfort, if you want to talk, or if you need to be held while you cry. We've only just met, but you're Virginia's granddaughter which makes you special to us."

Syd could feel the tears well in her eyes and she blinked them back. She was amazed at the outpouring of love and support from the two women she'd met less than a week ago. She already knew she'd miss them when she went back to Chicago. The funny thing, though, was that it was getting easier for her to imagine a new life in this small Iowa town. A slower life where she wouldn't be working long hours or hearing the sounds of the city.

But what would she do here if she did happen to stay, hypothetically speaking? She didn't happen to see any youth centers or investment banking firms when she was in town yesterday. Could she truly be happy here? What else would she do beside cook and feed the chickens? She knew nothing about living on a farm. She knew how to help buy and sell companies, and she knew how to be a mentor to inner city kids. The very thought of staying on the farm was just too ridiculous of a notion to even consider. Yet, looking across the table into Abby's bright blue eyes, that thought didn't seem ridiculous at all.

Two hours later, after they finished dinner, dessert, and more conversation, Abby and Bernice went home. Syd felt very lonely. She busied herself with washing the dishes and putting the food away. Abby had offered to help, but Syd didn't want to take time away from relaxing and talking with Bernice. Besides, after the fleeting kiss Abby had given her earlier, Syd wasn't ready to be alone with her, especially with her grandmother in the other room. Syd was confused by Abby's behavior.

Hadn't Abby said she didn't want to get romantically involved with someone who wouldn't be sticking around? Syd thought she'd been behaving and keeping her flirting in check even though it was more difficult than she had anticipated. There was something about Abby that made Syd want to throw caution to the wind and go with her gut. She recalled the times she'd spent with Abby since her declaration, and she couldn't recall any words or actions that could be misconstrued. Well, there was that kiss on the cheek when Syd took Abby home the other night. But that was just a friendly peck, really. No heat behind it at all. Not that Syd didn't want there to be. But she'd respected Abby's wishes.

Was Abby changing the rules and forgot to tell Syd? Did she decide that she did want to fool around? Why? And should Syd talk to her about it and put everything on the table, or should she just ignore it like it never happened? Syd definitely wouldn't be disappointed if she had the chance to sleep with Abby. Syd was very attracted to her, had been really, since the day they met. But there was more that drew Abby to her. Something indescribable. Something that actually had her thinking of staying in Iowa.

Syd shook her head as she climbed the stairs to shower then go to bed. She stopped at Virginia's bedroom door and looked around the room. It was time to rip off the Band-Aid and get started on going through it. Syd suddenly felt very tired as she thought of the daunting task she'd start in the morning.

## CHAPTER ELEVEN

Syd woke up already feeling lazy and had a feeling she wouldn't be getting much done in the way of cleaning out Virginia's room. She could at least do some cleaning and pack the living rooms and dining room. She luxuriated in the sheets and spent time stretching her limbs. This had been the most active she'd been in quite some time. With all the cleaning, packing, and her little horse ride the day before, her muscles were pleasantly sore. She closed her eyes and grinned when she recalled the dream she had about Abby.

*Syd and Abby were riding horses through a grassy field at a full gallop. The blistering yellow sun was a stark contrast against the deep blue sky. Syd found it amusing that she rode the horse so expertly since yesterday had been the first time she'd ever ridden one. Abby wore a straw cowboy hat, a blue and green flannel shirt, well worn faded jeans, and brown cowboy boots. Syd had never seen anyone look as sexy as Abby did atop the large animal.*

*They slowed their horses when they got to a wall of trees and found their way to a trickling stream. They dismounted and allowed the horses to wander to the water to drink. Abby spread out a blanket and held out her hand as an invitation for Syd to join her. They faced each other on their sides and remained silent, smiling and gazing into each other's eyes. Abby had removed her hat, and Syd tucked a wisp of hair behind Abby's ear, letting her fingers drift down Abby's neck, just inside the collar of her shirt. Syd felt the shiver run through*

*Abby, but she wouldn't make a further move unless Abby indicated that was what she wanted. She wouldn't embarrass herself again by making an unwanted advance.*

*Abby's voice was low and husky when she finally spoke. "How are your legs feeling?" she asked as she slipped her hand to the inside of Syd's leg, just above her knee.*

*Syd's breath hitched and her heart hammered in her chest. "A little sore," she managed to squeak out.*

*Abby's hand began to squeeze the muscles, and Syd felt her clit begin to throb.*

*"Here?"*

*Syd felt her vision dim and eyelids grow heavy, along with the pit in her belly. "A little higher."*

*Abby moved her hand a few inches higher and massaged the muscles a little slower, a little harder, and Syd automatically opened her legs to allow Abby easier access.*

*"Here?"*

*Syd gasped as she answered, "Just a little higher."*

*Abby continued to massage and squeeze Syd's tightening muscles as she inched closer to where Syd needed Abby's touch the most. Wetness flooded Syd's panties, and she was on fire just as Abby's hand reached the desperate destination, and she cupped and squeezed Syd's sex.*

*"Here?" Abby asked, her voice sound strained and her chest heaving.*

*"Oh, yes. Right there. Jesus, right there."*

*Abby's weight pushed Syd onto her back and Abby aggressively kissed Syd's waiting mouth while Abby's hand continued to massage Syd's swollen center. Syd moved her hips in rhythm, but it wasn't enough. She needed more. She needed Abby's fingers inside her while her thumb stroked Syd's clit. She unbuttoned her jeans and slid down the zipper, and Abby slid her hand inside Syd's panties, and she found her wet heat.*

Syd woke, panting and trying to catch her breath. Syd could still feel the thrumming of arousal between her legs, and it wouldn't take much to relieve the pressure that had built up. But it had been so long since she'd been that aroused, and she wanted to feel it for a little while longer. She idly thought what Abby would be like in bed. Would she be assertive? Take her time? Fuck Syd hard and fast? Or would Abby let Syd take control? Lie on her back and let Syd explore her body with her fingers and mouth? Shit.

That line of thinking wasn't helping Syd cool down. She slid her hand in her underwear and wasn't surprised to feel the slickness that awaited her. She stroked her clit between her index and middle fingers up and down a few times before moving them easily inside. Syd moved her fingers in and out slowly at first then increased the speed as she moved her thumb over the tightened bundle of nerves, just as Abby had done in her dream. Her breathing quickened and she pictured Abby hovered above her, sucking Syd's hardened nipple into her mouth. Syd moved her free hand to her breast and pinched her nipple, picturing Abby's teeth biting it, and the sensation traveled to her clit, making it even harder. Her orgasm built rapidly from the depths of her belly until she felt it in her entire body and exploded as she cried out Abby's name.

She lay there for several minutes trying to slow her breathing and come down from the rush she felt from the climax. She was just about to fall back to sleep when her phone buzzed. She blindly reached for it and smiled when she saw the name across the screen.

"Good morning, Vanessa."

"Hey, Syd. How's my temporary farm girl?"

Syd laughed at her teasing. "I'm good. Working hard and learning a lot."

"Learning? What the heck is going on there?"

"Well, I've learned how to feed chickens and I rode a horse yesterday."

The silence on the other side made Syd look at her phone to make sure the call hadn't been disconnected. "Hello? V? You still there?"

"Uh, yeah. I thought you said you were feeding chickens and riding horses."

"I did. I am. Virginia has chickens that I'm taking care of, and Abby took me for a ride on her horse, Bevin."

Vanessa laughed and Syd could almost see her shaking her head. "And who is Abby?"

Just hearing her name made Syd smile and her skin tingle. "Abby is the granddaughter of Virginia's neighbor and best friend, Bernice. Abby has been helping me clean out the place and she's been keeping me company."

"Company, huh? Is something going on between you two?"

Syd hesitated to answer. Was there something going on? At times, it seemed it was heading that way, but others, Abby was keeping her distance. "Honestly, I'm not sure. There seems to be some sort of attraction between us, but she told me she's not interested in getting together with someone who won't be staying."

"Hmm. Sounds like she's looking for a relationship and that's something you can't give her."

Syd felt her hackles rise and her face grow hot. "Why can't I? Don't you think I'm capable of being in a relationship?"

"Whoa, Syd. Slow your roll. I just meant that she lives in Iowa and your life is here in Chicago. Do you want to have a long-distance relationship with this woman?"

Syd knew Vanessa was right, but wouldn't it be worth trying? Syd had never met anyone like Abby, and that had to count for something. She would definitely consider dating her if Abby was up for it, but that wasn't something she wanted to ask her just yet. Other than some mild flirting and a few chaste kisses, nothing else had happened and it might not ever. Vanessa's voice brought Syd back from her ruminations.

"Tell me about her. She must be special if you're getting pissed at me."

Syd took a deep breath and let it out slowly while she ran her hand through her hair. Why was she angry with Vanessa? She had been her best friend for most of her life and Vanessa knew everything about Syd. "I'm sorry. You're right. Abby is special and I can't really describe why, but I'll try. First, she's really cute. I wouldn't exactly say she was femme but definitely not butch. Sportier, I would say. Blond hair, blue eyes, tall, terrific body that feels solid from the work she does on the farm. She lives with her grandmother, and I can tell they have a close bond. She was very close to Virginia as well, and I can see how much her death has affected Abby. She's been welcoming to me since I arrived. She taught me about the chickens, she's helped me go through Virginia's stuff, and she's told me about Virginia so I'm able to know more about her. We've shared meals, including a couple of dinners with her grandmother, who is also very sweet."

"Well, she sounds cute and nice, but what's the connection you feel with her?"

Syd took her time to answer Vanessa, not really knowing what to say. "Honestly, I'm not sure. I can't put a name to it or put my finger on any one thing, but something about her draws her to me. She's thoughtful, smart, down-to-earth, considerate. Her parents died when she was young so all she has is her grandmother."

Syd wasn't sure why she brought that up or what bearing that had on how Syd felt about her. Maybe it was because despite that, Abby had become a caring, loving woman. Or maybe it made Syd want to protect Abby from having to deal with anymore hurt in her life, but that wasn't anything Syd could control. "Anyway, I think you'd really like her."

"Am I going to have a chance to meet her?"

"I don't know. Like I said, things are up in the air with us, and unless you come visit me in the next week, probably not."

"Well, why don't you bring her home for a few days. Then she can meet me and your parents, and you can show her our fair city."

"I'm not sure that's a good idea, V. It's not like she's my girlfriend or anything. Wouldn't it be weird to bring her home to meet my family?"

"I don't think so. Not if you consider her to be a friend."

Syd was quiet for a moment, trying to picture Abby coming home with her, staying with her at her condo, meeting her family, maybe seeing the youth center where Syd spent so much of her time. "I'll think about it. She might not want to even come."

"It doesn't hurt to ask, if you're comfortable with the idea. How are things going at the farm? Do you still think you'll be done and back home in a week?"

"Probably. I only have a few more rooms to go through and I'll have to contact a real estate agent to get this place on the market. It's a really fantastic property, V. There's a barn, a pond, tons of land, and the house is really beautiful. This is a really great place to relax and escape crowds and stress."

"Sounds like you're considering keeping it. Are you?"

Syd hesitated again. Was she considering keeping it? It would be a great getaway, and it was already paid off. She could hire Abby to keep an eye on the place, or an agency to rent it out. "I hadn't thought about it, but that could be a possibility."

"Well, just make sure you come back soon, at least just to visit."

Syd could hear Vanessa's teasing in her voice, but she could also hear some trepidation.

"I miss you, Syd."

"I miss you too, sweetie. I promise I'll be home soon. I'll have you and my parents over for dinner and we can all catch up, okay?"

"That sounds great. Love you, sister."

Syd smiled and realized once again that despite being an only child, it was nice to have Vanessa in her life, who was so much like her sister. "Love you too, sis."

Syd looked at the time and was surprised to see how long she'd been on the phone. She needed to get dressed and get the chickens fed. The morning had started off lazy, but she had a sudden burst of energy and was determined to get the living room packed up. If she got enough done, she would reward herself by having lunch by the pond.

Abby sat staring at the blinking curser on her computer screen wondering what had happened. Once she finished her morning chores, she had sat at her desk and had a productive morning working on her manuscript. She had managed to not think about Syd once during that time, but now the words eluded her and all she could think about *was* Syd.

They'd had a lovely dinner together, her gran and Syd mon-opolizing the conversation, but Abby had been perfectly fine with that. It gave her an opportunity to look at Syd unabashedly while she spoke with her grandmother. Abby noticed most of her time was spent watching Syd's mouth when she spoke, when she smiled, when she laughed. The same mouth she'd thought of kissing since the moment they met. God, she had a gorgeous smile. The way the corners of her mouth turned up, her perfect, straight teeth, unlike her own. Abby's teeth were a little crooked. Not grossly so, but noticeable.

She got up from her chair and walked over to the mirror hanging on her wall. She smiled and studied her mouth. One of her front teeth was slightly longer and angled away from the one next to it. They weren't perfectly white like Syd's but pretty enough, she guessed. Abby took in the rest of her body and tried to imagine how Syd saw her. Her hair was growing lighter the closer they got to summer, as she was spending more time outside. Her blond hair was escaping her ponytail and looked a little messy. Her clothes were dirty and grungy from mucking the stalls and taking Bevin for a quick ride first thing in the morning. She hadn't taken the time to shower after; the words for her novel were shouting at her to write them down.

Was that how Syd saw her? A grungy farm girl? Granted, most of the time they'd spent together was going through Virginia's things, and she got a little messy with that. But the two times they'd had dinner with her gran, Abby had kept her hair down and dressed nicely. That was probably how Syd's dates dressed. They probably wore nice slacks or skirts, silk blouses, high heels, and makeup. Abby dressed like that only when she was doing a reading and signing. Out here on the farm, it was Carhartt jeans, flannel shirts or T-shirts, and her cowboy boots. This was what she was comfortable in. And if Syd didn't like it, then forget her.

Wait. Where was this all coming from? Abby's self-esteem was usually not in the gutter the way it was now. And she'd never seen Syd look at her with disgust when she wore her working clothes. She did look a little taken back when she saw Abby dressed up, maybe even a little lustful. Abby laughed at herself. She was being ridiculous. It was when Abby was her filthiest in the garage when Syd looked like she was going to kiss her. Maybe Syd did find the real Abby attractive.

Did it really matter though? Syd wasn't going to be hanging around once she had Virginia's place ready to sell. She'd be here for only another week or so. What would it hurt to fool around with her while she was in town? They were attracted to each other and mature adults, so what would it hurt? Abby's sex life had been made up of one-night stands. Would it make a difference if she was able to stretch that into a weeklong stand if Syd was interested? After all, it had been over six months since her last tryst. It was a pity though. Syd was a woman Abby could see having a long-term relationship with. She was gorgeous, smart, thoughtful. She wished she had more time to get to know her, but why not take advantage of the time she did have?

Abby nodded in resolve and stripped down before showering. She wouldn't get any more writing done for the time being so she might as well make herself useful and see if Syd needed any help going through the house. And if she was lucky, maybe she could talk Syd into fooling around a little. She dressed in a pair of her nicer but still comfortable jeans, a light blue button-down sleeveless shirt, and her cleaner boots, ones she didn't dare wear when cleaning out the stables.

Abby said good-bye to her grandmother then hopped in her truck for the half-mile ride. Normally she'd just walk, but it was starting to get warmer and she didn't want to arrive sweaty. When Syd didn't answer the front door, Abby walked around the house to the back and looked around. She finally spotted Syd sitting on the bench overlooking the pond. As she got closer, Syd turned and smiled brightly. That one simple act made Abby's heart flutter, and she realized she'd made the right decision. Now if she could only get Syd to agree.

"Hey."

"Hey, yourself. What's going on?"

Abby sat next to Syd on the bench and looked out across the pond. "I was thinking about you and thought I'd come by, see if you needed any help with anything." Abby hoped to hell she sounded calmer than she felt. Her insides were shaking and she felt a little breathless. Fear gripped her as she was about to put her pride on the line, but she wasn't going to turn back now. She rubbed her hands along her jeans to try to dry her sweaty palms and continued to look over the water, afraid that if she actually looked at Syd, she'd lose her nerve.

"You were thinking about me, huh?"

The playfulness in Syd's voice caused Abby to turn, and she was rewarded with Syd smiling at her. God, that smile. It was enough to turn Abby's insides to mush. She stared deeply into Syd's chocolate-colored eyes. "Yes, I was."

"What were you thinking about?"

Abby heard the flirtation in Syd's voice, could see it on her face. She hesitated. Could she do this? Would Syd respond in kind? *Now or never, Abby.*

"I was thinking about kissing you. What it would be like to really kiss you. The way I've wanted to since the day we met."

Syd's gaze never wavered as one eyebrow arched in question and her eyes darkened. "Well? What are you waiting for?"

Abby slid closer and cupped Syd's cheek with her palm. She held Syd's stare for just a second more before she leaned in, a whisper's breath away, then claimed Syd's mouth. She was gentle at first, then she kissed Syd like it would be the last thing she'd ever do. Syd's mouth was more than Abby had imagined—soft, giving, accepting, and she would never tire of having Syd's lips on hers. Abby slid her hand to the back of Syd's head and she pulled her closer, not wanting any space between them.

Syd opened her mouth slightly and allowed Abby's tongue to enter, to tease Syd's. Abby's head began to spin and she broke the kiss. She had been aroused before when she had been with other women, but no kiss had ever made her feel so dizzy or breathless. She felt Syd's arms around her shoulders, pulling her body to Abby's. Abby kissed her way from Syd's cheek to her ear and she sucked on Syd's earlobe. The loud sigh that came from Syd further emboldened Abby to continue her quest down Syd's neck. Abby felt

Syd's pulse beat against her lips in time with her own, and she felt her heart might burst through her chest. She felt Syd's skin grow hot against her tongue as Syd threw her head back and allowed Abby more access, and her continuous licks, nips, and kisses made Syd moan louder.

Syd broke away and moved into Abby's lap, straddling her legs and grabbing Abby's face before resuming their kiss. Abby grabbed Syd's ass and pulled her closer as her own hips began to thrust. Abby craved the contact with Syd. It'd been so long since Abby had had sex with another woman, but she'd go through the drought again if it meant being with Syd that very moment. She wanted to slow down, act like a woman in control, not some horny teen-aged boy full of raging hormones, but Syd made her want to lose control. Syd made her want to do a lot of things that were out of character. So far, kissing her had exceeded Abby's fantasies about what her lips would feel like, how she'd taste, what her tongue would feel like against her own. And Abby had had *many* fantasies about Syd. There was so much she wanted to do to Syd, wanted Syd to do to her, but she felt her holding back, as if she was fearful of moving too fast, too far, without Abby's consent.

"God, Syd. I want you to touch me." She grabbed Syd's hand and brought it to her breast, and Abby thought she'd lose her mind when Syd squeezed. Abby's nipple hardened and the jolt it sent to her clit set her on fire. She looked at Syd through hazy eyes and saw her chest heaving.

"Let's go inside," Syd panted.

"No. I can't wait that long. I've always wanted to have sex outdoors." Abby kissed Syd soundly on her lips. "Be my first."

The smile Syd rewarded Abby with indicated she didn't mind one bit. Syd moved her fingers to Abby's blouse and slowly unbuttoned it until it was open and exposing Abby's white lace-covered breasts. Syd stared at Abby's chest reverently and brought both hands up and started teasing her nipples through the rough fabric. Abby leaned against the bench and dropped her head back, letting the sunlight filtering through the tree branches warm her already scorched skin.

Abby looked up when she felt teeth replace fingers to see Syd's mouth on her, and she felt like she was about to lose her mind. Her head swam and blood raged as Syd took control. She needed to touch Syd like she needed air to breathe. Abby reached for Syd's pants, unbuttoned them, then slid the zipper down. She slipped her hand inside Syd's black silk panties and found her swollen and wet. Abby slowly moved her fingers up and down until a new flood of wetness coated her fingers. She barely resisted removing her hand and sticking her fingers in her mouth to get a taste of Syd. She'd get to that later.

Syd's hips began to move back and forth, slowly gliding her clit between Abby's fingers. Syd seemed content with the lazy pace until Abby reached her hand up Syd's shirt, under her bra, and fondled her breast. Syd's movements increased, and Abby pushed up Syd's shirt and bra before latching onto Syd's nipple and sucking it hard. Syd yelled out and held tighter to Abby as her hips moved frantically. Abby's own hips were thrusting and the seam in her jeans was quickly swelling her clit. Abby vacillated between biting and sucking Syd's nipple. She was too far gone in her own growing climax to have any sort of rhythm. Syd froze, then shook as she screamed out Abby's name and scared off a flock of birds from the tree behind them. Abby came at the same time as Syd and groaned as her climax released.

This was something she had been missing all her life—the ability to make her partner come at the same time she did, and it didn't really surprise her that it was Syd that was able to come with her. Even though the last bit was a little flailing, she felt in sync with Syd throughout the entire time, from their first kiss to their mutual release. Syd collapsed against Abby and shuddered with every pass of Abby's fingers over her clit until she coaxed out the last of Syd's orgasm. Abby gently withdrew her hand out of Syd's panties, generously coated with her essence, and stuck them in her mouth to lick them clean. Syd tasted better than Abby could've imagined, and her mouth watered at the thought of going down on her and drinking her in.

❖

Syd leaned against Abby, trying to regain control of her breathing. Her orgasm hit her hard and fast before she even had the chance to really enjoy it. Oh, she'd enjoyed it, but Syd wouldn't have minded if it had been prolonged a little more. She had been simmering since she woke up from her dream—from the moment she met Abby, actually, if she was being honest. Although she had brought herself to climax earlier that morning, the fullness and throbbing in her clit never dissipated. The whole encounter with Abby didn't last long, but once Abby started kissing her, she quickly lost control. That was all it took. Abby's lips on hers, her tongue against Syd's, Abby's hands exploring Syd like she'd been doing it all their lives. The familiarity of Abby touching her, as if Abby was touching her own body, was scary and exhilarating all at once. She didn't want this moment to end—the closeness she felt with Abby, not only physically but emotionally. But she had to ask.

"I thought you didn't want to get involved with anyone who wasn't local. What changed?" Syd leaned back to look into Abby's eyes. She'd discovered over the past week how expressive Abby's eyes were, and she saw a myriad of feelings swirl through the now indigo colored eyes—a little bit of confusion, a little bit of lust, and a little bit of resignation. She knew that Abby would speak her truth.

"You, Syd. You changed my mind. I'm so incredibly attracted to you, and I had to know what it would be like to be with you, otherwise I would've regretted it once you were gone. I felt we should make the most out of our time that we have left together. I got the impression that you might be up for having some fun together. Would that be okay?"

The hopeful look in Abby's shining eyes made Syd want to weep with joy. She knew already that this would be incomparable to the other times she hooked up with women. She also knew that being intimate with Abby, then having to leave her behind would rip her heart out, but that was something she'd be willing to deal with later. Now that she'd had a taste of what would come over the next week, there was no way she would deny herself the pleasure of being pleasured by Abby. Right now, she wanted nothing more than to take Abby inside and spend the rest of her time on this farm worshipping every inch of her body, getting to know her better than she knew herself.

She held Abby's face in her hands and closed her eyes as she kissed Abby soundly. She searched Abby's eyes to make sure that this was what she wanted, and when she saw the surety, the fire, the desire flashing back at her, she nodded. "That would be more than okay."

Syd yelped when Abby stood with her still in her lap. Syd's legs automatically wrapped around Abby's waist as she carried her inside. Abby's strength of being able to carry Syd up the stairs and to her bedroom turned Syd on even more, and she desperately needed to feel Abby's skin on hers, needed to be topped by her, and worshipped by her. She stripped off her clothes and leaned back to watch Abby do the same. Syd's arousal returned when Abby was finally naked and standing in front of her. She wanted to laugh at the stark contrast of her dark arms and face versus the white, white skin of the rest of her body. It was obvious by the farmer's tan on her arms that that was the only part of her body that saw the light of day.

Being able to finally see Abby naked had been worth the wait. Syd had an idea of what her body would look like because of the clothes Abby had worn to dinner, ones that fit her like they were specifically tailored for her, unlike her baggy farm clothes. Abby didn't really have curves, not like the other women Syd had been with, but her muscles were lean and tight and strong. Abby had the body of someone who physically worked hard every day, with broad shoulders and a tapered waist. Syd continued to study Abby's gorgeous body and felt her insides grow hotter while Abby stood before her, allowing Syd to continue her perusal. Abby's breasts were full and round, her areolae small and pink, and her hardened nipples even darker. Syd's hands itched to fondle, squeeze, and pinch before sucking them into her mouth.

Abby must've seen the fervor in Syd's eyes, or she was able to read Syd's mind, because her hips twitched forward and Syd's eyes dropped to the thatch of blond hair that covered the place Syd most wanted her mouth to be.

"Come here," Syd commanded as she reached out her hand. Abby took it and Syd indicated for Abby to straddle her pelvis. Syd sat up and kissed Abby hungrily as she dug her fingers into Abby's hips and ass. Syd's mind was spinning with all the things she wanted to do with and to Abby, and she didn't know where to start. She had to remind herself that she had time to do everything she wanted. But would it be enough time for them both? Syd didn't want to think of that since she had more pressing matters to tend to. Syd broke the kiss and cupped Abby's breast, bringing it to her mouth, and sucking it in until her nipple hit the roof of Syd's mouth and Abby cried out. She put her hand on the back of Syd's head and held her there, and Syd was happy to continue lavishing Abby's breasts. Abby's hips began to move back and forth, coating Syd's mound with her essence. Syd grabbed Abby's hips and raised her up a little, breaking the delicious contact and making Abby moan her disappointment.

"Don't worry, baby. I'll take care of you." Syd slipped her hand between them and lightly stroked Abby's stiffness. Abby sighed and started moving again, back and forth over Syd's fingers.

"Oh, God. Syd, put your fingers in me. I need you inside."

Syd happily obliged and easily slid two, then three fingers inside and let Abby adjust to the girth. Slowly, Abby rose up then back down onto Syd's fingers and kept up the movements. The look of blissful pleasure on Abby's face made Syd want to continue giving her that pleasure. She used the palm of her hand to add pressure to Abby's clit with each down stroke on her fingers. Syd wanted so badly to pull Abby's other nipple into her mouth, but she couldn't tear her eyes away from watching Abby fuck her hand. Abby's eyes slammed shut as her breathing quickened, and Syd knew Abby was close. Syd was in awe of the wondrous beauty astride her; it made her heart swell.

"Oh, God, Syd. I'm gonna come. I'm...coming...so hard."

Abby's pussy clinched around Syd's fingers and her body shook over and over as Syd pressed her palm harder against Abby's clit. Abby fell forward onto Syd, knocking her to her back with Abby lifeless on top of her. Syd loved having all of Abby's weight on her, nothing but their skin and breath mingling. Syd withdrew her fingers and wrapped her arms around Abby, holding her tight.

"You were amazing," Syd declared before licking a trickle of sweat off Abby's neck. She tasted like salt and vanilla and sunshine. Syd decided this was her new favorite flavor, and she wished more than anything she could bottle it.

Abby chuckled near Syd's ear, the breath sending shivers throughout her body. "I think that's my line. I don't think I've ever come that hard."

Syd rolled them over and hovered above Abby. "Let's see if we can beat it." Syd started to slide down Abby's body, hungry for more, when Abby stopped her.

"Hang on. I'm going to need a minute. Come back up here."

Syd lay on top of Abby, resting on her forearms, looking into Abby's eyes. Abby grinned and her dimples appeared. Syd kissed each one before kissing Abby's lips. Simple kisses that could tell so much. Syd wanted nothing more than to spend the rest of her time in bed with Abby, having sex, basking in the afterglow, then having more sex.

Abby's hand cupped Syd's face and she brushed Syd's hair behind her ears, massaging her scalp, neck, and shoulders. Syd felt herself starting to drift off, and Abby must've felt it too.

"Turn over. I'll cuddle you from behind and we can take a little nap."

That was one of the best ideas Syd had heard in a really long time and she obliged. The feeling of Abby pressed up against her backside and her arm wrapped possessively around Syd's body quickly knocked Syd into dreamland.

## Chapter Twelve

Syd woke up a couple of hours later feeling sore but rested. She reached behind her to feel for Abby's body, wanting to resume where they'd left off, but she felt nothing but sheets and a blanket. Great. Syd must have scared her off, or Abby decided that she didn't want a fling after all. What a shame, she thought as she sighed heavily. Syd had felt they really connected in bed, and she would've enjoyed the rest of the week with her. She guessed the best thing to do would be to finish cleaning out the house, get the farm listed with a real estate agent, and return to her life in Chicago.

She looked around the room, and with the exception of the rumpled sheets on her bed, there was no evidence that Abby had even been there. No evidence of the mind-blowing sex they'd had except the smell that still permeated the room. She brought her fingers up to her nose and could still smell Abby on them. She salivated just at the scent and grew wet thinking about having her fingers buried deep inside Abby, her head thrown back, and eyes clinched shut in the throes of passion. Oh, how Syd wanted a repeat performance along with all of the other ways she wanted to make Abby come. She moved her arms above her head and lengthened her body in order to stretch her muscles, then shook her head. Syd threw on a T-shirt and shorts and headed to the kitchen to heat up some soup for lunch.

She took her bowl to the kitchen table and was surprised to see a note from Abby.

*Dear Syd,*

*Our time together today was beyond remarkable, and I wanted nothing more than to remain in bed with you, but I had to get home to do the afternoon chores. If it's all right with you, I'd like to have dinner with you tonight. Call or text me when you get this to let me know.*

*—Abby*

Syd smiled as she read the note again, and the relief washed over her body like a warm waterfall, making her feel a little lighter. Abby hadn't been spooked after all, and Syd immediately texted her to tell her yes to dinner and that she'd make it. After she finished her soup, she opened her laptop and logged in to her email. She had done so every morning just in case there was something that needed her attention, but her inbox had been empty. Today, there had been an email for a grant she had applied for to start up her own youth center. Her hands shook as she moved the cursor to open the letter.

*Dear Ms. Carter,*

*I am pleased to inform you that your application has been chosen for the grant through the Sundance Group. Our committee had received many applications, and as you may know, we are looking for programs that will engage and build leadership among low-income families and people of color, and that will prioritize principles of equity and social justice in their work. We have all agreed that the youth center you plan on opening meet those criteria. We would like to schedule a meeting with you soon to finalize your grant. Please call us at your earliest convenience to make an appointment. Congratulations.*

*Sincerely,*

*Anne Palmer*

Syd took a shaky breath and wiped the tears from her eyes. They had chosen her application. She'd be able to start her own center. She read the email over and over to make sure she wasn't misinterpreting the letter, but no matter how many times she read it, it continued to say the same thing. She dug her phone out of her pocket and called the number Ms. Palmer had included. The phone call had lasted all of five minutes, but she had a meeting scheduled in a few days in Chicago. This was definitely a cause for celebration. She couldn't wait to tell her parents and Vanessa. And Abby. Syd really wanted to tell Abby the wonderful news.

She rummaged through the refrigerator, freezer, and pantry to figure out a special meal for tonight. She remembered seeing candlesticks and holders in the living room where Virginia's china had been stored, but she had packed them up earlier. She retrieved them from the boxes she had placed in the garage earlier in the day, but she frowned as she realized she still had a lot to go through to pack up or donate. She was really going to have to be diligent and not let herself get distracted by the blond-haired, blue-eyed, sexy farm girl down the way. Thinking of Abby pushed the thoughts of packing aside, at least until morning. She was determined to fix a delicious meal for Abby, then go upstairs for dessert. Maybe they could have some strawberries and whipped cream later. Syd shivered when she thought of licking the whipped cream off Abby's nipples and other delectable areas of her body.

She placed the candles on the table, found some matches, and set the table for two. She did most of the prep work so she wouldn't have to worry about it later, then she poured a small glass of wine and took it upstairs to sip while she got ready. She returned to the kitchen an hour later dressed nicely and smelling pretty. She had dabbed a little of her perfume behind her ears, hoping it would lure Abby's mouth to her most sensitive erogenous zone. There were a few things Syd wanted to use her mouth for on Abby too.

She was just putting the finishing touches on dinner and lighting the candles when there was a knock on the door. Syd looked at her watch and noted Abby was right on time. In fact, she'd been punctual every time she said she'd help her with something. That was a huge issue with Syd. Tardiness was a turn-off for her, and when someone continued to arrive late, that was a deal breaker because it showed disregard for her and her time. Thankfully, she'd never experienced that with Abby. She opened the door to find Abby standing there holding a bouquet of wild flowers that looked like she picked them herself. Syd didn't recognize any of them. The color blend of pink, orange, and purple was absolutely gorgeous and reminded her of the sunrise and sunset she'd gotten to experience since being on the farm. The flowers were tied together with a royal purple ribbon that matched one of the flowers. Syd placed her hand over her heart, taken aback by the chivalry of Abby. No one had ever brought her flowers for a date. Ever. Did people still do that? Obviously, Abby did, and it made Syd feel warm all over.

"For you," Abby said as she handed over the bouquet.

"Oh, Abby. These are so lovely. Thank you."

Syd stepped into Abby's arms once she was inside, and she couldn't wait another moment to kiss her. It was a nice kiss, not meant to fan the flickering flames that had lingered with Syd since earlier in the day. Syd snuggled into Abby's neck and inhaled her earthy scent. "You look very nice. You taste nice too," Syd noted as she kissed her way down Abby's neck.

Abby moaned and pulled Syd into her. Abby's mouth found Syd's, and she kissed her like a lover who'd been away far too long. Syd wanted Abby to back her up against the door and take her where she stood, but she broke the kiss instead, putting her forehead against Syd's, breathing hard.

"I'm sorry. I couldn't help myself."

Syd chuckled shakily. "Don't be sorry, just please promise me you'll kiss me like that again later."

Abby smiled and kissed the tip of Syd's nose. "I promise. It smells great in here."

Syd grabbed Abby's hand and led her to the kitchen table. Syd was nervous about Abby's reaction to the candles. She wasn't sure if it would be something she'd appreciate, maybe it was too romantic, but the smile on Abby's face reassured Syd she'd made the right decision.

"Come, sit. Dinner's almost ready. Would you like a glass of wine?"

"Please."

Syd poured a glass and set it on the table in front of Abby. She cupped Abby's face in her hand and she leaned down to kiss her.

She felt Abby's legs spread and her hands on Syd's hips, pulling her closer. The kiss deepened, and Abby's hands moved to Syd's ass, squeezing, making Syd throb. She broke the kiss and stepped back, instantly regretting the move and feeling the loss of being so close. But if she remained where she was, dinner would be forgotten and they would need sustenance for what Syd had planned for later. She smiled and shook her head before turning her back to Abby, feeling her eyes bore into the back of her. She plated their food and took a seat across from Abby.

Syd was quite pleased when Abby took a bite of the chicken stir-fry and moaned appreciatively. The sound reminded Syd of Abby making similar sounds just mere hours ago while in the midst of climax. Syd planned to elicit more of those sounds until she had Abby screaming her name as she came. She noticed the temperature increasing, sure it was just internal, and she took a sip of wine.

"So, I got some news today," Syd said after she finished chewing her food.

"Oh, yeah?"

Syd nodded. "I got the grant that I applied for so I can start my own center."

Abby dropped her fork on her plate, stood, and pulled Syd into a tight hug. "That's so great! Is there anything else you have to do?"

Syd laid her head on Abby's chest and relished the way she felt in her arms. She was pleased that Abby was so happy for her and genuinely interested. "I have to go back to Chicago in a couple of days to meet with them officially." Syd leaned back in Abby's arms and looked into her eyes. "Do you know how great this is going to be for the kids?"

"I do know. They're very lucky to have you on their side looking out for them. I'm so happy for you, baby."

The term of endearment surprised Syd, and by the wide-eyed look Abby had going on, it surprised her too. But Syd loved the way it sounded coming from Abby's mouth and the smile that accompanied it.

"Thank you." Syd moved closer to kiss Abby. A short, sweet kiss. Another. And another. Then Syd ran her tongue along Abby's upper lip until she opened her mouth and allowed Syd to enter. The longer the kiss went on, the more control Syd lost, and she frantically started unbuttoning Abby's shirt. Dinner forgotten, Abby quickly blew out the candles and grabbed Syd's hand as they ran upstairs and tumbled into Syd's room. They stripped their clothes off but couldn't bother with their bras and panties. Syd pulled Abby on top of her and held on for dear life as Abby sucked and bit her nipple through the lace of her bra at the same time her hand slipped under Syd's panties and into her hot, wet center. Syd scratched her nails down Abby's back as Abby thrust her fingers in and out of Syd.

The roaring in Syd's ears started the same time she felt her orgasm build deep in her belly and explode out of her mouth as she cried out Abby's name. Abby sat up and practically ripped the panties off Syd before she moved lower and took Syd into her mouth. Abby licked, flicked, and sucked Syd's clit, and she put her hand on the back of Abby's head, holding her there. Syd's hips rolled back and forth until she froze a moment before bowing her body and crying out.

Syd was spent. Two quick orgasms, so quick that she barely had time to form a thought before she was crying out in ecstasy. She wanted to reciprocate. She wanted to make Abby feel as good as she did, but she was so wasted, she felt like she couldn't move a muscle. Her eyes were closed, but the feeling of Abby's soft lips lightly kissing her inner thighs made her smile. In one day, Abby seemed to know exactly what Syd needed. There was one thing that Syd wanted though, and she wanted it now.

"Take off your bra and panties and come up here."

Abby did as she was told and crawled on the bed. Before she could lie down next to her, Syd grabbed her hips and guided her until Abby was straddling her face. Syd looked up to see the hunger clouding Abby's eyes, and she gave Abby a knowing smile before taking her in her mouth. Abby moaned and sighed before she started moving her hips back and forth, slowly, grazing her hardened clit over Syd's protruding tongue. Abby tasted salty and sweet, and Syd felt she could stay like this for the rest of the night, drinking all of Abby in. The feel of Abby's growing and hardening clit in her mouth had quickly become one of Syd's favorite sensations.

"Oh, God, Syd. That feels so good."

Syd reached up and fondled Abby's breast, squeezing and pinching her nipple, making Abby cry out. Her nipple was rigid and tickled Syd's palm as she brushed it across the hard point.

"Keep doing that, baby." Abby's movements sped up and she reached forward to grab the headboard. "Fuck, Syd. I'm going to come in your mouth." Syd had never heard Abby say "fuck" before, and she found it pretty hot to hear and feel Abby let loose. Abby shuddered as her juices flowed into Syd's mouth and she welcomed all of it.

Syd caressed Abby's back while she continued the pressure on her clit until Abby stopped trembling. She loved that Abby felt so comfortable with her that she could do or say anything. She looked up and found Abby staring down at her, looking spent but satisfied, a tired smile ghosting her lips. Syd flicked Abby's clit with her tongue one more time before moving her mouth away.

"You okay?"

Abby laughed. "That was ridiculously fantastic." She lay next to Syd and traced little patterns on Syd's chest and breasts, and brushed across her nipples, turning them hard once more. "You wore me out."

She leaned over and kissed Abby soundly on the lips. "Can you stay the night?"

Abby nodded and pulled Syd closer. "I'd like that."

Syd hesitated, then decided to take a chance. "Would you want to go to Chicago with me? We'll only be there for a few days."

"I'd like that too."

Syd smiled and laid her head on Abby's chest, feeling her heartbeat against her cheek. They fell asleep in each other's arms and didn't wake until morning.

# CHAPTER THIRTEEN

Abby woke facing Syd and studied her peaceful, lovely face. She was on her stomach, arms tucked under her pillow. The white, crisp sheet was pulled down to her lower back and made her light brown skin look creamy and smooth. Abby couldn't remember seeing anyone so lovely, and she had the sudden predilection to move closer, to be in the same air that Syd was breathing. She was tempted to reach out and skim her hand over Syd's flawless skin, or run her fingers through her hair. Unfortunately, she had to get going soon and she regretted having to leave.

Yesterday and last night had been the most amazing sex she'd ever had. Syd was an outstanding lover, so free, so knowing, so giving. If Abby hadn't been so wasted after her orgasm last night, she would have had sex with Syd all night long. She wanted to explore every inch of Syd's body, taste her skin, know her inside and out. And she didn't have much time to do it. Syd would be leaving soon, going back to her life in Chicago, and Abby didn't know if she'd ever see her again. That thought left a sour taste in her mouth and a heaviness in her chest.

"Why do you look so sad? Do you regret last night?"

Abby must have been really deep in thought because she hadn't noticed Syd had even opened her eyes. Abby had to reassure Syd and erase the look of doubt that marred her face. She reached over and gently brushed a lock of hair off Syd's forehead.

"The only thing I regret is not being able to stay in bed with you all day. Why are you awake so early?"

Syd turned on her back, stretched her arms above her head, and all Abby could do was stare at Syd's exposed perfect breasts. Her mouth watered at the thought of taking a nipple and sucking on it for hours.

"Eyes up, Price."

Abby looked at Syd's face and laughed when she saw an eyebrow arched and a crooked smile. Busted.

"I can't help it," Abby said as she crawled on top of Syd. "You have the most gorgeous breasts and I was just thinking of how much I want to suck a nipple into my mouth."

"Well? What's stopping you?"

Abby didn't have to be told twice. But rather than suck hard, she lightly brushed the tip of her tongue across and around it until it grew rigid. She bit gently which got Syd writhing beneath her. Abby knew she had to get home soon to do her chores, but she'd be nuts to leave now with Syd so ripe and willing. She'd also be nuts to leave Syd wanting, and Abby could never do that to her. She slid her hand between Syd's legs and found her wet and ready.

She slipped two fingers into her slick walls and stroked in and out slowly as she started sucking Syd's nipple. She felt Syd's legs wrap around her, opening herself farther. Abby continued to take her time, wanting to draw out Syd's impending orgasm and try to make it last more than five minutes, but the way Syd was moving, Abby knew she wouldn't make her goal. She released her mouth from Syd's breast and watched as she continued to pleasure her. Syd's lips were slightly parted and pursed, eyes closed and brows furrowed as if she, too, was trying to make it last.

Syd began panting, her walls tightening, and Abby knew she was close. She felt herself hard and throbbing, and she wanted to come with Syd. She withdrew her fingers, spread her lips to expose her clit to Syd's, and began moving against her, back and forth, intermingling their lust. She felt Syd's fingers dig into her back, pulling her harder, closer. After just a few thrusts, Syd came and pushed Abby over the edge. Their skin glistened with sweat and mingled when Abby collapsed onto Syd.

"Well, that was a hell of a wake-up call."

Abby chuckled in the side of Syd's neck and licked a trickle of sweat once her breathing slowed. "I couldn't help myself. You're so damn sexy."

"You're not so bad yourself, Abigail."

Abby looked into Syd's eyes. "I like the way you say my name," she said before kissing her long and soft. *Uh-oh. Starting to get a little too serious.* "Like I said, I'd love to stay here all day, but I have to get home to get some stuff done." Abby got out of bed and looked around the room for her carelessly discarded clothes from the night before. As she dressed, she made the mistake of looking over to Syd to see her intently watching Abby.

"Stop that."

Syd's smile was so provocative that Abby was this close to getting back into bed.

"What?" Syd continued to leer while tracing her fingertip around her nipple and moving it south.

Part of Abby wanted to wait and watch to see how far Syd would take that finger. She had a feeling Syd would give her a hell of a show and torture her all at the same time. Abby hurried over and put her hand over Syd's to stop the progression. "I really have to go, and if you keep doing that, I'm never gonna leave."

"Okay, I'll be a good girl."

"Let's not get crazy now. Just until I get back, then you can go back to being bad." Abby smiled and winked. "Um, may I come back later?" She didn't want to be presumptive even though she had an inkling of what Syd would say.

"Of course. We'll see if we can eat the entire dinner tonight. I guess I better get up too so I can feed the chickens. Never in my life did I expect that phrase to be uttered from my mouth on a regular basis," Syd said as she giggled.

Abby laughed and gently pushed Syd back onto the bed. "No, I'll feed them. I want to remember you lying here, looking flushed and sated so I can think later about the way you look right now. I'll call you later to let you know what time I'll be back."

"Sounds good. Give me one more kiss before you go."

Abby leaned down and met Syd's lips. When Syd lightly nibbled Abby's lower lip, she whimpered and pulled away. How the hell was she going to get anything done today knowing Syd was only half a mile away? She walked to the door, then retreated back to Syd and sat on the side of the bed.

"Hey, would you like to go for a ride later?"

"I thought that's what we were going to do," Syd said as she tickled Abby's side.

She squirmed away from the assault on her ribs. "I meant for a horse ride."

"Uh, no."

Syd looked at her like she was crazy and it made Abby smile. "Come on. We'll just walk the horses. No galloping will be involved. I promise to keep you safe."

"Are you nuts? Did you not hear me when I told you I've never been on a horse?"

"You rode Bevin."

Syd threw her arms in the air. "Yeah, with you walking him. All I had to do was sit on him. What you're asking me to do is actually *ride* the horse."

Abby put her hand in front of her mouth to smother her giggle. "At least come see the horses, meet Pokey. Once you see how sweet and tame she is, you won't be afraid to ride her. I want to share this part of me with you, and just think, it will give you a heck of a story to tell your friends back in Chicago."

Abby watched Syd chew on her bottom lip. She had seen her do this before when she was thinking about something. The fact that Syd was even contemplating going for a ride made Abby feel a little victorious.

"I'll come by and meet the horse. But that's all I'm promising."

"Thank you." Abby kissed her again and started for the door.

"By the way, is there a stream anywhere near here?"

"No. Why do you ask?"

Syd's fingertip was slowly teasing her nipple again, and Abby could do nothing but watch. She had a feeling that Syd would be teasing her a lot over the next week, but she also knew she'd follow through and thoroughly satisfy her. What was a little suffering if it eventually led to a happy ending? If it was good enough for her characters on the page to go through, then it would be good enough for her. Karma sure was a bitch.

"The other night, I had a dream of us riding then stopping at a stream so the horses could get a drink. You placed a blanket on the ground and once we were on our sides facing each other, you started massaging my very sore muscles on my inner thighs."

Abby audibly gulped. "Tell me more."

"Well," Syd said as she stood in her naked glory, nipples peaked, and body flushed as she pressed up against Abby. "I kept telling you to go a little higher until you reached the area that was aching a lot more than my muscles."

Abby gripped Syd's hips, squeezing the hardened muscles and pulled her closer into her. "Then what happened?"

"You just slid your hand in my panties and found me swollen and wet for you," Syd explained as she slid her fingers into the front of Abby's pants and Abby's legs nearly buckled.

"And I woke up," Syd said as she removed her hand and stepped back, out of reach from Abby.

A bead of sweat formed on Abby's upper lip and she ran her fingers through her hair. "Jesus."

"Uh-huh. So, I was just wondering if there was a way for you to help me finish my dream. That might make me more inclined to risk my life by riding a large animal."

"I'll think of something," she blurted out. Christ, when did Abby revert to being a teenaged boy raging with hormones? She really needed to leave and tend to her responsibilities before she spent the day in bed pleasuring Syd. Not that that would be a bad way to spend her day, but she had to get her chores done so she would have plenty of time later to play "Make Syd's Dreams Come to Life."

She kissed Syd once more and meekly waved before going out to the barn. When she finished feeding the chickens, she looked up to Syd's window and saw her standing there completely naked, smiling down on Abby. She laughed, blew Syd a kiss, and went home to get some work done.

Abby walked into the house to find her gran sitting in the living room reading the newspaper. It wasn't late, in fact it was barely seven thirty, but they were both early risers, and Abby was willing to bet her grandmother had been awake since before the sun rose. She peered around the paper and looked Abby up and down.

"I guess I don't have to ask how dinner went last night."

"Uh…" Abby felt her face burn, and she had no idea what to say to that. It's not like her gran didn't know Abby was a lesbian. When Abby had figured it out early in college, she had told her grandparents. They weren't exactly thrilled, but they didn't give her a hard time about it either. After her grandfather died, her grandmother started asking Abby more questions, telling her she was interested in her life and she didn't want Abby thinking she couldn't talk to her about anything. But Abby obviously hadn't talked to her grandmother about her sexual trysts. That would just be weird.

"I may be old, Abigail, but I'm not blind. I know you and Sydney like each other and since you didn't come home last night, it didn't take a genius to know what you did. I don't want to know the details; I just want to know if you had a nice evening."

Abby took a seat in the chair opposite her grandmother. She knew she must smell like sex and Syd, and she didn't want to get too close until she had a chance to shower and brush her teeth. "We had a nice evening, Gran. Syd cooked us a chicken stir-fry and we had some wine. She told me last night that she got an email saying she was being awarded a grant to get her own youth center started. She was very excited so we did a little celebrating." Abby could feel her face turn hot, and she knew she wasn't fooling her grandmother.

"Well, that's terrific news. What do the two of you have planned for today?"

"I'm going to do some work around the house and get some writing done. Syd's coming over later and we're going to take Pokey and Bevin out for a ride. Did you need me to do anything for you today?"

"No, dear. I'm going into town in a little bit to have breakfast with some friends then get my hair done. I'll be back later this afternoon."

"Okay. I'm going to take a shower and get started. Oh, before I forget, Syd has to go to Chicago tomorrow for a few days and she asked me to go. Do you need me for anything around here?"

"Really? Why does she need to go back to Chicago?"

"She needs to meet with the lady who contacted her about her grant. I figured I could keep her company on the drive."

"In that case, I'll be perfectly fine."

"Thanks, Gran. Love you."

Abby showered then went to feed the horses, promising them she'd be back later to take them out, then went to her office and booted up her computer. She ignored her email and pulled up her manuscript. After her and Syd's recent sexual activity, Abby was feeling inspired. She always felt writing sex scenes was her weakest link in her craft. Maybe it was because she didn't have a lot of experience. Well, maybe not so much experience as adventure. Maybe it was the inconsistency of having sex. After all, she hadn't had a girlfriend since college.

She and Karen had a nice relationship, vanilla, really. Neither was experienced; they were each other's first girlfriends, and Karen was satisfied with keeping it status quo. She never wanted to experiment beyond what Abby called "finger jobs." In the almost-year they'd been together, Karen never went down on her, they never used toys, never tied each other up or blindfolded the other. Vanilla. Abby had never experimented much beyond that either, mostly because every other woman she'd been with was only for one night. She had to be comfortable with a woman if she were to bring out her toy—singular—to use with someone. Would Syd be willing to go there? Had she gone there with anyone else?

She didn't know anything about Syd's history with other women. Had she had many girlfriends? Did she ever have time to have a serious relationship? From what she'd said, she worked long hours and didn't have much free time. Maybe Abby would "pack" tonight, see if Syd would be interested. In the meantime, Abby had writing to do. Her two characters had met at a bar and were leaving together. She knew they were going to have hot monkey sex that night, and Abby knew how it was going to happen. The foreplay, the actual sex scenarios, the afterglow. She now knew what it felt like to have earth-shattering, toe-curling sex, and she was now able to describe every feeling her characters were going to experience from her firsthand knowledge.

Abby had never gotten aroused while writing a sex scene, but she was now. She recalled having Syd's mouth on her, her fingers inside her stroking that special spot, her nipples being teased, and the direct current that led to her clit. Abby shifted in her chair more than a few times, the seam of her pants applying occasional pressure to where she wanted Syd's tongue to be. When she was done writing the scene, she had a strong urge for a cold shower and a cigarette even though she'd never smoked a day in her life. She wiped a bead of sweat off her forehead and laughed at herself.

Well, her characters were definitely sexually satisfied, something she knew more about thanks to Syd. She was shocked when she looked at the time in the bottom right corner of her computer, and she saved her work to her Dropbox. She needed to get moving. Syd was going to be at her house in thirty minutes.

Syd arrived wearing jeans and a form-fitting tank top, and Abby felt her libido rise, as it always did whenever she was close to Syd. She took her in her arms and kissed her hard up against the door. Abby groped Syd's breast as she continued to explore her mouth until Syd gently pushed her away.

"Where's your grandmother?"

"She's in town," Abby said as she closed the distance on Syd, only to be stopped by her outstretched arm.

"Are we going riding, or are you going to fuck me right here? I wouldn't mind skipping the ride, you know."

Hearing Syd ask her if she was going to fuck her nearly made Abby's legs give out. Abby blew out a deep breath and stepped away. She didn't seem to have any sort of control when Syd was around, and it was making her just a little bit crazy. "No, I promised them we were taking them out. Come on." Abby grabbed Syd's hand and led her out to the barn. They stepped up to the first stall where Bevin was waiting. Abby handed Syd an apple. "Here. Feed this to him and he'll be your best friend for life."

"Are you crazy? His mouth is huge! He'll bite off my hand."
Abby laughed. "No, he won't. He's gentle when you feed him.
Watch." Abby placed her hand under Syd's and brought the apple
up to Bevin's mouth, and he delicately took the fruit from her hand.
Abby reached out and rubbed his nose. "That's my boy."

They moved to the next stall where Pokey was, and she handed
another apple to Syd. This time, she did it by herself, and once the
apple was in Pokey's mouth, Syd rubbed her nose.

"This is Pokey. She was your grandmother's horse, and I
promise she'll be very careful with you."

Pokey moved her head up and down and curled her lips to
show her teeth as if she was agreeing with Abby and smiling, and it
made Syd laugh.

"Okay. First, I'm going to show you how to groom Pokey."

Abby pulled the older horse out of the stall and tied her with
crossties to keep her still. She placed the brush in Syd's hand and
covered it with her own to teach her the proper brushing strokes.
"This is to remove any dirt or grit from her. If there's dirt and we put
the saddle on, it will cause her pain."

Once Pokey was properly groomed, Abby grabbed a hoof pick
and cleaned her hooves, sparing Syd from having to do that. She
took Syd through the rest of the steps until Pokey was ready to ride
then she repeated the process with Bevin. Abby showed Syd how
to put on the saddle pad and saddle and buckle it, making sure it
was secure. She then showed her how to put the bridle over Pokey's
head and guide the bit into her mouth. Once both horses were tacked
and ready to ride, Abby grabbed a few water bottles from the small
refrigerator next to the tack room, along with a rolled-up blanket,
and placed the items in her saddlebag. She then untied Bevin and
Pokey and led them outside the barn.

"Do you remember how to mount?"

"I stick my foot in the stirrup, grab the horn on the saddle, and
pull myself up?"

"Yes. You're a quick learner," Abby said as she winked.

"I have a question. How do I drive this thing?"

Abby laughed heartily and handed her the reins once she was
in the saddle.

"What you want to remember is to hug Pokey with your legs by curving them inward toward her and keep your toes pointed upward. You want to hold the reins in your left hand like you're holding an ice cream cone and keep them loose. When you want to turn right, move the reins across her neck to the right and the opposite to go left. She'll know which way you want her to go when the reins touch her neck. When you want to stop, pull them back toward you."

Syd nodded in understanding. Abby was trying to keep the directions as simple as possible, but in all honesty, Pokey was such a great horse, she'd do exactly as Bevin would do while she was beside him. Syd could just hold onto the horn and Pokey would move identically to Bevin. But she wanted Syd as informed as possible so she could feel like she had a little bit of control during the ride.

"To get her to walk, kick or squeeze her. Relax your body and let it move with the horse. Watch me." Abby climbed into her saddle and squeezed Bevin's sides. As he started walking, she let her body move with him, and she also demonstrated how to use the reins. Syd watched every move, and Abby was confident that she would enjoy her first real horseback ride. She looked relaxed in the saddle. And sexy. Abby had thought about a special private place to take her after Syd told her about her dream, and her stomach fluttered as she thought of Syd's reaction to her little secluded paradise. There wasn't a stream, but there was plenty of grass and trees to provide shade and privacy. Abby wanted to please Syd, in any way she wanted.

"You ready?"

"As I'll ever be."

Syd let out a little startled yelp when Pokey started walking next to Bevin, but she quickly relaxed as they strolled through the pasture heading toward the back of Abby's property. The air was hot, the sun was shining down on them from the deep blue sky, and Syd couldn't believe she was thinking that it felt heavenly. There were no car horns, ringing phones, people shouting, no high-rise buildings. Just green grass, full, mature trees, wild flowers, birds flying overhead, and the sound of hooves clomping on the ground.

Syd didn't think she had ever felt that peaceful. She looked over at Abby who gazed back at her, and Syd could see the pride in Abby's eyes. She loved that she was the one that caused that emotion.

"You're doing great, Syd. A natural."

"That's because I have a great teacher."

"Virginia and I would ride together like this about once a week, maybe twice. It was a nice way to spend some time with her and discuss life. Your grandmother was a very intelligent woman who understood the ways of the world more than one would think. She seemed to know just the right thing to say if I was feeling sad about not having my parents around, or frustrated with life in general. She always listened, offered advice, and by the end of the ride, I would always feel better. I miss so many things about her now that she's gone, but our rides are near the top of the list."

Syd could see the sadness in Abby's eyes and on her face, and she wished she could lean over and caress her cheek, hold her until the feeling lessened.

"That sounds like a special time you two had. I'm glad she was able to help you and be your friend."

A few minutes later, they came to a grove of trees, and Abby brought the horses to a halt then dismounted. She draped the reins over Bevin's neck then helped Syd off Pokey. She grabbed the blanket and a couple of bottles of water before taking Syd's hand and leading her under the canopy of branches and leaves.

"There's no stream, but it's quiet and secluded." Abby smiled before spreading out the blanket.

"What about the horses? Won't they leave if they're not tied up?"

"Nah. They might wander a little, but they'll stick close by." Abby lay down on her side and extended her hand to Syd to come join her.

Syd's pulse raced as she realized Abby was trying to bring her dream to reality. She took Abby's hand and joined her.

"How did you feel riding Pokey? Piece of cake, right?"

Syd laughed. "I was scared shitless at first, but you were right. She's very gentle."

"And how are your legs feeling?"

The smoldering look in the darkened blue of Abby's eyes and her chest rising and falling turned Syd's insides molten. Her mouth was dry, which made it difficult to answer. "They're a little sore," she whispered. She felt Abby's hand touch the inside of her leg just above the knee, and Syd grew wet and hard as Abby began massaging her muscles.

"Here?"

Syd moaned, not wanting to wait, but enjoying the ride. "Higher." Her nipples hardened when Abby's hand moved higher up her leg, and Syd looked down to see them protruding through her tank top. She squirmed and pressed her mound into Abby's hand when it reached her center. Abby rubbed Syd's most sensitive place as she started kissing and biting Syd's ear, moving to her jaw, and finally down her neck. Syd threw her head back to allow more access to Abby's talented mouth. She unbuttoned her jeans and lowered the zipper with her trembling hands. When Abby had her hand just inside the waistband of Syd's panties, she hesitated. She looked into Syd's eyes, her vision dimming with arousal.

"I promise you won't wake up to find this a dream. I'm going to make you come, baby." Abby kissed Syd possessively and continued her hand into Syd's wetness. She thrust her hips into Abby's hand to get more pressure, more pleasure. Her legs spread farther, as much as her jeans allowed, encouraging Abby to take her, to take whatever she wanted because Syd wanted to give it all to Abby.

Abby slipped two fingers inside and stroked Syd's inner velvety walls before withdrawing to coat her bundle of nerves with her own wetness. She had been constantly aroused since the moment she and Abby had started innocently flirting, and it grew exponentially since they'd had sex near the pond. With the other women she'd slept with, there was never any urgency and her orgasm would come eventually. But with Abby, and maybe it was because of their limited time together, she always came so quickly that it was delicious and frustrating at the same time. She wanted each seduction, each climax to last for an eternity, but she also wanted to experience anything and everything Abby had to offer, and she only had six more days to have it. Syd opened her eyes to see sunlight streaming through the branches. She could smell the mixture of soil, grass, Abby's sweat, and her own arousal. That was her nirvana and she would commit every sensation of this moment to her memory.

She felt the tendrils of her orgasm building and fought to hang on, to make it last. She didn't want this feeling or moment to end, but she could do nothing to stop the powerful surge rage through her body as she pulled Abby closer, and she groaned into her shoulder. She convulsed repeatedly as Abby continued to apply pressure to her clit until Syd melted into Abby.

"Oh, God," Syd panted. She ran her fingers through Abby's hair and held the back of her head. "That was incredible."

"You're incredible, Syd. So responsive, so unguarded, so sexy."

Syd's body warmed and curled into Abby's. She'd never been that constantly aroused, so consumed with wanting to just be near Abby, needing to touch her and be touched by her. A week with her wasn't going to be long enough for everything she wanted to do to and for Abby. She pushed the melancholy she was beginning to feel far back to the recesses of her brain so she could be present and enjoy now. When she regained some energy, she rolled Abby onto her back and straddled her narrow hips. She unbuttoned Abby's jeans then pushed her shirt and sports bra above her breasts.

"I'm going to make you feel as wonderful as you just made me feel." She trailed her fingers over Abby's stomach and watched the muscles twitch. She leaned forward and took Abby's breast in her mouth and pleasured her nipples with her tongue while her fingers brought Abby to ecstasy.

Three hours later, Abby was back in the house once she walked Syd to her car, and she was ready for another shower. She spent a couple of hours checking and answering her email and jotting down some notes for her manuscript. Being around Syd was opening all kinds of ideas for her characters. She wouldn't exactly call Syd her muse, but she did feel her mind open to more creativity in regards to her character's sex lives. She smiled and shook her head. Since the first time Abby and Syd had sex, everything seemed clearer, like a fog had lifted from Abby's mind. Colors were brighter, sounds were sharper, smells more fragrant, words sounded smarter. She hoped that she would be able to keep this creativity when Syd returned to Chicago.

Abby decided against wearing her strap-on over to Syd's, but she put it in her overnight bag. She didn't bring it last night because she didn't want to assume she'd be asked to spend the night, but she felt pretty confident about tonight, especially after their morning together and their horse ride. Abby had to be careful of her heart though. She really liked Syd, and if geography were different, Abby could let herself fall in love with her. But Abby's life was in Iowa, with her gran, on the farm with her horses and chickens. This was the only life she knew with the exception of being away at Iowa State. Abby sighed. Why was she thinking about this now anyway? She had a gorgeous, sexy woman waiting for her, and she didn't want to waste a moment.

She grabbed her bag and practically ran into her gran, who was just getting home.

"Whoa, cowgirl. Is the house on fire?"

"Sorry, Gran. I was just on my way to see Syd."

She looked at Abby then noticed the duffel bag in her hand. "Am I to assume you won't be coming home again tonight, Abigail?"

Abby looked down at her feet, trying to buy time to figure out what to say. This was uncharted territory for her. The only thing she could do, the only thing she always did when it came to her gran, was she told the truth.

"Yes, Gran. I'll probably be staying the night with Syd."

"Come sit down, Abigail."

Abby followed her into the living room, oddly feeling like she was a child and her grandmother was going to explain why she shouldn't empty an entire bottle of bubble bath into a running bath tub. It had been an honest mistake for a nine-year-old Abby. Even though she was now in her early thirties, her gran still had a way of making her feel like a child, and that thought made her tense. She loved her gran, but she was a grown woman, capable of making her own decisions.

"I'm worried about you."

That simple yet complicated statement brought Abby up short. "Why?"

"I'm worried you'll be hurt by Sydney. She's a nice woman, but she's leaving soon to go home. I see you're fond of her and I'm afraid you'll have your heart broken."

"Gran, don't worry. I know exactly where Syd lives and that she'll be going back soon, but we enjoy each other's company and spending time together. I promise I'm being careful." Abby replayed her statement back in her head and thought it was self-explanatory without being disrespectful or too divulging. She would never knowingly or willingly treat her grandmother that way, not the woman who loved her and raised her, and had always been there for her.

Abby's grandmother sat staring at her with pursed lips, like she was trying to figure out what she would say next.

"I'm not going to get hurt. Syd and I have talked and we have an understanding." Abby looked at her watch then back to the woman who meant the most in the world to her. "I have to go, Gran. Syd's expecting me, and like Grandpa used to say, never keep a beautiful woman waiting."

Her grandmother smiled, probably recalling how affectionate her husband had always been to her. "I love you, Abigail. Enjoy your evening and tell Sydney I said hello."

Abby stood and kissed her on the cheek. "I will and I love you too." She looked back at her gran once more before closing the door behind her.

Abby understood why her gran was concerned, but she did have a grasp on her feelings for Syd and was already resigned to the fact that it was just a fling between them. Abby liked Syd, they got along well, and the sex between them had been amazing so far. She knew it would come to an end soon, but this was something she wanted. Something they both wanted. And when it came time for Syd to return to Chicago, Abby would kiss her good-bye and think of their time fondly.

Syd answered the door wearing a pale yellow sleeveless polo shirt that looked fabulous against her light brown skin and black, skin-tight jeans. Abby dropped her overnight bag just inside the door before taking Syd into her arms and kissing her passionately. Abby drifted her hands down and squeezed Syd's ass. Abby pulled her closer and nibbled on her neck. "We might not eat dinner tonight either."

Syd laughed and playfully pushed Abby away. "After I slaved away making a nice meal for you? Oh, no, lover. We're definitely eating dinner."

Notably admonished, Abby held her hands up in surrender. "I wouldn't think of wasting the delicious dinner we're about to eat."

"How do you know it's delicious?"

"Everything you've made me takes me to another place," Abby said before kissing Syd again.

"Oh, yeah? Well, Ms. Price, you seem to have the ability to take me to other places too." Syd turned and walked to the kitchen. No. She sashayed, Abby thought, and she willingly followed, unable to take her eyes off Syd's backside. She'd follow her to the ends of the earth just to see her from behind. The view was amazing.

When they sat down to eat, Abby noticed Syd looking at her contemplatively. "What? Do I have something on my face?"

"I was thinking about you while I boxed up some things this afternoon."

"Really? What were you thinking about? How great I am in bed? That I'm the best lover you've ever had?"

Syd smirked. "Beside that. I was thinking that I really don't know that much about you."

"What do you want to know?"

"Did I hear your grandmother say you went to college?"

Abby took a sip of her wine and wiped her mouth. "I did. I went to Iowa State and got my bachelor's in creative writing."

Abby tried not to look away while she answered, but it was difficult to look at Syd while not being completely truthful. There was a question in Syd's eyes. "I dabble a bit."

"Really? You like to write?"

Abby shifted in her seat. She didn't know why, but she didn't want to tell Syd that she wrote romance novels. It wasn't that she was embarrassed, but it wasn't something she was comfortable divulging at that time. "Eh, a little of this, a little of that. Whatever strikes me at the moment and allows me to be creative."

"That's so cool. I envy creative people. I was good at sports and I'm good with numbers, but I don't have a creative bone in my body."

"That's not true," Abby said as she took Syd's hand. "You're creative with your cooking. I'm sure you tweak recipes every once in a while, so you are creative. Just in a different way than me."

Syd squeezed her hand and took another bite.

"How about work? Do you have a job? I don't recall you mentioning anything other than volunteering at the animal shelter."

Abby was starting to feel a little scrutinized. She wasn't used to being interrogated. No, that was too strong of a word, but between her gran and Syd, Abby had answered more questions than she was used to, or comfortable with, in the past hour, and she was feeling a little out of sorts.

"Just around the farm and the shelter. I don't need the money so I might as well do something that brings me joy." When she saw the look on Syd's face, she knew she had to explain. "When my parents died, they left me a sizeable trust fund, one that leaves me never having to worry about money. My mom's family was rich and she was an only child, so she got her parents' entire inheritance when they died. I had a little distributed to me when I turned twenty-one, again when I turned twenty-five, and the rest when I turned thirty. I have a financial adviser that takes care of it for me, and as you've probably noticed, I don't live an extravagant lifestyle. I paid off Gran's farm and I pay all the bills. I indulge Gran and allow her to buy the groceries only because she thinks that since I'm the granddaughter, I shouldn't be paying her bills. But I explained to her that it was the least I could do to repay my grandparents for taking such great care of me."

"That's so sweet of you, Abby. I'm so sorry about your parents, but I'm so glad you have such loving grandparents."

"Me too. Was there anything else you wanted to ask?"

"No, that's it for now. I just wanted to know you better." Syd grinned and Abby felt herself relax.

They had finished dinner and Syd brought a slice of homemade cherry pie to the table. Abby wondered why only one slice until Syd sat in her lap and fed her a bite. Syd's eyes never left hers as Abby's lips closed around the sweet dessert. Abby moved her hands over Syd's hip and ass as she fed her another bite. Syd moved closer, and with the tip of her tongue, she licked a drop of cherry juice from the corner of Abby's mouth before kissing her fully on the mouth. Abby nearly growled then picked up Syd and carried her to the stairs. She felt like her legs would give out any second from the desire she felt throbbing between her legs, and she set Syd down before they both fell to the ground.

"Hang on," Abby said as she went to grab her bag and followed Syd to her bedroom. They frantically undressed and slid under the sheets, facing each other. Abby placed her hand on Syd's hip and pulled her to her. Whenever she was that close to Syd, she couldn't help but feel aroused and wanting. Apparently, Syd felt the same.

Syd closed her eyes and started breathing harder, making Abby dig her fingers into Syd's muscular leg, pulling her closer, meeting Syd's lips with her own, crushing them together. Abby reached between Syd's legs and stroked the length of her, feeling Syd get wetter and harder. Syd moved her hips back and forth slowly, letting Abby know she probably wasn't in any hurry to reach her destination, that she was just going to enjoy the ride.

"How do you feel about toys?" Abby whispered just before she sucked Syd's earlobe into her mouth.

"What kind are you talking about? Oh, God, right there."

"I brought a strap-on in case you're interested."

Syd smiled and nodded. "I'm very interested. Is that what you have packed in your bag?"

"Yep," Abby replied, feeling very pleased with herself for bringing it along.

"Put in on, baby. But I want you on your back so I can ride you."

It was ridiculous how just a few words could make Abby get so wet and hard. She groaned and sat on the side of the bed while she got all the straps buckled and the dildo in place. She always thought it looked ridiculous, but at this moment, she didn't care. All she cared about right now was having Syd on top of her, dominating her, fucking her until she came.

She turned on her back, the appendage pointing to the ceiling, and watched the slow smile creep up on Syd's pink lips. Jesus, she was sexy. In every possible way. Just when Abby thought Syd couldn't get any sexier, she licked the tip of the dildo and slowly rimmed it with her tongue before taking it in her mouth. Abby felt like it was a part of her, all the way to her core, and she thought she'd explode watching Syd's mouth move up and down the shaft, her hand gripped around it at the base, moving in the same direction as her mouth. Abby felt her clit swell and press against the base, but she didn't want to come before Syd.

"Come here, baby. I'm so ready for you." Abby handed a bottle of lube to Syd to apply to her cock. Syd put a little in her palm and covered the appendage, stroking it up and down, applying yet more pressure to Abby. "I'm going to come if you keep doing that, Syd."

Syd smiled again and straddled Abby. She moved into a half-kneeling position, grabbed the cock, and rubbed it up and down her clit. Abby was mesmerized by the site of Syd pleasuring herself.

"You're killing me," Abby squeaked out.

Syd let out a throaty chuckle as she lowered herself slowly until Abby was all the way inside her. Just as slowly, she raised up until only the head was in her. The dildo was coated with Syd's come, and Abby craved to have her mouth on her, drinking in her nectar. Syd continued at a leisurely pace, and Abby was in no hurry to rush her. This had to be the most erotic thing Abby had ever seen, the image burned into her mind for future fantasies—Syd straddling her, moving up and down on Abby's cock, eyes half closed and smoldering, breasts swaying with her movements. Abby reached up, tweaked Syd's hard nipple, and squeezed her breast then did it to the other.

"That's good, Abby. Keep squeezing my nipples. Harder."

Abby did as Syd told her until she leaned over, dangling her breasts in Abby's face. She took the hardened tip greedily in her mouth while she continued to knead the other breast. Syd's hips began gyrating back and forth, up and down, and her hand reached down to rub her own clit. Abby wanted to move Syd's hand so she wouldn't come so quickly and she could prolong her rhapsody.

"Oh, fuck, Abby. I'm going to come," Syd gasped. "Coming so hard." Syd cried out as her body jerked and shuddered. Abby didn't think Syd would ever stop. She didn't want her to. It was as if Abby could feel the same pleasure Syd had, and she never wanted it to end. Abby had been absently holding her breath and finally let it out. Abby realized that she would give or do anything to see Syd so sensual, so unbidden.

Syd collapsed onto Abby, her breathing labored, and gently bit Abby's neck.

"That was so fucking hot," Abby rasped out, her voice hoarse as if she had yelled out with Syd.

Syd laughed into Abby's neck. "It sure was. I don't remember ever coming that hard. This was the first time I've ever been fucked with a strap-on."

"You've never used one before? My God, Syd, you took command like it was second nature."

"I didn't say I've never used one before," Syd said as she traced Abby's lower lip with the tip of her finger. "Usually I'm the one doing the fucking." She winked and ground herself some more on Abby's cock, letting out a low, guttural moan. "I've always wanted to be on the receiving end, but the women I've been with wanted to receive so I always gave. Now I know what I've been missing."

Syd didn't seem in any hurry for Abby to pull out so they stayed in that position.

"What about you? Do you like to give or receive?"

Abby felt herself grow hot and was grateful for the muted light in the room. "I've only received since I've ever only used it on myself. I've never used a toy with anybody else."

Syd sat up and looked intently at Abby. "Really? That surprises me. Why is that?"

"Well, I tend to have flings, one-night stands, and I need to trust someone to make myself vulnerable like that."

Syd stroked Abby's cheek and she leaned into the pressure. "You trust me?"

"Of course. I know more about you than any of the women I've been with except for my college girlfriend."

"Hang on." Syd slowly pulled off Abby's cock, unbuckled the straps, and dropped it onto the floor. "Sorry. I love having that in me, but it's just weird to look at," Syd said while giggling. She cuddled up to Abby's side and placed her head on her chest. "Why don't you have a girlfriend?"

"Are you kidding? Does this town look like a hotbed for lesbian life?"

Syd laughed. "No, I suppose not, but aren't there larger cities nearby, ones that are more of a hotbed, as you put it?"

"No, not really. Not close enough that if I met someone, that we could see each other often."

"Have you ever thought of moving to a larger city?"

"Not really. Except to go to college, I've always been here on the farm. I'm not sure I'd be happy anywhere else. Besides, my gran is getting older, and I'd worry too much if she was alone."

Syd kissed Abby. "That's too bad. Any woman would be lucky to have you as their girlfriend," Syd declared before she kissed her way down Abby's body and brought her to climax with her mouth.

## Chapter Fourteen

Abby had gone home early in the morning to get her chores done and pack her bag. Syd pulled up to her house by ten a.m. and they drove to Chicago. There was still a little bit of time left before the sun would set, and Syd had promised her an amazing view if they made it back to her condo in time. They had stopped only a couple of times and they were both starving for dinner. Syd took Abby to a restaurant that Syd said had the best pizza in town.

After they ate, they drove to Syd's condo. They pulled into a parking garage and grabbed their bags. They walked through the garage until they came to double glass doors and were greeted by the doorman. Abby's gait slowed as she took in the opulent setting. White and gray marble floors, crystal chandeliers, floor-to-ceiling windows that allowed her to see the traffic outside. When Syd said she worked at a youth center, this wasn't what Abby imagined Syd's home to look like. She imagined Syd lived in a smaller, less fancy condo, maybe on the outskirts of the city, not directly in downtown. Abby looked over to Syd holding the elevator door open, and she hurried over. The doors closed and they began to ascend.

Abby stood still, surprised to feel how smooth and quick the ride was. She followed Syd down the hall, still remaining quiet, too shocked to come up with words. When they entered Syd's unit, she set down her suitcase and walked over to the windows that were, like the lobby, floor-to-ceiling. There was a gorgeous view of Chicago's downtown skyline, and Abby had quickly realized that Syd hadn't been lying about the view. The sky still had some deep purple, but soon it would be pitch-black.

"This is stunning, Syd."

"The view or my condo?"

"All of it." Abby turned and Syd was standing in front of her. Abby placed her hands on Syd's hips and pulled her closer. "You're stunning too."

"My meeting is at nine tomorrow morning. When I get back, I'll take you on a tour of my Chicago. But right now, I need a shower to wash the day off me. Want to join me?"

Syd didn't wait for Abby's answer, and she disappeared around the corner. Abby grabbed her suitcase and went to the room with the light on. She heard the shower running, and she quickly stripped out of her clothes. The glass door to the shower was already steamed, but Abby could see the silhouette of Syd's shapely body. Abby stepped in behind Syd and wrapped her arms around Syd's waist. Abby kissed her shoulder, and Syd leaned her head back. Abby took advantage of that position, and she kissed Syd's neck, licked the water that coated her skin, and brought her hands up to fondle Syd's breasts. Syd's nipples hardened against Abby's palms.

Abby turned Syd so her back was against the wall and kissed her hard. Syd put her foot on the built-in shower bench and Abby had clear access to Syd's sex. Abby pushed her fingers through the slick opening as Syd thrust her hips forward. Syd had slipped her thigh between Abby's legs and began rubbing her own clit against Syd's tight muscles. Abby felt Syd's walls tighten around her fingers. She pressed her thumb to Syd's clit, and the extra pressure sped up the impending orgasm. Syd threw her arms around Abby's neck, begging her to not let her fall. When Syd's body relaxed, Abby shut the water off and grabbed for a towel while keeping Syd in her arms. She wrapped the white, fluffy bath sheet around Syd's shoulders and back, then gave her a soft, lingering kiss.

"You're so beautiful when you come, Sydney. So fucking beautiful."

"You know just how to touch me, Abby. Now let's go to bed and I can see just how beautiful you are when I make you come."

❖

Syd drove home after meeting with Anne feeling like she was on Cloud Nine. Everything seemed to be falling into place. She got the funding needed to start her own center, she was having amazing sex with an amazing woman who was waiting for her back at her condo, and the weather was perfect to show Abby Chicago. She thought about calling Vanessa and her parents to join them, but she didn't want to overwhelm Abby with meeting the family. Besides, it wasn't like they were in a serious relationship. They would head back to Iowa tomorrow, Syd would continue cleaning out Virginia's home, put it up for sale, and she would return to Chicago to get started on developing her own center.

Syd walked through the front door and spied Abby outside on her patio standing at the rail looking out at the city. Syd stood there for a moment and admired Abby from behind. Syd couldn't think of one thing she didn't like about Abby. She was sweet, giving, adorably cute, and had a beautiful body. It really was too bad they lived so far from each other. Syd would exclusively date Abby if they lived in the same town. No sense in thinking about that right now, though. She approached the sliding glass door and Abby turned when Syd opened it. Abby had the type of smile that reached her eyes and made Syd feel like the sun was shining just on her.

"Hi. How'd it go?"

Syd stepped closer and gave Abby a kiss that made promises for later. "It went great. Anne was very nice and excited for my plan. Even more so when I told her that I wanted to include LGBTQ youth. When I get back, I'll start looking for a place, as well as hiring staff and volunteers."

Abby wrapped her arms around Syd's waist. "I'm so happy for you. You're doing a really great thing by opening up a place to include all kids."

Syd gave Abby one more kiss. "Let me change into more comfortable clothes and we can get going."

They walked two blocks down from Syd's condo to Navy Pier and grabbed a quick lunch. Syd bought them tickets to the Centennial

Wheel and they climbed into the gondola. When they reached the top, Abby gasped and squeezed Syd's hand.

"This view is spectacular."

Syd had lived in Chicago her entire life, and she never tired of looking at the skyline or Lake Michigan. It was the main reason she bought her condo, because of the fantastic views she had from her living room and bedroom.

"Wait until you see the view from the restaurant I'm taking you to tonight."

When the ride was complete, Syd took Abby's hand and walked to the front of the pier.

"Where are we going now?"

Syd led her down a ramp to a large boat. "We're going on a river architecture tour. It's a great way to see all the stunning buildings in Chicago."

They sat near the front and Abby put her arm around Syd's shoulders. "I'm having such a great time here with you."

Syd kissed Abby's hand that was draped on her shoulder. "I'm glad. I wish we didn't have to head back tomorrow so I could show you more."

"Me too. I'd love to see where you work."

"Actually, that can be arranged. We can swing by on our way out of town."

They listened to the tour guide talk of the different buildings along the Chicago River, who designed them, and why they were designed in a specific way.

Syd snuck glances at Abby looking up at the tall structures with wonder. She was pleased that Abby was enjoying herself. For some reason, that was very important to Syd. Maybe it's because Abby and Bernice had been so nice and helpful to Syd while she'd been in Iowa. She'd hoped that she would be able to maintain a friendship with them.

They arrived back to the condo and agreed to sit out on the balcony for a little while before they needed to get ready for dinner. Syd poured them each a glass of wine as they watched the sun start to slip behind the tall buildings.

Abby took a sip of wine then chewed on her bottom lip. Syd saw the action and placed her wine down on the small glass table between the two chairs.

"Is there something on your mind?"

"Well, I don't mean to pry, and you can tell me it's none of my business, but how can you afford this place and your car by working with children?"

Syd laughed and picked up her glass to take a sip. "I made a lot of money and gained some stock options when I worked for my firm. I was actually pretty responsible with my money. I had nice business clothes, my car, and my condo. I never took vacations, I didn't go out a lot, and I saved most of my paycheck and occasional bonuses I received. Just by cashing in my stock options, I was able to pay off my condo and car, and still had some left over to invest. I no longer need to wear fancy suits and silk blouses. Where I'm taking you to dinner tonight is a special treat. It's not something I would typically do."

Abby nodded as if she understood.

Syd continued. "Growing up, I was always focused on my sports and schoolwork, and after I graduated college, I worked my ass off to get where I was. I worked so hard and so much that I never stopped to enjoy what life had to offer. It was never about money for me. Well, not entirely. I grew up in a middle-class family and my parents taught me to work for what I wanted, not to expect handouts. And they also taught me never to lose sight of what was important. Working with those kids, giving back to my community is what's important to me. I just happened to make a lot of money when I was working my previous job and I allowed myself the two luxuries of my condo and car. Other than that, I live a pretty simplistic life and I'm much happier now. All that's important to me is giving these kids a safe place and a chance for a better life."

Abby's face relaxed and her eyes softened as she took Syd's hand. "I think what you're doing for these kids is wonderful, and I think you're very special."

Syd smiled and leaned in for a kiss. "Thank you. That means a lot to me. Let's go get ready so I can treat you to an unforgettable dinner."

They arrived at the Signature Room at the 95th floor of the John Hancock Center and were shown to a table at the window. The sun had just set and the dark purple and pink sky helped illuminate the building lights that seemed to go on forever. Once the waiter left to fulfill their drink orders, Syd pointed out the taller buildings to Abby and gave her a few fun facts about them. Syd never got to play tour guide because she didn't really know anyone outside of Chicago. She hoped Abby was enjoying this as much as Syd was. Although the food was delicious, it was the view of the city that made Syd want to bring Abby.

Syd sipped her glass of sparkling wine that was paired with the white and dark chocolate mousse cake, and she looked across the table to Abby, who was gazing back at Syd.

"Are you enjoying yourself?"

Abby smiled just as the rim of her flute reached her lips. She took a small sip and waited to answer until she set down her glass. The move and the slight upward curve of her lips was indescribably sexy. Syd felt a flutter in her belly and a twitch a little farther south.

"I'm having a great time. I wish it didn't have to end so soon."

Syd reached across the table and held Abby's hand. "You're welcome to come visit anytime you'd like.

Abby woke the next morning, feeling sore and satisfied. When they arrived back to Syd's the night before, they frantically removed their clothing before having sex that lasted into the early morning. Abby would love nothing more than to remain in bed with Syd and continue where they left off. Unfortunately, they had a long drive ahead of them and they still needed to stop by Syd's work. Technically, they didn't *need* to go to the center, but Abby wanted to see the place that was so special to Syd.

A cup of coffee and an hour later, they were in the car headed toward a different Chicago. One that wasn't all lights and high-rises. This other Chicago was old apartment buildings and old cars parked along the curb. Instead of tourists and fancy restaurants, there were residents and burger joints. The discrepancy between the two parts of Chicago was vast in Abby's opinion.

They pulled into a parking lot next to a rundown-looking building and walked through the front door. A young girl reading in the corner looked up and her face lit up with joy.

"Ms. Syd! You're back!"

Syd knelt and accepted a hug from the girl. "Hi, Alisa. I'm only here for a few minutes. I have to go back out of town, but I promise to be back soon. Have you been helping out around here while I've been gone?"

"Yes. Ms. Leah has been helping me with my homework and I help her straighten up the books. Who's that?" Alisa pointed at Abby.

"Alisa, it's rude to point. Please apologize."

"Sorry." Alisa looked down at her feet, clearly embarrassed at being called out on her manners in front of a stranger.

"This is my friend, Abby. Abby, this is Alisa. She's one of the best helpers I've ever had."

That compliment put the smile back on Alisa's face and she gave Syd another hug. Abby stuck her hand out and Alisa shook it. "It's nice to meet you. Ms. Syd has told me so many great things about you and the other kids here."

Alisa looked up at Abby. "You're pretty."

Abby knelt so she'd be closer to Alisa's height. "Thank you. I think you're very pretty, too." That earned Abby a hug and she felt like her heart might melt.

"Abby wanted to see where I worked. Would you like to give her a tour?"

Alisa nodded and grabbed Abby's hand.

"Make sure you introduce her to everyone, too."

Abby looked behind her and noticed Syd trailed a few feet behind them, the pride evident on her face. Being able to see Syd interact with the kids and staff was a beautiful sight. The kids obviously loved Syd. All of them were excited to see her and gave her hugs. Syd took the time to talk with each of them, asking them about school, and a particular project or test. She asked them how their parents or siblings were doing. Syd seemed genuinely interested in every aspect of the kids' lives. Syd laughed and joked with the adults on staff. Abby had known Syd for only a short week, but it was apparent from her interaction that this was where Syd belonged.

## Chapter Fifteen

Syd and Abby had arrived back to Virginia's farm late the previous night and they fell into bed completely exhausted. They woke early so Abby could get back home to start her day. Syd lingered at the door, taking her time kissing Abby good-bye. The sun had barely risen, the birds had just started chirping, and Abby had to get home to do her work. Syd reassured her that she would feed the chickens, that she was getting quite good at it. Her reason, however, was purely selfish. If she did the chore instead of Abby, it would give them a few more minutes to kiss and hold each other. Syd really liked Abby, and the more time they could spend together, the better. Her time in Iowa was quickly coming to an end, and the thought of saying good-bye to Abby was making her heart heavy.

Abby gave her one more kiss before extricating herself from Syd's arms. She stood in the doorway watching Abby drive away, then she poured herself another cup of coffee and fixed breakfast. She wanted to keep finding things to do other than clean out Virginia's bedroom, but she knew she couldn't put it off any longer. She had to go through her closet, dresser drawers, and nightstands, and she wasn't looking forward to it at all.

Syd decided to go through the bathroom first. That should be easy enough. She opened the medicine cabinet and found the basic staples—deodorant, face cream, a few small bottles of perfume. She smelled each one and liked the scents—light, not too flowery. Syd decided to keep them, and she set them off to the side. She spotted a prescription bottle for blood pressure and multivitamins and also set them aside to properly dispose of them. No other medications. Virginia must have been relatively healthy until just before she died. She found some nearly full bottles of lotion and shampoo, bars of soap, a couple of tubes of toothpaste still in the box, and she placed them in a donation box. She would ask Abby if there was a homeless shelter she knew of that she could give them too. She boxed up the linens, tissue, and toilet paper that could also go to a shelter. The rest of the items in the drawers, Syd dumped into a trash bag. With the bathroom cleaned out, she had no choice but to start on the bedroom.

She opened the closet door and was amazed at the amount of space it had. Virginia had left a few of Harold's suits hanging, but the rest of the clothing was hers. She took each dress, blouse, and pair of slacks off their hangers, folded them, and placed them in boxes for donations. Every article of clothing was in good shape—no tears, no stains, no missing buttons. It was obvious that Virginia took great pride in her appearance. Some of the outfits were appropriately stylish for a woman her age. Syd would have to ask Abby where Virginia liked to go, things she liked to do. Did she go to church every Sunday? Did she go out to eat often? Did she like to stroll down Main Street and visit the shops?

She pulled the shoe boxes down from the top shelf of the built-ins and checked inside. She found a few pairs of low heels that were cute, and if they weren't three sizes too small, Syd would've kept them for herself. She chuckled at the size of Virginia's feet. She knew she was a short woman, and she had very small feet, but it was one more thing that she had learned about her grandmother on that trip. Syd's mama's feet were small too, so she obviously got them from her mother. Syd definitely had her father's feet because they were a little larger than they should be for a woman her height. She smiled at the thought. The last box felt too heavy for shoes, and Syd found it full of photos. She sat on the floor and started looking through them. There was writing on the back of each one indicating who was in the picture and the year it was taken.

Syd was amused at the baby pictures of Virginia being held by her mother and grandmother. She had on a frilly dress and a bonnet on her head. The picture was taken in 1931. The next one was of Virginia as a toddler being held by her father and her mother standing next to them, taken in 1933. These were Syd's great-grandparents. Her great-grandfather was a tall, good-looking man, dressed in a sharp double-breasted suit that had oversized pockets and pointed lapels, and he was wearing a hat. Syd thought he looked quite dapper. Her great-grandmother was in a floral print dress that came to just below her knees with a matching thin belt high on her waist, and her hat and shoes matched. They made a striking couple. She wondered if her mom knew anything about them. She would have to ask her the next time they talked.

By the time she finished looking at all the photos, two hours had passed. She set the box aside so she could add it to the items she wanted to keep. Even though she didn't know any of the people in the photographs, they were part of her history, and they didn't deserve to be dumped in a trash can. Her pile of things she was keeping was growing, and she'd probably have to have some boxes shipped to Chicago because it all wouldn't fit in her car. To count, she had the china, photos and albums, candles, and some of her mama's belongings such as her high school yearbooks and report cards that she had found in the garage. She hadn't even cleaned out the kitchen yet, so who knew what else she'd keep.

Syd went through the dresser and chest of drawers, and again folded and boxed the clothing that she was able to donate. One drawer held antique-looking cloths and doilies. Maybe they had belonged to Virginia's mother. One more thing to add to the "keep" pile. In another drawer, she came across baby clothes. She recognized them from seeing her mama wearing them in her baby photos. She added those to the "keep" pile.

Syd moved on to the nightstand on one side of the bed, and when she opened the top drawer, she immediately knew it was Harold's. She found a pair of reading glasses and a bible that had his name inscribed in gold lettering on the front. She also found his wallet that held his expired driver's license and one credit card, a small notebook that contained bible verses, and a pen. Harold must have been a religious man because it appeared he had put a lot of thought into the verses and had to write them down. There wasn't much else of consequence. Was it always this tidy? Or did Virginia clean it out but left those few items remaining? Maybe it made her feel less lonely to keep his nightstand with a few of his things. She wasn't sure what to do with them. She could throw out his reading glasses and notebook, maybe donate his bible. She'd need to shred his driver's license and credit card, but it was a nice black leather wallet that was in excellent condition. She'd keep that too.

Syd's stomach rumbled and she looked at her watch. One thirty? Time had flown by, but her stomach was reminding her that she hadn't eaten anything in over five hours. She fixed herself a sandwich and bowl of soup to tide her over until dinner. As she ate, she realized that by going through her grandparents' possessions, she was learning a little more about them. Virginia liked to sew, cook, garden, and play cards. She was a stylish dresser and took pride in not only her appearance, but also her home. Syd knew less about Harold, only that he farmed, fished, was religious, and didn't want his daughter marrying a black man. And truthfully, knowing what she knew, she didn't really have any desire to learn more about Harold, but she felt a heaviness in her chest the more she learned about Virginia and a sadness that she never got to know her or spend time with her. But she still hadn't found the answers she was looking for. Why had they disowned their daughter? Why did Virginia hire a private investigator to find her but not contact her once she was found? Would Virginia have wanted her as a granddaughter?

She had four hours before Abby would be back. She had no idea what she would fix for dinner, but she was sure she had something she could throw together. She wondered how Abby's day was going and what she was doing. The more time they spent together, the more she liked Abby. The sex was out of this world phenomenal, but it went beyond that. Syd appreciated Abby's love for her grandmother, her work ethic, her sense of humor, her capacity for caring. Abby had everything Syd had wanted in a girlfriend yet hadn't found. Until now. Maybe she should talk to Abby to see how she felt about Syd. Maybe they could do a long-distance relationship if Abby was willing.

Syd pulled out her smart phone and Googled the nearest airport to Charville. Almost an hour from there to Des Moines. She then Googled flight time from Des Moines to Chicago. Almost another hour. A two-hour trip each way wasn't a long trip. Definitely doable. Since Abby didn't work, she could fly out and spend a few days, or a few weeks, which Syd would love even more. And she could fly here occasionally and spend a long weekend with Abby and Bernice. The more she thought about it, the more excited she got. She felt a giddiness inside her, like her heart was full but light. She couldn't wait to discuss it with Abby. But first, she had more cleaning to do.

Syd went back to Virginia's room and opened the top drawer to her nightstand. The contents were similar to Harold's—reading glasses, bible, five romance novels by Leah Griffin. *Go, Virginia.* Syd had to laugh because that was Vanessa's favorite author. She opened the cover and discovered it had been signed to Virginia from the author. How cool was that?

Syd decided to give these to Vanessa, sure she would love them. She probably had copies of those five books, but at least these were signed. Syd typically read non-fiction, but she felt she knew enough about Leah Griffin. Every time there was a new post on her website, Facebook, or Twitter, Vanessa felt it was her duty to read them to Syd.

According to Vanessa, Leah's sixth book was going to be released in two months, and she was currently working on her seventh novel. Syd turned the books over to read the blurb and they sounded a little racy. Maybe she should give one of her books a try. She was a little disappointed that there wasn't a picture of the author on the back cover.

Syd pulled out her phone again and Googled Leah Griffin. She read some of the posts on Leah's website, and they actually made Syd laugh. They were musings of what it was like when she wrote a book, going through edits, choosing a cover, and coming up with a title and names for her characters. Leah's humor was similar to Abby's, and Syd found it rather endearing. Again, she was disappointed there weren't any pictures of her on her website. Under the "Up and Coming" tab, she saw that Leah was going to do some book signings once her latest novel was released. Syd got excited when she saw Chicago was one of her stops. She couldn't wait to tell Vanessa. Of course, she probably already knew. Okay, enough of that. Syd had work to do. She put her phone on the bed without seeing a picture of the popular author and opened the bottom drawer of the nightstand.

Syd's breath caught when she saw a stack of letters addressed to her mama that were unopened. "Return to Sender" was written on the front in her mama's writing. Syd took off the rubber band holding the envelopes together and counted eight. Eight letters that Virginia had written to Syd's mother that went unread. She looked at the dates on the stamps. The first one was mailed out just a few months before Harold died. The last one dated two years ago. With shaking hands, Syd opened the first envelope, unfolded the single page of stationary, and began to read.

*Dear Jillian,*

*I know it's been too many years since we've seen each other or talked, and I regret that immensely. I understand why you haven't called. Your father said some awful things to you on that day you brought Isaiah and your daughter to the farm, and I didn't do anything to stop it. For that, I'm so sorry.*

*She's so beautiful, Jillian, just like her mother. I feel your father also regrets that day because whenever he looks at the photograph of the three of us taken the day you left for college, he gets moody and retreats to the barn. I wish we could turn back time to the day you brought Isaiah home to meet us. I wish I could do that and change your father's attitude. In my perfect world, we would have invited Isaiah in, got to know him, made sure his intentions toward you were honorable, then start planning your wedding over supper. But I can't change the past. I can only hope that we can move on to the future and become a family again.*

*Unfortunately, your father's future is coming to an end. I hate that I have to tell you this in a letter, but you keep refusing to take my calls. Jillian, your father is dying of cancer. He hadn't been feeling well, and by the time he went to see his doctor, it had spread. The doctor said it can be two months or two years, but he probably doesn't have that much time. It would mean so much to me, to both of us, if you would at least call. Maybe we could all forgive each other while there's still time. Not a day goes by that I don't think of you. I love you and I'm sorry.*

*Mama*

Syd read the letter again. Virginia must not have known that Mama had called the house and Harold hung up on her. Did her mama know that her father was dying? She must not have since none of the letters had been opened. Her eyes stung with the tears that were starting to form. She couldn't imagine what it would be like if she didn't have her parents in her life. Even when she came out to them, she was confident in their love and support to know that they would never disown her. Maybe her mama's estrangement from her own family made the process for Syd so much easier. She opened the next letter, dated just two weeks before Harold died. Again, the envelope had "Return to Sender" written on the front.

*Dear Jillian,*

*I was rather disappointed that you sent back my previous letter unopened. I'm hoping with all my heart that you'll open this one. Your father doesn't have much time left, honey. The cancer has ravaged his body, and he spends most of his time sleeping in a hospital bed on the first floor of our house. He's been placed on hospice care, and the staff have been really helpful, coming in every other day to make sure he's comfortable. It's so hard for me to watch him wither away, and I really wish you were here with me, with us. Your father has been contemplative over the past few weeks, knowing he doesn't have much time left. The thing he's expressed the most guilt over is being a "racist son of a bitch," his words.*

*He told me that he regrets sending you away. All of you. He wants to tell you in person how sorry he is. Please come, Jillian. And please bring your family. He really wants to meet his granddaughter, and he especially wants your forgiveness.*

*I love you, sweetheart.*

*Mama*

Syd wiped away the tears that were now falling down her cheeks. *Oh, Mama. I wish you had opened these letters. Do you regret not making up with your parents before they died? That I was deprived of a relationship with my grandparents?* Syd didn't blame her mama for being hurt by the racism and bigotry of her father, but she lost out on so much and Syd's heart ached for all the loss it had caused.

She read the rest of the letters, which were so different from the first two. In the third, Virginia had written that Harold had passed away and they had a memorial service for him at their church. In the others, Virginia would write about her new life as a widow, things she did to keep herself busy so she wouldn't miss Harold so much. She mentioned Bernice and Abby, and how helpful Abby had been in taking care of the work around the farm that Harold had done when he was alive and well.

Virginia spoke so fondly of Abby, the gratitude and love she felt for Abby had been palpable, practically jumping off the page. Syd's feelings for Abby grew with each praise Virginia had said about her. Syd appreciated the kind of woman and neighbor Abby had been to her grandmother, and now to her.

The last letter Virginia had written spoke of her resignation that she would never reconcile with her only child, that she would never know her son-in-law or her only granddaughter. That no matter how Jillian felt about her, Virginia would think of her every day and love her until the day she died. That she wouldn't bother her anymore.

Syd wrapped the rubber band around the pile of letters and held them against her chest. Her body slumped as she continued to weep. She never knew how her mama felt when she told her Virginia had died. She never gave any indication that it bothered her. Like she was a stranger, not her own mother. Syd wondered if her mama told Daddy. Did she cry? Was she relieved? Or was she regretful, as Syd was feeling. The big dilemma she was now facing was whether or not she'd give these letters to her mama. It could be cathartic for her mama to read them, to know of her parents' regret, how they wanted to reconcile and get to know her family.

It might be good for her mama to know they never stopped loving her or thinking about her. On the other hand, it could wreck her emotionally to think about all the time that had been wasted being estranged from them, that if she had not been so stubborn and read at least one of the letters, that she could have forged a new relationship, at least with her mother. Syd understood that her mama had been hurt, and that she was doing what she had to do in order to protect herself and her family.

As much as Syd loved her mama, she had been known to be quite a stubborn woman. There were times that she was so set in her beliefs and values that she was incapable of seeing an opposing point of view or forgiving when she had been wronged. Maybe sometimes that was a noble trait to have. Other times, it could be a downfall. Syd would have to consider the repercussions of giving those letters to her mama. She would talk to her father about it and see what he thought.

Next to where the stack of letters had been was a folder. She opened it to find an envelope addressed to her, and some papers and photos underneath. She set the letters aside and sifted through the photos. They had been of Syd, from what she could gather, taken almost two years ago. There was a picture of her walking in downtown Chicago dressed in her work attire. Another of her and Vanessa sitting on a park bench near Lake Michigan. Another of her visiting a museum with the kids. And a final one of her having breakfast on a patio of a café with her parents.

She read through the papers and realized it was a report completed by the private investigator Virginia had hired. It had a lot of her personal information—phone number, address, birth date, employment, education. Syd was conflicted. She felt violated that so much information could be obtained by a complete stranger. Overjoyed that her grandmother would go through so much just to find her. Sad that even though Virginia had her address and phone number, she didn't reach out to get in contact with her. Why would she spend all that money on a private investigator if she had no intention of using his information? She stared at the sealed envelope that bore her name, flipping it over and back, trying to gather up the courage to find out what her grandmother couldn't say to her in person or on the phone, that she felt the only way to say it was on a piece of paper. Syd took a deep breath and carefully opened the envelope. She pulled out pages of paper and ran her fingers over the writing as if she could actually touch her grandmother. After a few more moments, she unfolded the letter and began to read.

*My dearest Sydney,*

*If you're reading this letter, then I have passed on and my attorney contacted you. There is so much I want to say to you, I don't know where to begin. Maybe I should start with regrets. I regret that I never got to meet you or have a relationship with you. It's not that I didn't want to, but your mother and us, your grandfather and me, had a falling out, and our relationship never recovered.*

*I tried several times to contact your mother, but she was probably too hurt, too angry, and probably too stubborn (she got that from her daddy) to forgive us of the major mistake we made with her. I'll get back to that later.*

*I saw you in person only once. You were just a young thing, but I loved you with all my heart from that moment on. I don't know if you remember that day, but you and your parents arrived unannounced to introduce you to us. Unfortunately, my husband, your grandfather, was raised by a racist father, and that bigotry spilled down and tainted your grandfather. Please know that I didn't share his views in that manner. He wasn't happy that your mother married a black man. I'm sorry. I'll get back to that later, too.*

*I'm so nervous that I can't seem to keep my thoughts straight. Or it could just be a symptom of being an old woman. As I was saying, that day many years ago, when I first laid eyes on you, I thought you were the most beautiful little girl I had ever seen, and my heart nearly burst with pride because you were my granddaughter.*

*Seeing you now, even though it's only through pictures, and seeing your accomplishments, my heart wants to burst again. You've made this old woman very proud.*

*Please know that if we had been in your life, I would have gone to every sporting event, every award ceremony, every graduation, and I would have cheered the loudest, pointing to you and yelling, "That's my granddaughter!" If Harold hadn't been so stubborn, we both would have been there.*

*Back to your grandfather. As I said before, he was raised by a racist, spiteful man. I despised my father-in-law, but I loved my husband. I had honestly never heard him speak a racist word about anyone until the day Jillian brought your daddy home to meet us and informed us they were engaged to be married. We were both shocked by that announcement, as your mother never even told us she was dating anyone while she was away in college.*

*That was the first time I had ever heard your grandfather say the N-word, and to say I was shocked speechless would be an understatement. Another big regret is that I stayed silent while he told your mother and father to leave and never come back. A couple of days later, I thought he had cooled down enough where I could talk some sense into him about what he did and how I strongly disagreed with him, but he screamed at me and told me never to bring it up again.*

*He didn't hit me. In fact, he'd never raised a hand to me or spoken to me in that manner ever. That is why I was scared to say anything else about it again. I wished I had the courage to stand up to him, especially after your mother brought you to visit. If I had, things might have been different. But I wasn't. I went along with what my husband said and did. That is something I had to live with, and it's my biggest regret, along with not knowing you in person.*

*You're probably wondering why I didn't contact you when I obviously had your information. Truth is, I was scared. I wasn't sure how you or your parents would react to me getting in touch with you after all this time. That fear kept me from reaching out so I did what I thought was the next best thing—I left you my property.*

*My wish is that you'll love it as much as I do, and that you'll decide to keep it. I don't expect you would drop your life in Chicago to move to this small town and live in my house, but maybe you might find it as charming as I do.*

*We raised your mother in this house, and until that horrible day, our home was filled with laughter and love. I want that to return to our home, your home, and I would love for you to build new, happy memories. If you decide to sell, I've made arrangements for Bernice and Abby (they're my neighbors and two of the sweetest women I've had the pleasure of knowing) to take Pokey and the chickens so I know they'll be well taken care of.*

*Well, I guess these were the most important things I wanted to say—I regret being a coward, not standing up to your grandfather and allowing the estrangement between your mother and us. I regret not having you in my life and not being able to know you. And I regret not being able to ever tell you I love you. Because I do, Sydney. So very much.*

*I hope you can find it in your heart to forgive us, all of us, for being so stubborn and cowardly. Please tell your mother that I love her and that I never stopped. I love you and I'm so very proud of you.*

*Your grandmother,*
*Virginia*

Syd curled up on the floor and cried for the grandmother she never knew, yet loved Syd so much. She cried for all that her mama lost out on with her parents. And she cried for the son of a bitch grandfather who caused this whole mess.

• 168 •

## Chapter Sixteen

A bby had been knocking on the door for over five minutes with no answer. Syd must've been in the shower. Her car was in the driveway so Abby knew she was home. She had walked around to the back to see if Syd was there or sitting by the pond, but she didn't see her, so she used her key and let herself in. She found the downstairs to be empty. Syd wasn't in the kitchen, which surprised Abby. Syd had said she'd cook them dinner, but there was nothing on the stove. Maybe she had been busy packing all day and was running late. She went upstairs and didn't see Syd in her room or the bathroom. She was just about to call out for her when she noticed the door to Virginia's room was open.

She stood in the doorway and took in the boxes, trash bags, and utter disarray. The sun was just beginning to set, and there was little light in the room. She was about to turn around and head back downstairs when she heard a sniffle. She quickly made her way to Virginia's side of the room and spotted Syd lying in a fetal position on the floor.

"Syd? Baby? What's wrong?"

Syd didn't answer, but also didn't object when Abby picked her up off the floor and carried her to her room. She gently placed Syd on the bed, and when she turned on her side, again resuming fetal position, Abby got behind her and wrapped her arm around Syd.

"What happened, sweetheart? Why are you crying?"

"I found letters in Virginia's nightstand."

"What letters? Who were they addressed to?"

Syd took a shuddering breath that made Abby tighten her hold.

"There was a stack from Virginia to my mama that were marked "Return to sender.""

"Did she have the wrong address?"

"No. Mama sent them back without even reading them. I can't believe she didn't open any of them."

Abby dropped a kiss on Syd's temple. "Why would she do that?"

"The short version? Because Harold told Mama that if she married Daddy, she'd no longer be welcome in the family. She married him anyway. When I was a young girl, they brought me here to meet my grandparents and Harold told us to leave and never come back. That was the last time my mama saw or spoke to her parents."

"Jesus, Syd. That's awful. The Virginia I knew wouldn't have treated her own daughter that way."

Syd extracted herself from Abby's hold, and Abby felt it like a slap to her face. She watched Syd stand and look out the window, not bothering to look at Abby. "Are you calling my mama a liar?"

"Not at all. I believe what you told me. I'm just saying that I can't imagine Virginia treating *anyone* that way."

Syd's shoulders slumped and she turned around with her arms crossed over her chest. "Well, technically, Harold was the one that did all those things, but Virginia went along with it. She didn't stand up for her daughter or against her husband."

Abby moved to sit on the side of the bed so she could be closer to Syd but still give her the space she seemed to need. "Do you want to talk about the letters? What was in them? If you do want to talk, I'll listen."

Abby waited until Syd uncrossed her arms and sat in Abby's lap. She again wrapped her arms around Syd and waited for her to begin.

"I feel so bad for Mama and Virginia." Syd told Abby about the first letter, when Harold had been diagnosed with cancer, and every letter until the last, when Virginia had resigned that she had lost Jillian forever. "They both lost out on so much because they were all too stubborn to accept and forgive." Syd placed her head on Abby's shoulder and began to cry. "I lost out on so much by not knowing my grandmother. Did you know she'd hired a private investigator to find me?"

"Yes." Abby tightened her hold. "You mentioned it the first time you had dinner with Gran and me."

"Oh, yeah. I just can't believe she knew where I was and she didn't contact me. She wrote me a letter that I was meant to find after she died. I could've gotten to know her, Abby. I could have visited her."

"Would you have? Knowing your mother was estranged from her parents, would you have possibly gone against your mother's wishes and had a relationship with Virginia?" Abby asked the question as gently as she could. The moments of silence that followed led Abby to believe Syd wouldn't have.

"I'm not sure, to be honest. But I was never given the chance. And now it's gone. All I'm left with are photographs, stuff that belonged to her."

"What did your letter say?"

"She talked about regrets—of losing Mama, of not getting to have a relationship with me. How much she loved me. How proud she was of me."

Abby could feel her shirt become wet from Syd's tears. "I believe her, Syd. How could she not be proud of the woman you've become? How could she not love you? You are an incredibly smart, giving, courteous woman, and I'm willing to bet Virginia would have been a wonderful grandmother to you."

Abby hadn't meant to say anything to make Syd cry harder, but that's what Syd did. Her arms came around Abby's shoulders, and Syd held on like Abby was her lifeline.

"I'm so sorry, baby. I'm so sorry," Abby cooed as she held Syd and let her cry. Abby's heart broke for Syd and her never having the time to spend with Virginia like she'd had. She wished that Syd had had the opportunity to know and love Virginia, and vice versa.

Having had the opportunity to spend time with Syd over the past week or so, she was certain Virginia would have completely loved Syd, just as Abby was beginning to. She had meant for this time with Syd to be a fun, no-strings-attached affair, but the times they'd spent together had begun to attach those damn strings. Abby knew she was going to ache to her very core when Syd went back home. But she wouldn't have traded this time with her for anything.

Abby was surprised when Syd released her hold and stood, facing Abby with her red, swollen eyes and flushed cheeks. Syd lifted her shirt over her head, released the clasp of her bra, and shimmied out of her shorts and panties, standing gloriously nude in front of Abby.

"Make love to me."

That simple command unraveled all the protection Abby had tried to place around her heart. She stood and cradled Syd's face in her calloused hands and kissed her like there would be no tomorrow. Before tonight, all of their kissing was hot and heavy and meant to turn up the heat that would lead to even hotter sex. Tonight, her kisses would be slow, sensuous, loving. Syd parted her lips and Abby slid the tip of her tongue into her warm mouth. She felt Syd's hands move down her back and squeeze her ass as Abby deepened the kiss. A moan escaped, but she wasn't sure if it came from her or Syd. All she knew was that Syd was like no other woman she'd ever been with. She reined in her aggressive passion because tonight felt different. She felt different. There had been a shift in her feelings for Syd, and tonight they were going to make love.

Reluctantly, Abby broke the kiss but held Syd's gaze with her own. Their eye contact broke only with Abby pulling her own shirt over her head. When her clothes were discarded, she stepped slowly toward Syd and fully embraced her, reveling in the skin-to-skin contact—thighs, stomach, breasts. Abby resumed kissing Syd, first on the mouth, down her neck, and to her shoulder. Abby felt Syd shiver from the delicate contact of Abby's lips and tongue tasting Syd's warm skin.

Abby slowly turned Syd and walked her back until they reached the bed. Syd lay down in the center of the bed and reached out for Abby. She obliged Syd's request and stretched out on top of her, noticing for the first time how perfectly they fit together. Abby leaned on her elbow, caressing Syd's face with her free hand.

"You're so lovely, Sydney."

Abby tasted the salt from Syd's tears as she kissed her again. She kissed Syd like she'd never kissed another woman. Abby moved down Syd's body and captured her rigid nipple in her mouth and danced her tongue around before gently biting it. She sucked Syd's breast, taking her time to build up Syd's excitement before moving to the other. Repeating her performance, she felt Syd's chest rise and fall in staccato with her tongue flicking her nipple.

Syd grasped the back of Abby's head, silently pleading to take more—more of her nipple, more of her breast, more of Syd. Abby felt Syd's pelvis move beneath her, and she wanted to continue her journey down Syd's body, but more than that, she wanted to be staring into Syd's chocolate brown eyes when she came. Abby again kissed Syd as she slipped her hand between Syd's legs, to the wet warmth that begged for her. Abby slid her fingers in the slick wetness and spread it about Syd's sex.

Syd's clit grew with every excruciatingly slow stroke of Abby's fingers and more liquid was released from Syd's center. Abby gently slid two fingers into Syd's velvet walls and just as slowly, slid them out. After a few languid strokes, Abby brought her fingers out to circle Syd's growing bundle of nerves. Even though Abby's tongue was dancing with Syd's, she could practically taste Syd's excitement.

"Abby, I'm so close. Make me come, baby."

Abby returned her fingers into Syd's warmth and sped up her thrusts, curling her fingers to hit Syd's special spot. Abby couldn't not give Syd what she wanted, what she needed, what she hungered for.

"Open your eyes for me, Syd."

Syd opened her eyes and stared into Abby's, into her soul as she cried out and her walls contracted and squeezed around Abby's fingers. Abby continued to massage Syd's inner walls until her contractions subsided, but their eye contact never wavered. It was that moment Abby knew she had fallen in love with Syd. It was also that moment Abby knew her heart would be eventually shattered into a million pieces.

❖

Syd lay in the warm, comforting embrace of Abby's arms, the slow beating of her heart under Syd's ear. It had been an emotional day and night for her, especially when Abby had made love to her. Everything about it was tender and heartfelt. As Syd looked into Abby's eyes when she brought her to climax, Syd felt the change in feelings between them—deeper, stronger, soulful feelings that Syd had never experienced before. She wasn't sure if she could feel this with any other woman. How in the hell was she supposed to leave in a few days? Maybe she could call her boss to see if she'd consider giving her another week off. And what would that solve? One more week to fall faster, harder, deeper in love with Abby, then leave anyway? Syd had considered talking to Abby about having a long-distance relationship, but after what happened between them last night, Syd didn't want that. She wanted a full-time, no-distance relationship with Abby. She wanted to stay on the farm, keep her chickens, maybe learn more about how to care for and ride Pokey. She wanted to fall asleep every night in Abby's arms, and wake every morning looking into her bright blue eyes.

That was crazy, right? They hadn't even known each other for two weeks and Syd was considering giving up her job? Her life in Chicago? What would she do in Iowa? She had spent so many years in school, so many hours giving her life to the kids at Englewood Youth Center. She could just give that up? She felt Abby's warm, soft lips kiss her forehead, and the answer became clear as the sky was sure to be today. This was how she wanted to wake up every morning.

Syd lifted her head to kiss Abby properly. "Good morning."

Abby's smile made Syd's pulse race a little faster. "It certainly is. How are you feeling this morning?"

"Disappointed in myself," Syd said as she started teasing her fingers across Abby's chest. She smiled when Abby's nipples hardened.

Abby's voice was deep and husky. "Why is that?"

Syd drew her fingers across Abby's nipple and lightly pinched it, eliciting a gasp from Abby. "I didn't get a chance to reciprocate last night. But I intend to rectify that right now." Syd kissed Abby and explored her mouth thoroughly. She took Abby's hands and brought them above her head.

"You keep your hands right there and just enjoy the ride." Syd straddled Abby's hips and enjoyed the view from above. Syd's awe was renewed looking down at this gorgeous woman, looking so soft yet solid, compliant yet eager. Syd reached out and began massaging Abby's soft, supple breasts, continuing to tease her nipples. Abby's hands clasped, and she looked like she was struggling to keep them where Syd had told her. "Don't move, baby."

Syd leaned forward and licked her way up Abby's chest through the sweet valley between her breasts. Abby's pelvis thrust upward into Syd's, and she felt her own clit begin to swell and throb. She needed to release herself from the delicious pressure Abby was applying. Syd slid her body down to where she settled between Abby's muscular legs. The tantalizing smell and the glistening coat of Abby's arousal made Syd's mouth water, and she couldn't wait another second.

She parted the soft folds with her fingers and barely touched Abby's hardened clit with the tip of her tongue, causing Abby's body to jerk. She moved her mouth lower, flattened her tongue, and moved it upward, tasting all of her. She repeated the sequence then pulled the rock-hard bundle of nerves into her mouth, lightly tugging, feeling it grow in her mouth. Syd slipped her hands under Abby and squeezed her behind in rhythm to her tongue flicking over Abby's clit.

"Syd, please."

Syd released Abby and she moaned. "Please what, baby?"

"Make me come. I need to so bad."

Syd slid one finger, then another into Abby and stroked her slowly before taking her clit back into her mouth.

"Oh, fuck. Just like that, Syd, baby. I'm going to come."

Abby grabbed the back of Syd's head and held her there as her body shook with her orgasm. Syd had no intention of releasing Abby until she sucked every last tremor from her. When Abby's body finally relaxed, Syd crawled up and cupped Abby's cheek, feeling her lean into the pressure. Syd looked into her eyes and saw her soul.

"You're amazing."

Syd was surprised to see tears well in Abby's eyes, but before she could say anything, Abby kissed Syd so deeply, so passionately, so lovingly, that Syd couldn't help but think Abby felt the same about Syd as she felt about her. That kiss was a life-changing kiss that Syd would feel until the day she died. She wanted nothing more than to tell Abby she loved her and wanted to see where this could go, but it was too soon. And she wanted it to be special. Not that saying it after she brought Abby to climax wasn't special, but she wanted it to be romantic. Wine, dinner, candlelight. Besides, she knew Abby had to get going soon to do her chores and take care of the horses. That was one more thing that she loved about Abby—her reliability.

"I know you have to be going, but can I make you some coffee and breakfast first?"

"I'd love that. Any opportunity to spend more time with you is one I'll always take. But let me help. I'm not completely useless in the kitchen."

They dressed and made their way to the kitchen. Making breakfast took longer than usual with the many kissing and touching breaks. One such break nearly led to Syd backing Abby onto the table and having a different kind of breakfast.

Syd walked Abby to the door and kissed her with promises to come.

"If you need me, baby, I'm only a call away. Otherwise, I'll see you tonight."

Syd couldn't wipe the smile from her face or the love from her heart as she watched Abby get in the truck and drive away.

## Chapter Seventeen

Abby's day dragged on like a crawl through dry sand. She couldn't get Syd off her mind and couldn't wait to get back to her. Something changed between them last night and again this morning. This was no longer a fling for Abby. It had become so much more. But she always knew it would never be just a fling. Before she'd decided to take things in a sexual direction with Syd, she had already started to feel more. And now their time was quickly coming to an end. She wiped an errant tear from the corner of her eye and grabbed the bouquet of wild flowers she had picked while taking Bevin for a ride. Whatever time she had left with Syd, she'd make the most of. She'd worry about picking up the pieces of her broken heart once Syd went home.

She didn't bother knocking on the door since Syd was expecting her, and she walked quietly through the house and followed the sound of Syd's voice in the kitchen. She stopped in the living room when she noticed the bare shelves of the large oak cabinet against the wall. The shelves that had been adorned with family photos, books, and knick-knacks. She opened the doors on the lower part, and Virginia's china, silverware, and candles were gone. How had she not noticed the nearly empty room before? *It's because all you've been thinking about lately is getting Syd naked and into bed.*

"I'm not sure when I'll be back, Vanessa. Yes, I know I can help a lot of kids with that grant, but things have changed."

Abby stood silently, quietly listening in on the conversation and staring into the empty room that used to hold so many photographs and memories of Virginia.

"I know what a great opportunity this is, but things have changed, V. I want to talk to her about staying in Iowa. I finally met someone I really like and I can see a future with. Don't you want me to be happy?"

Abby's arm dropped to her side and the flowers fell onto the floor, causing Syd to turn around. *Did I just hear that correctly? Syd is thinking about staying in Iowa and not starting the youth center? I can't let her do that.*

"I'll have to call you tomorrow, Vanessa. I know. I love you too."

She looked at Syd who was suddenly standing next to her.

"I packed the room up, but I'm not sure if I'm going to keep any of the things that were in here beside the pictures. Was there anything you wanted?"

Abby shook her head and willed the tears not to fall but was unsuccessful. Over the past few days, Abby had almost forgotten why Syd was there. She had mourned Virginia's death but apparently, she wasn't done. Syd took Abby into her arms and held her, allowing Abby to cry. This wasn't how Abby pictured the evening to pan out, losing her control on her emotions. Seeing the bare living room, then overhearing Syd's conversation was the culprit. Too many emotions all at once were just too much for her to handle. Abby stepped back and angrily wiped her eyes. "I'm sorry. I don't know where that came from."

Syd put her hand on Abby's shoulder, then slid it down her arm until she was holding her hand. "Don't apologize. I know how much Virginia meant to you, and she hasn't been gone long. You probably miss her like crazy, and it doesn't make it easy to see me come in here and pack up her stuff."

Abby bit the inside of her cheek to try to prevent herself from crying again.

"I wish there was something I could do to ease your heartache."

Abby finally felt enough control of her emotions to speak. "I do miss her, and you've been great. You've offered me to help myself to anything of hers I might want and you've been respectful of her things. This probably hasn't been easy for you either—not knowing her but having inherited her property and figuring out what to do with it all. The one positive I can focus on though is meeting you. I've really enjoyed spending time with you and getting to know you better."

"I feel the same," Syd said before stepping closer to kiss Abby—a kiss of understanding, of sympathy and empathy.

Abby felt her emotions were raw and scratching the surface from seeing the empty living room and then overhearing Syd's conversation with Vanessa. She had trouble looking Syd in the eyes, so she cast her gaze downward. It looked like she wouldn't have to wait a few days to pick up the pieces of her broken heart. She could hear it already shattering. She wasn't going to cry anymore. If this was going to be her last night with Syd, she wouldn't spend it crying. She bent down, picked up the flowers, and handed them to Syd, trying her hardest to plaster a smile on her face.

"I picked these for you. I didn't mean to eavesdrop on your phone conversation, but is everything okay?"

Syd stepped into her arms and Abby held on tight, afraid to let go.

"Let's talk about it after dinner."

Syd took Abby's hand and led her into the candlelit dining room. The table was elegantly set, soft jazz was coming from a Bluetooth speaker, and the food on the plate looked like it had been prepared by a five-star restaurant. A bottle of champagne sat in an ice bucket, and two crystal flutes were filled halfway. Syd pulled out Abby's chair for her and she sat. The role reversal would've amused Abby if she could feel anything. All she felt was numb. She cleared her throat. "This looks amazing."

"Thank you. I wanted tonight to be special."

"Why?"

"I wanted tonight to be special for you." Syd took Abby's hand and kissed it. "For us. Abby, I have something to tell you."

Abby could feel Syd's hand shaking and she covered it with her other hand. "What is it?"

Syd looked into Abby's eyes, the flicker of the flames from the candles made Syd's skin look so smooth and flawless. Abby had never noticed the specks of gold in Syd's chocolate-brown eyes. The glistening of Syd's lips when she licked them made Abby lose all concentration, and she didn't hear what Syd had said. "I'm sorry. Could you repeat that?"

"I said, I love you, Abigail, and I want to see where this goes," Syd said as she moved her finger between them.

Abby let go of Syd's hand and took a drink of champagne. "But what about your life in Chicago? Your job? Your family? The kids you work with?"

"I haven't thought of all the logistics, but I know I want to be with you, Abby. Did you hear the part where I said I love you?"

Abby nodded, staring into the hypnotic flame. *She loves me and she wants to stay here to be with me.* Abby started to think that through. She wanted to jump up and tell Syd she loved her too, but something stopped her. The kids. Abby saw firsthand how much the kids loved Syd and how much she loved them. Syd couldn't leave them. They needed her and everything she had to offer to show them what could be possible in their young lives. Syd got the grant so she could start her own program. That was what Syd had wanted all along; she felt it gave her life purpose, she'd said. Iowa didn't need Syd. The kids in Chicago did. All that work, all that planning, and Syd was willing to let it all go for her? She couldn't let Syd do that. Just when Abby thought her heart was broken, the words that came out of her mouth completely crushed it.

"I'm sorry, Syd, but I don't feel the same way. I like you. You're an attractive woman and we have a great time together, but we agreed that this was going to be no-strings-attached."

"Don't say that, Abby. I know you felt it last night like I did. It was more than just sex."

Abby had somehow managed to put her armor up and continued the charade. "You were upset and I felt sorry for you, but that was it."

She flinched when Syd sat back in her chair like Abby had punched her. She watched Syd drain her glass and slam it down on the table so hard, the glass shattered. How apropos, Abby thought. The glass was broken into many pieces, just like her heart.

"So, last night was a pity fuck? You felt sorry for me?"

Abby stayed silent, not knowing how much longer she could continue to lie to Syd about her feelings.

Syd stood and grabbed Abby's cheeks in one hand, cupping her chin, and squeezed. "You're lying to me. Don't you fucking lie to me, Abby."

Abby took a deep breath and hammered home the final nail in her own coffin. "I'm not. Like I said, you're nice and the sex was great, but that's all it was—sex."

Abby was expecting a slap to the face, but what she got was far worse. She watched the light leave Syd's eyes and the tears start to fall. She couldn't take it anymore so she stood and walked out of the house, out of Syd's life, forever.

❖

"What. The. Fuck?"

Syd stared at the door long after it closed behind Abby. What the fuck just happened? Did Abby really just sit there and deny what she felt? What they both felt? Syd was so certain after last night and this morning that Abby had feelings for her too. How could she have been so wrong?

She sat at the table and drank the champagne that was meant for Abby. She refilled and gulped it down until the bottle was empty. She stared at the food—untouched—and wondered how this night went so horribly wrong. The phone call.

Abby had heard all of it, and Syd had seen the dejected look on her face, in her stance, in her posture. She had to talk to Abby. She stood to get her keys and stumbled. She was drunk and there was no way she could get behind the wheel even if it was just for a half-mile down the road. Maybe she could walk over to her house.

She took a few steps and the room spinning meant she was even less likely to be safe on foot. The phone. She'd call her. The call went to voice mail. She hung up and called again, desperate to talk to Abby and get this all straightened out. Voice mail.

"Abby, please call me. We need to talk." Syd hung up. She didn't know what else to say, and even if she did, she didn't want to leave a voice mail of everything she wanted to say. She'd have to wait for morning. She was certain that if they could just talk face-to-face, she could make it better. She could make Abby understand they belong together.

❖

Abby rushed through the door, vision blurred by the tears that wouldn't stop. She went to her room, pulled out her suitcase, and started to pack her clothes. She turned when there was a short knock before her grandmother opened the door.

"Abigail, what are you doing?"

"I have to leave town for a little while, Gran. I can't stay here. You'll be okay, right?"

"Honey, you're scaring me. What happened?"

"Syd and I had an argument and I can't see her anymore. If I stay here, I don't think I'll be strong enough to stay away."

Her grandmother sat Abby on the bed before pulling over a chair to sit in front of her. "Start from the beginning."

Abby told her of the phone call she overheard and that Syd was going to turn it down so she could stay here to be with Abby. "I can't let her do that, Gran. Those kids need her and she needs them."

"Do you love Sydney?"

Abby just nodded, unable to get the words around the lump in her throat.

"Then why do you want her to leave?"

Abby's tears started again. "It's because I love her that I want her to go. She does such great work for those kids, and it makes her so happy. I can't ask her to stay and abandon them."

"It sounds like she offered to stay. It sounds like she loves you, too. Why would you let her leave?"

Abby stood and paced the room, ready to pull the hair out of her head by the roots. "I told you, Gran. Those kids need her. I saw her with them. I saw how much they love her and respect her. She's a safe haven for them, and she offers a safe alternative to hanging out in the streets or getting into trouble. She needs to go back and concentrate on those kids. Now please, I have to go. I'll call you when I get to where I'm going."

"Okay, but do one thing for me, Abigail. Leave in the morning. You're too upset to drive right now, and you don't want your old grandmother worrying all night, do you?"

"No. I'll leave in the morning, but it's going to be early. I can't risk seeing Syd before she leaves."

"Are you sure she will? What if she decides to stay?"

Abby didn't have an answer, but she'd have to do something to make sure Syd went back to Chicago. After her grandmother kissed her good night, she finished packing, then sat down to write a letter.

Syd woke to the feeling of a jackhammer trying to get through her skull. Between drinking an entire bottle of champagne and crying herself to sleep on the couch in an awkward position, Syd wished she could go unconscious for another few days. But she had things to do—most importantly, going to talk to Abby. She made a cup of coffee and quickly showered and dressed, not wanting to wait any longer before seeing Abby.

She took a couple of deep breaths to quell the butterflies in her stomach before knocking on Abby's door. Surely, she could figure all this out with her. If Syd had thought for one minute that Abby felt *nothing* for her, she'd just pack up and go home. Her instincts from two nights ago couldn't be that wrong, could they? She wasn't completely surprised that Bernice answered the door.

"Good morning, Mrs. Price. Is Abigail available?"

"I'm sorry, Sydney, but Abigail left town early this morning."

Stunned, all Syd could do was blink. She was lightheaded and grabbed onto the doorframe to steady herself. "Oh. I see. I'm sorry to have bothered you." She turned to go but stopped when Bernice called her name.

"Sydney, please come inside for a few minutes."

She followed Bernice inside, every step feeling heavier than the last, and she sat at the opposite end of the couch from her.

"I'm not usually a meddling old woman, but Abigail told me you had an argument last night."

Syd wasn't sure what to say so she just stayed silent.

"She told me about your grant to start your youth center. Congratulations, my dear. I'm sure Virginia would've been very proud of you."

"Thank you." To hear that from Virginia's best friend made her more emotional. After reading her grandmother's letter, Syd fervently wished she was there to talk to about this.

"I'm not exactly sure what's going on with you and my granddaughter, but she left this on the counter and it was addressed to you." Bernice handed over yet another envelope that bore her name.

"I'm not sure either, ma'am. But I want you to know that Abby has become very special to me and I enjoyed our time together. Thank you for being such a great friend to my grandmother and looking after her."

"Virginia was a very special lady, Sydney, and I'm sorry you never got the chance to know her. But know this. Whenever she talked about you, the pride in her voice was evident."

Syd blinked back the tears that filled her eyes. "Thank you for saying that, ma'am." Syd stood to leave and was surprised to be embraced by Bernice.

"You take care, Sydney. Keep making Virginia proud."

"Yes, ma'am. Thank you again. And please thank Abby for me."

Syd left with Abby's letter in her back pocket, and she fought back a wave of nausea as she thought of reading it once she got back to the farm, and what Abby had to say. She sat on the bench beside the pond where she and Abby had shared their first kiss, and she opened the letter. Before she read it, she took a deep breath and rubbed her eyes. She inhaled the scent of hay and earth, listened to the birds sitting in the tree behind her, and looked to the sky.

*Dear Syd,*

*I have so much to say, but I'm not sure how well this will come out. I'm so sorry about last night. I knew the day would come that you would return to Chicago, but that day snuck up on me too quickly. It was truly one of my greatest pleasures in life meeting you, getting to know you, and helping you. I wish we'd had more time together.*

*Syd, you're destined for great things. Special things that you probably wouldn't find here in Charville. That's why it's necessary for you to go back to Chicago—so you can do what you love so much. I know how much you love working with your kids, and I can't think of a better person for them to have as a role model. That's why it's so important that you return to set up your own center for them.*

*I wish you all the best life has to offer, and if you ever need anything, I'm only a call away.*

*—Abby*

*Oh, Abby, baby. I* need *you.* Syd traced her fingers along the writing and felt her eyes sting with tears. Fine. If that's what Abby wanted, Syd would go back to Chicago. She folded up the letter and stuck it in her back pocket, pulled her shoulders back, and walked back to the house with a determined gait. She called her grandmother's attorney to get recommendations for a Realtor, a mover, and a charity that would pick up her donations. It was time for her to finish packing up the house so she could get back to her life in Chicago. Her life without Abby.

## CHAPTER EIGHTEEN

In between bouts of crying and two bottles of Scotch, Abby had killed two birds with one stone. She had finished her manuscript, and she had learned from her grandmother that Syd had left town. Mission accomplished, Abby thought as she threw back the rest of her Scotch.

When she left Charville, her only plan was to escape her feelings for Syd. That worked well. She put her sadness and aching for Syd into her writing, and she was finally able to finish. How good it was remained to be seen. She had holed herself up in some dank motel room and ate all her meals at a Denny's down the road. It was *Leaving Las Vegas*-light. She managed to brush her teeth every day but showered every other day. Now, the coast was clear. She'd be able to return home without the risk of running into Syd. The images of her, like a slide show, ran through Abby's mind, and it made her want to throw up.

The For Sale sign in the front yard of Virginia's home would be burned into her memory forever. A memory of what she'd had and what she'd lost. Both Virginia and Syd. Gone from her life.

She pulled into her driveway and tiredly dragged her suitcase through the front door.

"Gran? I'm home."

"I'm in the kitchen, honey."

Abby left her suitcase just inside the front door and went to see her grandmother. Abby had made sure to call her every day while she had been gone to check in on her and see if she needed anything.

"My word, Abigail. You look a fright. You have dark circles under your eyes and your clothes are hanging off you. What in the world have you been doing?"

"Good to see you too, Gran. I'm fine, by the way. Oh, and good news—I finished the manuscript," Abby said sarcastically. Her agitation had been at high level since she walked out on Syd nine days ago. The only time it lowered was when Abby had a couple of drinks to numb her heartache. She needed love and caring from her grandmother right now, not criticism.

She went to the living room and dropped onto the couch, kicking her feet up, and draping her arm across her eyes. She felt her gran come into the room, her perfume she always wore accompanying her. No matter how Abby was feeling, the scent was like a comforting blanket being wrapped around her.

"Syd put the house up for sale." It wasn't a question she needed answering. The sign still burned in her mind.

"Yes. She came by last Saturday on her way out of town to say good-bye. I think she was hoping to see you one last time."

"How did she look?"

Her grandmother sighed. "Sad. Tired. Resigned, I suppose. She left a letter for you. I put it in your room on your dresser."

Abby remained quiet. She had no aspiration to read that letter. She wouldn't blame Syd if she tore her a new asshole, but Abby did what she felt was the right thing to do, the noble thing. Those kids needed her and she needed them. A farm in a small town in Iowa was no place for a woman like Syd. It was too slow, too quiet, not anything like she was used to.

"Did she say anything else?"

"She asked if we could take care of the chickens until the farm was sold and I agreed. She gave me a box of some of Virginia's things she thought I might like, including some photographs."

Abby went quiet again, her mind cluttered with thoughts and images of Syd and her together, and she let out a sob. She had trouble breathing, the tears were coming so quickly. She felt the whole world closing in on her and she was suffocating. The only thing that could help was Syd, but she was long gone and back in

Chicago, where she should be. Abby's grandmother sat next to her and took Abby into her arms.

"Oh, sweetheart. I understand why you did what you did, but are you sure? You obviously love her and I could tell how much she cares for you. Why don't you call her?"

"I can't, Gran. I have to be strong, and if I call her, it will be too hard. I just need more time, is all."

Her grandmother gave Abby a kiss on her forehead. "Why don't you go take a shower and lie down for a bit? I'm making your favorite dinner tonight."

"Pot roast with mashed potatoes, gravy, and cooked carrots?"

"Of course," she said with affection. "And there might be a carrot cake too. We need to put a little weight back on you."

Abby hugged her again. "I love you, Gran. So much."

"I love you too, sweetheart. Now go get some rest while I finish dinner."

Abby lugged her suitcase to her room and dumped every article of clothing into the hamper, including the clothes she was wearing. She turned on the shower as hot as she could stand and stepped under the powerful spray. She wanted to stay there all day. The shower in her motel room had low water pressure and never got hotter than a tepid warm. Abby felt like she hadn't been clean since she left here. She let the hot water soothe her tired and stiff muscles, used her body wash and loofah to scrub every inch of her body. She had lost a lot of weight while she was gone, and her hard-earned muscles she got from working on the farm had all but disappeared. The hard planes of her stomach were now soft and flabby and her bones were protruding from her pelvis and ribs. But she was confident that it wouldn't take long to get her muscles back.

She dressed in a clean T-shirt and boxer shorts, and she spotted the envelope from Syd on her dresser. She contemplated reading it and decided to put it on her nightstand. She lay down on her bed and stared at the ceiling, resuming the slide show in her mind of her and Syd. Meeting her in the barn, teaching her how to feed chickens, helping her clean out the garage, watching her make magic in the kitchen. The romance between them, sitting together by the pond, their first kiss, the first time Abby made Syd come, the first time Syd made Abby come, the many kisses, even more touches, the night they made love and their feelings were silently revealed. That was a magical night for Abby. She never knew she could feel so much, so deeply that only one woman could consume her every thought.

She pounded the bed with her clinched fist and turned on her side. She shouldn't have allowed herself to fall in love with a woman who lived in another state. *Like I had a choice.* From the first moment Abby saw Syd, she was completely, utterly captivated. Her beauty, her confidence, at times her defiance, her compassion, her humor, her passion. Syd had it all, and Abby thought she'd never find that again. Her soul ached from the loss of Syd, and Abby wasn't sure she'd ever recover. She would die a single, old, washed-up author, cat lady with nothing to show but the brief glimpse of being in love and being loved by such a remarkable woman.

She obviously wasn't going to be able to nap, and she might as well add to her misery and wallowing. She opened the letter from Syd, and she could almost smell her. She stared at the words, afraid what they might say, but felt she deserved everything Syd had to say to her.

*Dear Abby,*

*I'm lying here in bed, alone, and all I can think of are the times we shared in this bed. It feels so lonely without you here with me, so much so that I wish we had one more night together. We would laugh, we would cry, we would make love, and we would stay awake all night long, holding each other, coming up with ways to stay together. You don't know this, but I actually researched travel time from Charville to Chicago (it's about two hours each way, in case you were wondering). I thought that what we were getting to in our relationship was worth seeing where it could go, but you obviously didn't feel the same way.*

"Oh, God, Syd, but I did. I felt exactly the same, but I just couldn't tell you. I did it for you, baby. Your life is in Chicago. You wouldn't be happy here."

*Despite how it ended, I want you to know that I wouldn't change the time we spent together. Well, except for that last night when you walked out on me. When you walked out on us, and left town without even saying good-bye. That hurt me, Abby. More than I've ever been hurt before.*

"Christ, Abby. You are such a cowardly asshole."

*Anyways, I'm grateful that I got to know you and Bernice. Thank you for being such great friends to Virginia and looking out for her. She loved you so much, Abby. She talked about you in her letters to my mother. I'm glad she had you and Bernice. I really appreciate all the help you gave me sorting through Virginia's property. I'm not sure if I could have done it without you.*

*I'll never forget you, Abby. You gave me my first horse ride, taught me how to care for the chickens, and I could never forget that first kiss near the pond. I can almost still feel your lips on mine, your hands on my body, you bringing me to orgasm better than anyone. Damn it, Abby. I miss you so much.*

"Oh, Syd. I miss you too, baby. More than I ever thought I could miss anyone."

*I just wanted to tell you that I think you're so special, honey. You have a heart of gold, and anyone would be lucky to have you in their life. I know I feel lucky, even if it wasn't for forever like I had wanted. Every time I think of you, I'll remember you fondly. If you're ever in Chicago, or just want to talk, I'm only a call away (sorry for stealing your line, but it's just too good). I hope we can remain friends, but if you don't want to, I'll understand. You take care of yourself, Abby.*
*All my love,*
*Syd*

Abby pulled her pillow up to her face and screamed into it, muffling her voice so she wouldn't scare her grandmother. How could she have been so stupid? To let someone like Sydney Carter go? She mentioned something about continuing to see each other. Abby scanned the letter. *It's about two hours each way, in case you were wondering.* Abby took a deep breath and frowned. And then what? Continue commuting for the rest of our lives? She couldn't leave her life in Chicago, and Abby couldn't leave her grandmother all alone in Iowa. Why did love have to suck so bad?

Abby curled up in fetal position and gathered one of her pillows in her arms, imagining it was Syd she was holding.

## Chapter Nineteen

Syd was painting the walls inside the new building she bought that would be the community center for the kids. In addition to providing services for the inner-city youth, she was adding a program for LGBTQ youth. A safe place for them to come and hang out. It was going to be an all-inclusive program that was going to provide tutoring, a library, field trips, and counseling.

She had used her grant and the proceeds from the sale of the farm, as well as a substantial loan to buy the building, furnish the place, and pay the utilities. She was working normal hours at the youth center, but it was still her full-time job, so the work she'd been doing on her center was after-hours and the weekends. The new building was close to Englewood, but it was in much better shape. She talked with her boss, Christina, and Anne, and they all decided it would be in the best interest of everyone involved, especially the children, to move the old center to the new building.

Syd and Christina would be able to combine resources to make the center even more successful by offering more services. Syd fell into bed exhausted every night from all the extra work she had been putting in, but she didn't care. This had been her dream and it was finally coming true. Besides, the more she worked, the less time she had to think about Abby.

Her drive home from Iowa had been brutal. Every song that played on the radio had some lyric that brought Abby front and center to Syd's mind and left her with tears in her eyes. Leaving Iowa and not being able to see Abby one last time was the hardest thing she'd ever had to do. She couldn't believe how wrong she'd been about Abby's feelings for her. The last time they'd been together, she could've sworn she'd seen the love in Abby's eyes, felt it in her touch, in her kiss. Syd had brought her fingers to her lips. It was as if she could still feel them against Abby's.

Syd couldn't count the number of times she considered turning around, taking the farm off the market, and staking her claim—in Iowa and with Abby. But that wasn't what Abby wanted. She said herself that she didn't feel the same for Syd as she did for Abby. Syd wouldn't and couldn't stay where she wasn't wanted.

She didn't hear the door open and nearly had her heart stop when she heard her best friend's voice.

"Wow! This place is looking good. I love the colors you picked out."

"Jesus Christ, Vanessa. You scared the shit out of me." She eyed Vanessa's ratty shirt and cut-off shorts. "What are you doing here?"

"What does it look like? I came to help."

Syd put down the paint roller and embraced Vanessa. "That is so sweet of you. Thank you."

Vanessa laughed as she let go of Syd. "I'm not doing it totally out of the kindness of my heart. I have a favor to ask."

"Uh-huh. What is it?" Syd picked up where she left off on the wall. She smiled when Vanessa started painting another wall.

"Leah Griffin is going to be signing her book next Saturday at the Barnes and Noble, and I want you to go with me."

Syd had no interest in going to a book signing, especially for an author whose books she didn't read. And especially when she still had so much to do before the center's grand opening next month. "I don't think so. I still have a lot to do here and I can't afford to slack off."

"Who's slacking? I'm talking one hour, two tops. I've barely talked to you or seen you since you've been home, and I miss my buddy."

Those words were enough for Syd to agree, but the pout and puppy dog eyes Vanessa displayed sealed the deal, and Syd laughed.

"Okay, *buddy*, I'll go with you, but you're buying me dinner after," Syd said as she swiped a strip of sage green paint on the tip of Vanessa's nose.

"Deal. I've missed you, Syd. How are you doing really?" Syd had called Vanessa from the road the day she left Iowa to let her know she was on her way home. She was shocked and pleased to walk into her condo to find Vanessa cooking her dinner. After they ate and unloaded Syd's car, they sat on the couch and shared a bottle of wine while Syd cried on Vanessa's shoulder. She told her how she fell for Abby and wanted to be with her and that Abby shot her down. The rest of the night had been spent with Vanessa holding her while she cried, handing her Kleenex, and refilling her wine glass. That was the last time they'd spent time together.

"Oh, that reminds me. Virginia had five Leah Griffin books autographed, and I brought them home for you."

"Seriously? Oh my God, Syd. That's terrific. Thank you." Vanessa was quiet and her eyebrows scrunched together. "Your grandma read romance novels?"

Syd laughed at the look on Vanessa's face. "I'm not sure since I didn't see any other books in that genre, but she had these and they were signed. I'll give them to you next week."

They were able to get two rooms painted before calling it a night, with a promise to see each other the following weekend.

## Chapter Twenty

Syd rushed home after spending eight hours at the center touching up the paint, putting bookshelves together, and stocking them with all kinds of books from the classics to the vampire books that had been turned into movies, to gay and lesbian young adult books. She'd also placed orders for the office supplies they would need and drafted a letter that she would send out to different organizations for donations of time and/or money. Her former boss from the firm had already agreed to some of the company's time for observations and minor internships for the kids to learn about investment banking. She only had an hour to get ready before Vanessa arrived to take her to Leah Griffin's reading and book signing. She wasn't sure why, but she'd taken extra time to pick out the right outfit for tonight. She'd just finished fastening her earrings when Vanessa called out to her.

"Whew, you're looking snazzy tonight. Are you ditching me later to meet someone?"

Syd playfully punched Vanessa in the arm as she walked to the kitchen to get a glass of water. The thought of dating anyone but Abby made her feel a little nauseous, and she placed her hand over her stomach to try to settle the queasiness. No other woman held any sort of appeal to her, and she had refused a few offers of sleeping with the women she used to hook up with. "Of course not. But I didn't know what to wear to something like this." She looked Vanessa up and down and noticed she was dressed a bit more casually than Syd, wearing blue jeans and a button-down cotton shirt. Syd had opted for dress slacks, a silk blouse, and low heels, and she was suddenly feeling very overdressed. "Maybe I should change."

"Don't you dare. You look fantastic. Besides, we need to leave now if we're going to get a good seat. I want one up close so I can see my favorite author and listen to her every word."

Syd laughed at Vanessa's enthusiasm. "I'm sure she's a normal person who puts her pants on one leg at a time, just as we do."

"You don't understand, Syd. This is my favorite author and I finally get a chance to meet her."

Syd's feelings softened and she hugged her. "You're right, sweetie. I know how important this is to you, and I didn't mean to make light of it. Oh, that reminds me." Syd hurried into her room and returned with the books Leah had signed to Virginia. "Here you go. I know they're not as good as having them signed to you, but I wanted you to have these." The look of awe in Vanessa's eyes as she read the inscription warmed Syd's heart, and she was glad she was able to give the books to her.

"I love them, Syd. And I love you. Now let's go."

Syd had to pick up the pace to keep up with Vanessa as they walked from the parking garage to the bookstore. Syd hadn't spent much time in a bookstore lately. At all, really. She was surprised how many people were milling about in the aisles, looking at magazines, calendars, books, and other items. She saw a sign for a coffee house and was about to suggest to Vanessa that they go get a cappuccino, but Vanessa grabbed her by the hand and pulled her toward the back of the store. So much for getting a beverage. She noticed signs announcing Leah Griffin appearing tonight for a reading and signing, but she noticed there wasn't a picture of her on the sign, just the cover of her latest release.

They managed to snag two seats in the third row and Vanessa expressed her displeasure of not being able to get seats in the front row. Syd thought about teasing Vanessa but thought differently when the crowd hushed and a woman stepped up to the podium and spoke into a microphone.

"Good evening, ladies and a few gentlemen." That got a few chuckles from the crowd, and Syd looked around to see four or five men in the crowd, probably dragged there by their wives or girlfriends. Syd mentally rolled her eyes at the look of anticipation on the women's faces, and boredom on the men's.

"Leah and I would like to thank you for coming out tonight to listen to her read a passage from her latest novel, *Open to Love*. After the reading, we'll have time for some questions. And if you're interested, her other novels will be for sale and she'll be happy to sign them for you. We request that no pictures be taken and that you turn your phones to silent."

Every face Syd saw in the crowd was riveted to the woman at the podium.

"Now, without further ado, Leah Griffin."

The crowd burst into applause with a few whistles thrown in. Leah Griffin stepped from behind a curtain and smiled at the crowd as she approached the microphone.

Syd felt her jaw drop open and her eyes widen as she gasped and grabbed onto Vanessa's arm, then she muttered under her breath so only Vanessa could hear her. "Holy fucking shit." The room started to spin and she felt a little disoriented.

Vanessa whipped her head toward Syd and she stared back with trepidation. "What?"

"That's Abby."

Syd watched Vanessa's face fall then she turned back to Leah—Abby—only to see Abby staring back at Syd. Abby looked as shocked as Syd felt as the color seemed to drain from her face.

Abby stood behind the partition waiting to be announced. She took a quick peek and was pleased to see such a large turnout. She normally didn't like speaking in front of large crowds, but as Leah Griffin, she became another person, one who was admired by her readers. It was that thought that enabled her to do public readings. She had picked a passage early in the story, one that was sure to grab the reader's attention, or in this case, the listener's attention. Hopefully, they would like it enough to want to buy her latest release.

Being in Chicago brought conflicting feelings to Abby. One was that she wanted to call Syd to see if they could get together. Abby thought about her every damned day, and missed her so damned much that her heart truly ached. She had been irritable with her gran, then felt ashamed that she would treat her one remaining family member the way she'd been. But her gran never said anything about her behavior. She seemed to take it in stride, knowing how depressed Abby was.

Abby would wake early, do her chores, ride Bevin and Pokey, and work even harder around the farm in the afternoon. She'd be so tired that she'd had just enough energy to eat dinner before falling into bed for a fitful night's sleep. It was the only way to keep thoughts of Syd at bay.

On the other hand, she wanted to get in and out of Chicago as quickly as possible to reduce the chances of seeing Syd. The odds of that happening were ridiculously low in a city that big, yet she still didn't want to take that chance. The thought of accidentally running into Syd made her insides tremble, and not in a good way. Not like they had when she was being intimate with Syd. Besides, what would she say to her? They'd each written a letter and said all there was to say. But there was more to say. She wanted to tell Syd she loved her, that she was in love with her, and she never wanted to live another day without her.

It had been two months since they'd last seen each other, and Abby was sure Syd would've moved on by now. Found a lover that lived in this amazing city of culture and nightlife, someone who had more in common with her than the farm girl from Iowa.

The applause roused Abby out of her thoughts, and she quickly regained her focus on why she was there. Those people out there were waiting to see Leah Griffin and hear a passage from her latest book. Normally, after an appearance like this, Abby would go to the happening lesbian nightclub in the area and find some company for the night before flying home the next day. But since having been touched by Syd, the thought of anyone else touching her held little appeal. She would just go back to her hotel room alone, maybe raid the mini bar to help dull the pain of being in Syd's hometown. So close to her, yet so far. Abby brushed her damp hands along the front of her trousers, took a deep breath, and let it out slowly before stepping out from behind the partition.

Abby stepped up to the podium and smiled as she looked out into the crowd. Mostly women, which she expected, but also a few men. Her gaze froze on the woman who'd invaded every waking thought, the woman with the chocolate brown eyes and a look of shock on her face. Shit. She grabbed the podium to prevent from falling over. On the other hand, if she fell over, she might lose consciousness and would be taken away from this place.

Abby could feel her mouth drop open when she spotted Syd sitting in the third row next to an attractive woman who looked almost as shocked as Syd. Abby had never felt so trapped in her life, but she couldn't just take her book and leave. All of these people came to hear and meet Leah Griffin. Time to suck it up and give them what they wanted. She cleared her throat and shook the fog from her mind.

"Good evening, ladies and gentlemen. Thank you so much for coming out tonight. I'll be reading from my latest release, *Open to Love*. I hope you enjoy it." Abby opened the book to the marked page and began reading. It was amazing how five minutes could seem like five hours, especially when the love of her life was sitting in the third row, clearly avoiding looking at Abby.

She'd glance over toward Syd and her companion every so often, but Syd was looking down into her lap. She wondered what Syd was thinking of at that very moment. Abby had struggled to pull her attention back to the audience and to her reading, but she somehow managed. She had finished her reading and was greeted by a thunderous applause by everyone. Well, almost everyone.

Syd continued to sit quietly, avoiding looking at Abby. Abby allowed fifteen or twenty minutes of thoughtful questions from the crowd, and she tried to be present and engaged, but in the back of her mind was Syd. That had to be the longest night Abby had ever experienced, and it wasn't over yet. She still had to sign books, chat with people, and pretend that her world hadn't just upended. She loved interacting with her fans; it was her favorite part of being a published author. But tonight, she wanted to run—into Syd's arms or back to Iowa—she couldn't decide which.

Abby had taken a seat at the table where stacks of her latest novel sat, waiting for the readers to hand them over to sign. When the last person bid her a good night, she reached down to get the bottle of water next to her chair to quench her thirst. When she looked up, Syd was standing in front of her, and her mouth went dry again.

That had been some of the sweetest torture Syd had ever experienced. It was too hard to look at Abby during her reading so she had closed her eyes and listened to the honey-thick voice speaking the words. The same voice that had talked dirty to her during their throes of passion, had whispered sweetly in Syd's ear after making love, who soothed her when she had been so upset after reading Virginia's letters. She had contemplated walking out, but one, she didn't want to be rude, and two, she didn't want to risk never seeing Abby again. So she stayed and let the torture continue. When people started lining up to have Abby sign their books, she told Vanessa that she could leave once Abby had signed her book, and she begged Vanessa not to say anything to Abby about her. She was going to grab a coffee and wait until Abby was done. She had to talk to her. Syd missed the slow pace of Iowa, the peacefulness she experienced in the early dawn while feeding the chickens, but she missed Abby more.

She rubbed her chin and bit her bottom lip as she thought of what she would say. Syd felt she laid out all her feelings in the letter she wrote to Abby. Had she even read it? She was hoping, but not expecting her to call Syd, but after a month of constantly checking her phone for a message from Abby, she had given up hope. She knew she had to keep the conversation platonic. After all, they had started out becoming friends before it became sexual. Abby was someone Syd wanted in her life, even if it was just as a friend. It might be hard at first, but Syd was hoping it could be done.

"Hello, Leah." It felt so strange calling her that, but obviously keeping her real identity a secret from her readers was important to her, and she would respect that.

"Hi, Syd."

"You should have called me to tell me you were coming to town."

"I know, and I'm sorry. I should've called you after I read your letter, but I didn't know what to say."

Syd nodded, taking Abby's words at face value...for now. She stood still and just stared at Abby. Now that she was that close to her, she had no idea of what to say. All she knew was that she might never have that chance again and took a leap. "Do you have plans for dinner?"

"Actually, I was just going to order room service. I have a flight back tomorrow morning."

"Why don't you come back to my place and I'll cook us dinner. I've discovered a few recipes since we last saw each other." Syd forced a smile. *Please say yes, Abby. I have so much to say and I just want some more time with you.*

"Are you sure? We could just go to a restaurant and let the other people do the work."

"That would be nice, but considering it's Saturday night, we would have to wait forever for a table. Really, it won't be that much work, especially if you help me prep."

Abby laughed and shook her head. "Sure, I'd love to help."

Since Vanessa had driven them to the bookstore, Syd hailed a cab which was quicker than taking the train. They arrived at Syd's building in less than fifteen minutes.

"Good evening, Ms. Carter. Welcome home," the doorman said as he opened the door.

"Hi, Sam. This is my friend Abby. Abby, this is Sam, one of my most favorite people in Chicago. He wasn't on duty when you came to Chicago with me."

"Go on now, Ms. Carter. Ms. Abby," Sam said as he tipped his hat.

"It's a pleasure to meet you, Sam."

They walked across the marble floor to the elevator, and Syd could feel Abby's gaze on her.

"What?" Syd couldn't help return the smile Abby had.

"I love the way you treat people. I've never met anyone as respectful as you."

Syd shrugged. "I just treat people the way I want to be treated."

They stepped into the elevator and Syd's skin tingled being in such close proximity to Abby. The electricity between them hadn't waned. Did Abby feel it too? How was Syd going to keep her hands to herself? All she'd wanted to do since she saw Abby in the bookstore was take her in her arms and kiss her until she came to her senses. Her hand shook and she had trouble getting the key in the lock. This was going to be more sweet torture, Syd was sure, but it was something she was willing to go through in order to spend just a few more hours with Abby.

She flipped on the lights and watched Abby take in her home, like it was the first time she had been there. She glanced at the art that hung on her walls, the coffee table books in front of her sofa, and she stopped in front of the window. Syd stood beside her, wondering what she thought of the view.

"Still breathtaking," Abby whispered.

Syd looked at Abby's profile, unable to tear her gaze away. "Yes."

Abby looked at her, and a wistful smile belied the sadness in her eyes. "I've missed you."

"I was only a call away," Syd said, borrowing Abby's signature good-bye.

"It wouldn't have been enough, Syd. It just would have made me miss you more, and I didn't think my heart could have taken that again."

"Wait. You told me you were just having fun, that it was just sex, and you didn't love me back. Was that a lie?"

Abby returned her attention back to the view of the skyline, and she wiped away a tear. She nodded.

"Abby, let's go sit down. My legs are suddenly feeling weak." Syd took Abby's hand and led her to the couch. "Would you like a glass of wine? Or I have Scotch."

"Wine, please."

Syd took her time opening the bottle, which allowed her to consider what Abby had said. So Syd wasn't wrong when she thought Abby had feelings for her. But why would she lie? Syd took a deep breath and squared her shoulders. She had every intention of finding out. She set the glasses on the coffee table and sat next to Abby.

"Why did you lie to me?"

"I did it so you'd come back here to help the kids. They need you, Syd."

"So you did it for them?"

"Yes. I saw the excitement in your eyes every time you talked about them and the center you wanted to start for them. You got the grant to start it. How could you have done that if you stayed on the farm?'

"I thought maybe we could try the long-distance thing. I would've tried anything to stay together with you."

"And how long could we have done that? Your life is here. Mine is in Iowa. My gran is getting older and she's the only family I have left. I can't leave her."

Syd took Abby's hand in hers. "No, of course you can't. I thought I had all the answers. At least some of them."

Abby brought Syd's hand to her mouth and kissed it. "It was a good idea, but it's just not possible. We would eventually get tired of traveling back and forth, and we'd stop spending so much time together. I felt it was best to end it then while we still had a chance at being friends. I didn't want there to be any resentment down the road."

It made sense. Syd didn't like it, but it made sense. "All right. I understand what you're saying. I'm going to go get dinner started." Syd stood and put more distance between them. She put her hands on the counter and hung her head. She wouldn't cry. She. Would. Not. Cry.

"Syd," Abby said as she put her hands on Syd's shoulders. Syd let out a wracking sob and turned to bury her face in Abby's chest. She felt Abby's arms engulf her and strengthen the hold. "I'm so sorry, baby. I really am." Abby's soothing voice was the same Syd had heard when Abby comforted her, and it gave her the courage to lift her head.

Syd looked into Abby's eyes, then at her lips. She cradled Abby's face in her hands and kissed her sweetly. A kiss of apology and understanding. "I know. Me too. I've never met anyone like you or felt so much for another woman, and I really wanted to be yours and for you to be mine. But I understand your reasoning. I could never ask you to leave Bernice. Let's just enjoy our time together tonight. Maybe we could work on being friends again." She kissed Abby once more before stepping back to put space between them. If she didn't, she'd never stop kissing her, and she was sure they'd end up in Syd's bed. "Come on, let's get you fed."

They moved in the kitchen like they had back at the farm, when things were easy and light. They sat down to eat, and Syd asked Abby about Bernice, the horses, and how her book tour was going. Syd didn't want their time to end, but it was getting late and Abby had a flight back home in the morning. She placed their dishes in the sink and grabbed her keys and wallet. "Come on, I'll take you back to your hotel."

"You don't have to do that, Syd. I can catch a cab."

Syd looked at Abby forlornly. "I want to spend as much time with you as I can. Besides, I want to show you something."

Ten minutes later, Syd was unlocking the front door to the center she'd been working so hard on. She flipped on the lights and guided Abby in. "This is it."

Abby was silent as she took in the room, moving around in a slow circle. "Syd, this is fantastic."

Feeling proud of the work she'd done and what this center was going to do for some of the children of Chicago, she stood tall and felt her chest puff out. "Thanks."

Abby took Syd's hand and looked into her eyes. "I mean it. This place is going to be amazing. When are you opening for business?"

"Grand opening is in three weeks. I got the inside painted this week and some of the furniture put together. I'm still waiting for a few more pieces of furniture and supplies, but I've been assured they'll be delivered next week. My boss, Christina, and I have decided to combine our centers, so the kids I'm working with now will start coming here since it's a bigger space and it's newer. Let me give you a tour." The front room held two couches facing each other with a coffee table in between on one side of the room and the other side held four accent chairs that were arranged for socializing.

They walked down the hall and stopped at every doorway. Syd pointed to the room on the left. "This is going to be where the kids can be tutored, or do their homework. It's basically a quiet space for the kids to learn." There was a white board on the wall with different colored markers, and two six-foot long tables and six chairs for each table. There were also three computer stations in the corner. She pointed to the room on the right. "This is the library. This is another quiet zone for the kids to read or study. In these two rooms, their cell phones have to be turned off. If they want to text their friends or play on social media, they need to go out to the front room.

Syd led Abby down the hall. "This is the break room where the kids and staff can keep their food. I'm also considering giving cooking lessons," Syd said with a smile. There was another table with chairs, a full-sized refrigerator and freezer, a stove, microwave, oven, and sink.

"Across the hall is the staff office and at the end of the hall is the game room." They passed two bathrooms and entered the game room. This and the staff office were the two rooms that still needed to be furnished. "There's going to be a foosball table, Ping–Pong table, board games, and cards. Out back, eventually, I want to level the ground and have it paved to put in a basketball court, but we'll have to see how much we get in donations."

Now that the tour was done, Abby stayed silent and Syd was anxious to see what she thought. Abby turned and faced her then took Syd's hands in hers.

"This is why you had to come back, Syd." Abby dropped Syd's hands and raised her arms as if she was showcasing the room, and she turned slowly in a circle. "This is what you've been dreaming of and you did it." She wrapped her arms around Syd and picked her up off the ground. "I'm so proud of you for achieving your dream and what you set out to do. The young people of Chicago don't know how fortunate they are to have you in their corner."

Abby placed Syd back on the ground and they stood there staring into each other's eyes. Syd wanted nothing more than to take Abby back to her place and make love with her until she had to leave for the airport. But she couldn't. It had nearly killed her when Abby had walked out on her in Iowa. She couldn't go through that again. Her heart might not survive a second time.

"Come on. I'll take you back to your hotel."

They pulled up to the front of Abby's hotel and Syd put the car in neutral. Abby covered Syd's hand as it rested atop the gearshift and she faced her. "Do you want to come up to my room?"

Syd's heart wanted to shout, "Yes! I want to be with you!" But her head prevailed. Sometimes, she hated being so rational and at that moment, she really hated her head. "I can't, Abby. You have no idea how much I want to, but I think we should just say good-bye here."

Abby looked down into her lap and nodded. "I understand. Thank you for tonight. For everything."

"I'm glad we got to say what needed to be said, Abby. I wish you nothing but the best." Syd leaned over and kissed Abby's cheek, letting her lips linger on her soft, warm skin. "Give my best to Bernice.

Abby got out of the car and walked through the glass doors of the hotel and looked back at Syd, giving her a short wave. She then continued through the lobby. Syd watched until she could no longer see her, and that, Syd decided, was the second hardest thing she'd had to do. Watch Abby walk out of her life. Again.

## Chapter Twenty-one

A bby boarded the plane that was going to take her back to Iowa and away from Syd. She'd barely slept last night. She kept replaying her time with Syd and wished she'd had more. But it was time to get back to her reality. Syd was her fantasy. Abby had been impressed with the center Syd was putting together.

Abby had allowed herself to fantasize last night when she was alone in her room about coming home to Syd every night after spending the day at the center as an operating manager. Abby thought she would enjoy partnering with Syd to run it, and Abby had enough money to keep the place going, even if Syd never got another grant again. She had already decided as soon as Syd gave her the tour that she was going to be an anonymous donor for the center. She thought that Syd would never accept the money if she knew it was from Abby so she was going to let her accountant take care of it.

She had nearly cried when Syd told her it was going to be called the Virginia Adams Youth Community Center. Abby knew that Virginia was looking down on her granddaughter, full of pride. She could imagine Virginia smiling from ear to ear, and it warmed Abby inside.

Abby turned down her street and waved to the little girl playing out front. It still saddened her to see Virginia's house, as it had reminded her of two very important women she'd lost. The family that had bought the place was nice. The little girl was eight years old, and she had a little brother who was almost a year old. The girl, Stephanie, reminded Abby of herself at that age. Blond pig tails, big blue eyes, and an adventurous soul. Stephanie was always running around the yard or playing on the tire swing that her father had hung from the large oak tree in front of the house. Abby and her grandmother had taken them some cookies to welcome them and sat for a while talking. This was exactly the type of family Virginia would have wanted living on her farm.

Stephanie had told Abby that she wanted to get a horse one day, and Abby promised to teach her how to tack and ride, after getting it okayed by her parents. Abby had taught Stephanie how to ride Pokey, and Abby had to admit that Stephanie had been a quick learner.

Abby pulled into the driveway and pulled her overnight bag from the front seat. The smell of beef stew hit Abby as soon as she walked through the door. Her grandmother had been trying like crazy to put weight back on Abby, and she was succeeding with the stick-to-your-ribs type of meals she'd been cooking.

"Hi, Gran."

"Hi, sweetheart. How did it go? Was Leah Griffin a hit?"

It amused Abby that her grandmother talked about Abby and Leah as if they were two different people. She supposed they were, as almost no one knew who Abigail Price was. But a lot of people knew who Leah Griffin was, as her publisher made it a point to always remind her.

"There was a pretty good-sized turnout and I sold a few books." More like in the fifty to sixty range, but that didn't matter to Abby. She was just happy to have the opportunity to take people away from the stresses of the real world for a little while and give them a happily ever after. She wondered if she would ever have her own.

"I'm so proud of you, Abigail. It's quite a feat to just write a book, but the fact that you're so popular is such a kick."

"Thanks, Gran." She grabbed a glass of water and leaned against the counter, watching her grandmother make homemade biscuits. "So, I had something funny happen yesterday."

"What was it?"

"I saw Syd."

She put down her wooden spoon and faced Abby. "I didn't realize you called her."

"I didn't. Seems her best friend is a huge fan of Leah's and dragged Syd with her to the signing. Imagine my shock when I stepped up to the podium to begin my reading and saw her looking back at me from the third row."

"Did you never tell her that you wrote romance novels?"

"No. I didn't get around to telling her."

"Oh, honey. How did it go? Were you able to talk to her?"

"Yes. She waited until I was done signing books. We went back to her condo and talked. It was really difficult, but I told her the truth about why I left."

"What did Sydney say to that?"

"She was angry, then hurt. But eventually, she told me she understood. We got a lot of stuff out in the open, cried, hugged, then we ate dinner."

She hugged Abby. She was much shorter than Abby, but Abby always felt like she was a little girl again whenever her grandmother hugged her.

"When she took me back to my hotel, she stopped to show me the youth center she's starting. It's so amazing, Gran. She's thought of everything to help not just the inner-city youth, but it's also going to include the LGBTQ youth." Abby was embarrassed that her eyes filled with tears and she quickly wiped them away. "I'm so proud of her, Gran. She's such an incredible person."

Her grandmother hugged Abby again as the tears continued to fall. Abby loved Syd so much, and it was breaking her heart not to be with her. "That was why I had to let her go, Gran. Imagine all the young people she's going to help. I wish I could do something like that."

"Why don't you, Abigail? You'd be great working with young people."

"In case you haven't noticed, Gran, Charville is a little less populated than Chicago. There's no need for it here," Abby said as she wiped her eyes again.

"No, but there is in Chicago."

"Gran, I already told you. I'm not leaving you."

"Abigail, you listen to me. You have found a woman that you were able to fall in love with. A woman who reciprocates that love. Finding the person you want to spend every day with doesn't happen very often, and when you find that special love, you need to covet it. I was lucky enough to have had a lot of wonderful, loving years with your grandfather, and I want the same for you. You need to go to Chicago, tell Sydney you're in love with her, and that you never want to spend another day apart. If you're lucky enough, she'll forgive you for being so stubborn and tell you the same thing."

"But what about you, Gran? I can't leave you on this large farm by yourself. I don't mean to be rude, but you're not a spring chicken anymore. I won't be close enough to get to you in case anything happens."

"I've been thinking about that for a few weeks, and I love you so much for wanting to take care of your old grandmother. But I think I've been on this farm long enough. I've never lived in a big city, and I think I'm ready for a change. I've always wanted to go to Chicago." She smiled at Abby like the cat that ate the canary.

"Are you serious? You want to sell your farm?"

"Honey, it's our farm. But no, I don't want to sell it. I'd like to keep it so we have a quiet place to escape to if we feel the need. It can be our little getaway from the city. I know how fond of this town Sydney had become. I'm sure she'd love to get away with us."

Abby's head was swimming. This wasn't at all a conversation she ever thought she'd be having with her grandmother. She'd lived there on the farm for most of her life. Would she like living in a big city like Chicago? She thought about it for a few minutes and smiled back at her. She'd live anywhere as long as it was with Syd. She kissed her grandmother's cheek and wrapped her up in a hug. "I'll be back soon, Gran."

"Where are you going to, honey?"

"I need to see a girl about a couple of horses."

❖

Syd and Vanessa had put the finishing touches on the staff office and there wasn't much left to do while they were still waiting for the items for the game room. All the walls had been painted, tables and chairs set up, computers linked, and books lined the bookshelves. They were ahead of schedule, and with the exception of the unfurnished game room, they were ready for the grand opening in two weeks.

This past week had been difficult for Syd. Seeing Abby had further rocked her slightly off kilter world. Syd had been trying to get over Abby, and she thought she had been succeeding, but in reality, she was just pushing her feelings to the back of her mind. Seeing her last Saturday night brought those feelings back to the forefront. She'd lost count of the amount of times she wanted to call her, but she'd remained strong. And stayed busy. Syd and Vanessa were done for the day and now she had nothing to do. Nothing except think of Abby.

"Hey, how about we go grab a drink? Maybe go to a club and go dancing?"

Vanessa had heard Syd's sob story from last Saturday night and how hard it was to watch Abby walk away again. Syd had called Vanessa Sunday morning and told her the abbreviated version over the phone. She got the in-depth version when she met Syd at the center with bagels and coffee. Syd appreciated Vanessa's outrage of Abby leaving and not willing to give their relationship a chance, but Syd had talked her off the ledge. She did agree with Abby that it would eventually be too hard to continue the distance. She didn't like it, but she agreed.

"Not tonight, V. I finally have a chance to go to bed early. I've been working nonstop for the past couple of months, and I'm going to enjoy a nice glass of wine and a hot bubble bath."

"Are you sure? You're not going to debate whether or not you should call Abby, are you?"

Syd winked at her. "I'm not making any promises, but that's not my intention."

"Do me a favor and call *me* if you get lonely. I'm not the one who'll break your heart."

Obviously, Vanessa was still a little miffed. "I know you won't, sweetie. I'll be fine. Thanks again for all your help on this project."

Vanessa hugged Syd. "If it's important to you, it's important to me. Love you, buddy."

"Love you, too."

Syd waved to Sam as she walked to the elevator and looked to the woman sitting in the chairs to her left, watching Syd intently. Syd did a double take and stopped in her tracks. She forgot to breathe for a moment before her heart accelerated and thudded in her chest.

"Abby?"

Abby stood and approached Syd. "Sam said I had to wait down here for you to arrive. He remembered me, but since I wasn't on your guest list, I couldn't go any farther. I'm happy to see they don't let just anybody in this joint."

"I was at the center." Syd couldn't think clearly, but she remembered the most important question. "What are you doing here?"

Abby shoved her hands in her pocket and rocked back on her heels. "Can we go upstairs? I need to talk to you."

"Um, sure."

Abby grabbed her carry-on that was next to the chair she had been sitting in and followed Syd to the elevator. Syd didn't know what to say, and she had to keep looking over at Abby to make sure she wasn't dreaming. She almost pinched herself, but if she was dreaming, she didn't want to wake up. Having Abby here was like a dream come true. The ride up was interminably long, and Syd let out a sigh of relief when she heard the ding, indicating they had finally arrived at her floor.

They entered the condo and Syd flipped on the lights. "Would you like anything to drink?"

Abby had left her suitcase by the door and looked around. "Just water would be fine."

Syd returned and handed Abby her glass. "Let's go sit down and you can tell me why you're here."

Once they were settled on the couch, Abby took a small sip then placed the glass down.

"I'm miserable without you, Syd. I can't sleep, I can't eat, I can't concentrate. From the first day I met you, I fell under your spell, and the more time we spent together, I continued to fall deeper. That last night we made love, I knew then that my life wouldn't be the same, and I couldn't imagine being with anyone but you." Abby grabbed Syd's hand and Syd remained speechless. She couldn't believe the words coming out of Abby's mouth. That was what Syd had longed to hear.

"I don't want to spend another day without you, Sydney Carter. I love you and I want us to be together."

Those were the words Syd had been waiting for and they hung in the air like a child's mobile. "But you told me you didn't want a long-distance relationship."

"I don't. I'm moving to Chicago if you'll have me."

"But you didn't want to leave Bernice all alone." Was Syd missing something?

Abby laughed, and it was the sweetest sound to Syd's ears.

"I'm not. She's moving here, too. She told me she had lived on the farm long enough and she wanted to experience living in a big city."

"Chicago's a big city," Syd said excitedly.

Abby laughed again and Syd could feel the tears fill her eyes.

"I know, baby."

"Are you being serious? You and Bernice really want to move here?"

"Gran gave me a good talking-to when I returned from seeing you last week. She told me that when I met the person I want to spend the rest of my life with, I need to do everything in my power to make it happen. I want you, Syd. I want to go to sleep in your arms every night and wake up with you every morning. I want to begin and end my days telling you how much I love you. I want to grow with you, experience good and bad times with you. Please say yes, Syd. Please tell me you want that too."

Syd wiped away her tears then cupped Abby's cheek while she stared deeply into her eyes. Abby was the woman she wanted to spend the rest of her life with, and Abby felt the same about her. This was way better than any dream or fantasy she'd ever had.

"Yes."

"Yes?"

Syd laughed and threw her arms around Abby. "Yes, Abby. I want all of that."

"I love you so much," Abby declared before kissing Syd breathless. "I need you, baby. I want to make love to you."

Syd stood and led Abby to her bedroom. They stood next to the bed, undressing while never breaking the eye contact that was binding their souls. Syd had wished and hoped for this moment since the night Abby walked out on her, and suddenly, she feared it would happen again. Could Abby truly be happy living anywhere but on her farm? Was Syd being selfish for wanting Abby to stay? As much as she wanted to be with Abby, it didn't feel right for her to make this sacrifice. She took a step back from Abby and looked into her eyes.

"Are you sure this is what you want? Can you be happy living here? And what about your horses?" Syd couldn't believe the horses came into her thoughts at this moment, but she knew how much Abby loved to ride Bevin, how it cleansed her soul.

Abby stepped toward Syd, erasing the gap she had put between them. "The horses are going to be well cared for by the family that bought Virginia's place. Their daughter had always wanted a horse, and I've been teaching her how to care for them, cleaning their stalls, tacking them for a ride, and how to ride safely. She promised me that when we come back to visit, she'd let me ride Bevin. I know they'll be in great hands with Stephanie, and they'll get lots of attention. As for me being able to be happy in a big city? I'll be happy anywhere as long as we're together. You are my home, Syd. You and Gran. And with her being in Chicago with us, my life will be complete." Abby took Syd in her arms and kissed her soundly on her mouth. "I'm exactly where I want to be with the woman I want to spend the rest of my life with. I'm going to show you every day how much I love you, starting right now."

Abby guided Syd back to the bed, and when they were finally naked, Abby hovered over Syd before kissing her again. "I love you, baby."

"I love you, too. Now make love to me."

Abby happily obliged.

❖

Abby woke the next morning expecting to hear the call of a rooster or the chirping birds welcoming a new day, sounds that had greeted her nearly every morning for most of her life. Those sounds were absent, but the soft breathing of the woman she was madly in love with, the woman that was snuggled up against Abby's side, was the sweeter sound. Abby couldn't imagine a more wonderful way to wake up. She felt Syd begin to stir and Abby tightened her hold on her.

"I'm not dreaming, am I? You're really here?"

The soft, husky tone of Syd's sleepy voice brought a sense of peace to Abby that she'd never experienced before.

"I'm really here, baby. For as long as you'll have me."

Syd moved on top of Abby and kissed her with her soft, full lips. "Will forever be long enough?"

Abby wrapped her arms low on Syd's waist and caressed her back before sliding her hands over Syd's perfectly round backside. "I may need a little longer than that, but it's a start."

"It feels amazing to wake up with you and not dread you having to leave to go do your chores."

Abby laughed. "Agreed. So, what are your plans for today? I know I showed up unexpectedly, and I don't want to disrupt anything you have going on."

"I'm supposed to have brunch with my parents, but I can call and cancel."

"No, don't do that. May I come with you? I'd love to meet them."

The tears that welled up in Syd's eyes along with her watery smile nearly undid Abby.

"I'd love for them to meet you. We still have a few hours before we have to meet them, so we can discuss what's going to happen next."

Abby laughed and turned them both on their sides. "I'm glad because there are a few things I'd like to talk to you about. If it's okay with you, I'd like to accompany you to the grand opening of the center, and I'd like for Gran to be there. She was absolutely tickled that it was named after Virginia."

"I'd love for both of you to be there."

"Good. I figured I could fly back to Iowa in a couple of days so we can start packing up some of the house. Gran and I can fly back here a few days later and start looking at places for her to live. I can get us a room at a nearby hotel so we won't be in your way."

The look of outrage on Syd's face frightened Abby a little, and she almost expected to be smacked.

"You'll do no such thing. You and Bernice will stay here. I have a nice guest room she'll be comfortable in. Unless she'd be uncomfortable knowing you and I were sleeping in the same bed across the hall."

Abby laughed and shook her head. "I'm pretty sure she won't mind as long as we keep it quiet."

The sultry look on Syd's face got Abby wet and she considered continuing the conversation later, but what she wanted to ask next was very important to her and she was hoping Syd would agree to her request.

"Syd, would you consider allowing me to help you run the center? Since I'm a writer, I can make my own schedule. What you're doing for the kids is so amazing and I really want to help."

"I'd love for you to do that. Thank you, baby."

"No, thank you. I've always wanted to be able to do something meaningful, and now you're giving me the opportunity."

"Abby, volunteering at the animal shelter was meaningful. I told you that before. And you helped out my grandmother with her farm. You are an incredibly giving woman, and I'm so happy you'll be here to help. The kids are going to love you."

Abby could feel the blush creep up her neck and into her face. She was ecstatic that she'd be able to help Syd help the kids, and even more so that they wanted to spend their life loving each other. It was unbelievable that within one day, all of Abby's dreams had come true, and it was all because of the woman in her arms whose hand had parted Abby's wet folds and was languidly stroking her. Abby's hips began moving back and forth slowly, matching the rhythm of Syd's strokes. She felt the beginning of her orgasm start low in her belly and she sped up the thrusting of her pelvis. Syd slipped two fingers inside while her thumb continued to increase the pressure against the hardened bundle of nerves. Abby cried out Syd's name as she climaxed over and over until the tremors had subsided and her breathing returned to normal.

"I love you so much, Syd."

"I love you too, Abigail. I'm going to spend every day making sure you know that."

## CHAPTER TWENTY-TWO

"Come on, Syd. We're going to be late to our own grand opening," Abby yelled from the living room.

"Abigail, calm down. We have plenty of time," her grandmother said as she sat patiently on the couch.

Abby looked at her watch for the third time in five minutes and continued her pacing. "We need to be there early, Gran. We have to be there before the caterers arrive and show them where to set up." Abby had pleaded with Syd to allow her to pay for the catering, and Syd conceded only after Abby agreed to keep it low-key.

Syd's explanation was that she didn't want the investors and donators to think they had plenty of money to spend on expensive hors d'oeuvres and flutes of champagne. She settled on a taco bar with chips and salsa, quesadilla quarters, and taquitos as appetizers. Syd, Abby, and Vanessa had spent all morning at the center setting up tables and chairs, and decorating with colorful tablecloths and streamers hanging from the ceiling.

Abby had gone to the florist and grabbed up a bunch of carnations that were inexpensive but colorful, and placed two in a vase on each table. Vanessa had forgiven Abby for her earlier treatment of Syd after Syd told her how Abby had shown up declaring her love and that she wanted to spend their lives together. Vanessa had spent the early morning fan-girling that her best friend was in love with her favorite author, but after a couple of hours together talking and laughing and joking around, Vanessa accepted Abby as Abby who also happened to write romance novels. The whole center looked festive by the time they locked up to go home and get ready.

Abby was just about to look at her watch again when she heard their bedroom door open. She looked up to see Syd emerge in a stylish yet simple black dress that hugged every mouth-watering curve. Her hair was pulled up in a twist; she had on light makeup and strappy three-inch heels. She also wore the simple diamond earrings and matching pendant Abby had given her in private the night she and her gran had arrived in Chicago. She promised Syd, before they made love that night, that they would soon pick out a ring that would match the design. Abby's mouth had gone bone-dry at the gorgeous vision walking toward her, and she had to clear her throat to find her voice.

"You look stunning."

"Thank you. You look pretty spiffy yourself," Syd replied as she adjusted Abby's tie. Abby had rented a black suit for the night, but she wore her own white linen blouse and she bought a silk tie patterned with different shades of blue to bring out her eyes. When she had shown the tie to Syd, she showed her the different ways she could use that tie once they were home from the opening. As enticing as those options were, she asked for a rain check for when her grandmother was in her own place. If they were going to get a little creative in their lovemaking, she wanted it to be uninhibited.

"You look lovely, Sydney."

"Thank you, Bernice. You look quite exquisite yourself." While they'd been at the center earlier, Abby's grandmother had gone to have her hair and nails done. She had explained that since that night was going to be the first time in many years she'd had an opportunity to get gussied up, she was pulling out all the stops.

They arrived to the center by five o'clock and the caterers were to arrive at five thirty, half an hour before the shindig was to start.

"See, baby? Right on time."

Shortly after they arrived, Vanessa and Syd's parents came in.

"Hey! What are you doing here so early?" Syd asked as she hugged them hello.

"We're here to do any last-minute things you may need," Jillian responded.

"Thanks, but everything is set. The caterers are setting up the food and drinks, and as you can see," Syd raised her arms, "we're all decorated and ready to go."

Isaiah threw his arms around Abby and squeezed her shoulder. "How about I try to calm this young lady down? I think you're more nervous than Syd, Abby."

Abby nervously laughed. The butterflies had long ago started fluttering in her stomach, and at this point, she was just trying not to throw up or sweat through her suit. "I just want everything to be perfect, Mr. Carter. Syd has worked so hard for this and her dream is finally coming true."

Isaiah squeezed her again and smiled down on her. He was a good six inches taller than Abby and about seventy-five pounds heavier. "I think her dream came true when you decided to move here. I've never seen my daughter as happy as she's been these past two weeks. I'm thrilled to see her in love."

"Thank you, sir."

Abby's grandmother came back into the reception area after touching up her lipstick in the bathroom. Abby held her hand out to her grandmother as she made her way toward them.

"Mr. and Mrs. Carter, this is my grandmother, Bernice Price."

Jillian stepped forward and gave Abby's grandmother a hug. "It's so nice to finally meet you. I'm Jillian and this is my husband, Isaiah. We want to thank you for being so kind to Sydney while she was in Iowa. She said you and Abby were a big help."

"Oh, I don't know about that. Besides, Abigail is the one who did all the work. I'm very fond of your daughter. You both did a wonderful job of raising her and you must be very proud."

"We are extremely proud of her. I also want to thank you for your friendship with my mother. Syd gave me the letters to read." Jillian dabbed the corner of her eye before a tear could escape. "I wish I had read those letters when she sent them. There was so much hurt and misunderstanding between my parents and me, and I wasted all those years when I could have had her back."

Bernice took Jillian's hand in hers and gently patted it. "If it makes a difference, your mother loved you until the day she died. She was aware that you and Isaiah had been successful educators and loving parents to Sydney. She was also very proud of Sydney, and the young woman she grew up to be."

"Thank you." Jillian pulled a tissue out of her purse and dabbed her eyes before wiping her nose.

"Now, no more crying. This is a special night for Sydney and Abigail, and there should be happiness and laughter, not sadness and tears."

Once the invited guests started arriving, Syd and Abby made introductions, then gave the group a tour of the center. They received a ton of compliments on what they were going to offer, and a few even took out their checkbooks to add a significant amount to the center. Syd might be able to build that basketball court out back sooner than she thought.

The rest of the evening had been spent eating and mingling. Syd had brought her high-end docking station speaker and cued up the playlist she had made specifically for that night, and she was overjoyed when some of the people moved the furniture out of the way and started dancing. One of the highlights of the night was when Syd's father asked Bernice to dance and they moved across the floor, turning and twirling, dancing like they'd been partners for years.

Syd was finally able to get Abby alone off to the side of the dance floor and she held her hand. "So, what do you think? Tonight went pretty well, right?"

Abby looked at Syd with eyes that shone with pride and awe. "Tonight was perfect, my love. I'm so proud of you."

"I'm proud of us," Syd said before kissing Abby. "We're going to do amazing things with this center. There's no one I'd rather take this journey with than you. I love you, Abby."

Abby took Syd in her arms and held her close. "I love you, too, baby. Let's dance."

Syd, Abby, and Bernice got home a little after midnight, and Syd went to the refrigerator to pull out a bottle of champagne. She brought three flutes into the living room and poured, then handed a glass to Abby and Bernice. She held up her own to theirs and toasted. "Here's to a fabulous evening and a wonderful new adventure."

"Cheers."

Bernice set her glass on the table and sat back into the couch. "I haven't had that much fun in ages. I never knew what I was missing by not being in a big city."

"Mm-hmm." Syd looked over the rim of her glass and winked at Bernice. "I saw you and Mr. Abrams talking quite a lot this evening. Care to share?"

"Oh, Sydney." Bernice waved her hand as her face turned red.

Syd laughed at Bernice's reaction, then Abby's.

"Share what?" Abby asked, looking to Bernice and Sydney.

"I think Mr. Abrams took a fancy to your grandmother."

"Sydney," Bernice warned her, which made Syd close her mouth, but she continued to grin.

"Gran? Was he hitting on you?" The smile that crept up on Abby's face was enough to make Syd and Bernice laugh.

"Please, Abigail. We're much too old to be 'hitting,' as you put it. He asked me out for coffee and I agreed. We exchanged numbers and he said he'd call to set up a date and time."

"Oh, my God. Gran has a date." Syd and Abby laughed.

"It's not a date. It's more like a meeting. If I'm going to live here in Chicago, I need to meet some people my own age. I can't be spending time with you two all the time. Speaking of, I'm going to put an offer in on a place I like."

Syd looked at Abby, unaware that Bernice had already found a property.

"There's a building on the next block that I really like. It's for fifty-five and older." Bernice went to her room and returned with a flier that she handed over. "It's a two-bedroom, two-bath with an updated kitchen and baths. It's a nice building, but it was the amenities that sold me. They have monthly excursions to museums and tours, movie night every Thursday, Bingo every Monday, and other random activities. It also has a workout room, indoor pool and spa, and a concierge service. And get this. They even have a salon and dry cleaner next to the building. That place is perfect for me."

The excitement bubbled over like a shaken soda over to Syd and Abby.

"This place looks great, Gran. And you're still close enough to be within walking distance to us."

"I'm really happy for you, Bernice. And I'm really happy you'll be close by."

"Sydney, I really appreciate your hospitality and letting me stay here with you two, but it's time I get out of your hair and let you girls start your life together without me intruding on you."

Syd hugged Bernice then kissed her on the cheek. "You'll never be an intrusion. You're part of my family now."

"That makes me happy. I love you, Sydney. And I love how happy you make my granddaughter."

"The feeling is mutual, Bernice. Let's go to bed so I can treat you Price women to breakfast, then we can all go take a look at that condo."

Abby and Syd undressed and climbed into bed after brushing their teeth. They lay on their sides facing each other, smiling.

"What a night, huh?"

"You were great tonight, baby. You sure know how to schmooze the checkbooks out of pockets. They teach you that in business school?"

Syd chuckled. "Nope. It's just the Carter charm. It's how my daddy got my mama to fall in love with him, and it's how I got you to fall in love with me."

Abby laughed. "Is that right? You think it was your charm that got me hooked?"

"Well, yeah. What else could it have been?"

"Your cooking." Abby smiled and let her hand drift down and squeeze Syd's behind. "And how your ass looks in jeans."

Syd feigned outrage and pushed Abby's shoulder, but she was quick enough to pull Syd on top of her.

"Maybe it was all of the above. No matter what it was, I did fall and I am hopelessly, madly, forever in love with you. And I will spend every day showing you how much I love you."

Syd kissed Abby and let their lips linger. "You're such a romantic."

Before kissing Syd again, Abby said, "That's why I write romance novels, baby."

## Epilogue

*Six months later*

Syd left work at lunchtime in order to get some errands run. The new hours she was working were much more conducive to having a personal life, and it allowed her to be home at a reasonable hour to have dinner with Abby and spend some alone time together. They worked together at the center, but they remained professional with each other. Syd was finding it very difficult to not be able to show affection to Abby while they were at work, so it was important to have that time together at home. One Friday a month, however, she taught a cooking class at the center in the afternoon. The teens who were interested cooked their own dish, and it ended up being a "family dinner night" for the staff and young people who wanted to stay. They would set up some tables and chairs together in the lounge, and they would all sit down to eat and discuss how their month had gone.

On good days, they would hear about the accomplishments—a good grade they received, an award, a good deed they performed. But since they were dealing with mostly teenagers, there were also problems that came up. Sometimes a kid got a bad grade on an assignment, or they were being bullied at school, or home life wasn't going well. The great thing about the "family night" was there was a roomful of people ready to cheer, listen, offer some helpful advice, whatever they needed to hear. Syd loved these nights, and she wouldn't miss them for the world.

She arrived at the center after picking up groceries and called on Reggie and Dwayne to help her bring the bags into the kitchen. In one of the corners of the room, she spotted Bernice playing chess with Chandra. Once she and the boys had put the groceries on the counter, she thanked them then returned to see Bernice.

"Better be careful, Bernice. Chandra is a really good player and she'll make you win fair and square." The pleased look on the thirteen-year-old's face indicated Syd hit the mark with her compliment. Chandra was a shy girl who had trouble making friends, but being at the center and interacting with the other kids had helped build her confidence.

Bernice accepted Syd's kiss on her cheek. "I've been playing this game a lot longer than she has, so if she wins, it won't be easy for her." Bernice moved her piece and Chandra's face lit up.

"Check mate!"

Syd busted out in laughter. "Nice job, Chandra. Are you going to help with dinner tonight?"

"Yes, Ms. Syd."

"Great. Go on and wash your hands and I'll meet you in the kitchen. Please find Alisa for me. She wants to help out too." Syd turned to Bernice. "Where is that granddaughter of yours?"

Bernice looked at the clock on the wall. "She had a late lunch with Edward Robinson to discuss the funds we need to start that new program. She should be back anytime."

"Good. Are you staying for dinner tonight?"

Bernice stood and pulled her sweater on. "Not tonight, dear. I'm having dinner with Jeremiah then we're going to see a movie."

"You sure are seeing Mr. Abrams quite a bit. Is he ready to make an honest woman out of you?" Syd teased her.

"We're just friends that enjoy each other's company, so mind your own business."

The twinkle in Bernice's eyes indicated she was teasing.

"I could ask the same of you about my granddaughter, Sydney. Are you going to put a ring on it soon?"

Syd burst into laughter at the lingo Bernice was picking up when she hung out with the kids. Syd was going to have to keep a closer eye on her to make sure she stayed in line. "As a matter of fact, we're going ring shopping next weekend, so I promise, it will be soon."

Bernice placed her palms on the side of Syd's face. "Good. You girls give me so much joy to be able to witness your love growing."

Syd wrapped Bernice in a gentle hug. "I'm so happy you're here, Bernice. I don't think I ever thanked you for talking sense into Abby and getting her to come back to me."

"No need to thank me. You just make sure you do right by my Abigail. She's very special to me."

"Yes, ma'am. I promise. Have a nice evening and we'll see you on Sunday for brunch with my parents."

Syd went back to the kitchen and was pleased to see two other kids arrived, Nicole and Bobby, to help with dinner. "Hey, guys. You ready to cook? We're going to make lasagna, salad, garlic bread, and chocolate cake for dessert. Alisa and I will make the lasagna. Bobby can make the salad. Nicole, I'd like you to prep the garlic bread then make the frosting for the cake Chandra is going to make."

They all got busy and Syd was just about to spoon the meat mixture onto the noodles when she heard the all too familiar voice coming from the doorway.

"It sure smells great in here. I can't wait to eat."

Syd turned around to find the love of her life smiling from ear to ear. Her heart raced, just as it did every time she saw Abby. She wondered if that feeling would ever go away, maybe when they were old and had been married for fifty years. *God, I hope not.*

"Hey. Let me just finish up here and I'll come find you."

When Syd had placed the lasagna in the oven once the cake came out, she told the kids to clean the mess they'd made and she'd be back in a few minutes.

The door to the office was ajar and Syd knocked before entering. The site of Abby sitting behind the desk stirred something primal inside Syd, especially when she had her reading glasses on. Syd thought she looked so sexy like that, which always made Abby laugh when Syd brought it to her attention.

Syd closed the door and Abby greeted her with open arms and soft, yielding lips.

"Hey, baby. How did the meeting go?"

Abby continued to hold Syd against her, missing the feeling of her in her arms. The days seemed to drag on when they were at work until they were alone together every night.

"It went great. I told him how we do a family night dinner one Friday a month and how useful it would be to have our own community garden. He agreed to fund the whole thing as long as we invite him to the first dinner using our own vegetables."

Syd laughed and kissed Abby again. "That's incredible. I can't believe you got him to pay for the whole thing."

"Well, he's very impressed with what we're doing here that he sees it as an opportunity to keep making strides in the right direction. He said he wished there was something like our center when he was growing up."

Syd felt her chest swell with pride. The center was Syd and Abby's pride and joy, and she loved seeing the positive impact it had on the youth in that part of town.

"We do great work, baby. I love you."

"I love you, too, sweetheart. Now go finish dinner and I'll get Reggie and Dwayne to help me set up the tables and chairs."

Thirty minutes later, they all sat down to eat and share their week. Syd looked around to the eight teens, three volunteers, and Abby sitting by her side. The smiles, laughter, joking, and interaction between everyone was the perfect end to her week, and this truly was Syd's dream come true.

# About the Author

KC Richardson attended college on a basketball scholarship, and her numerous injuries in her various sports led her to a career in physical therapy. Her love for reading and writing allows her to create characters and tell their stories. She and her wife live in Southern California where they are trying to raise respectful fur kids.

When KC isn't torturing/fixing people, she loves spending time with her friends and family, reading, writing, kayaking, working out, and playing golf.

KC's second novel, *Courageous Love*, was a 2017 Goldie Finalist. You can reach KC on Facebook, Twitter @KCRichardson7, email kcrichardsonauthor@yahoo.com, or her website, kcrichardson author.com.

# Books Available from Bold Strokes Books

**A Call Away** by KC Richardson. Can a businesswoman from a big city find the answers she's looking for, and possibly love, on a small-town farm? (978-1-63555-025-2)

**Berlin Hungers** by Justine Saracen. Can the love between an RAF woman and the wife of a Luftwaffe pilot, former enemies, survive in besieged Berlin during the aftermath of World War II? (978-1-63555-116-7)

**Blend** by Georgia Beers. Lindsay and Piper are like night and day. Working together won't be easy, but not falling in love might prove the hardest job of all. (978-1-63555-189-1)

**Hunger for You** by Jenny Frame. Principe of an ancient vampire clan Byron Debrek must save her one true love from falling into the hands of her enemies and into the middle of a vampire war. (978-1-63555-168-6)

**Mercy** by Michelle Larkin. FBI Special Agent Mercy Parker and psychic ex-profiler Piper Vasey learn to love again as they race to stop a man with supernatural gifts who's bent on annihilating humankind. (978-1-63555-202-7)

**Pride and Porters** by Charlotte Greene. Will pride and prejudice prevent these modern-day lovers from living happily ever after? (978-1-63555-158-7)

**Rocks and Stars** by Sam Ledel. Kyle's struggle to own who she is and what she really wants may end up landing her on the bench and without the woman of her dreams. (978-1-63555-156-3)

**The Boss of Her: Office Romance Novellas** by Julie Cannon, Aurora Rey, and M. Ullrich. Going to work never felt so good. Three office romance novellas from talented writers Julie Cannon, Aurora Rey, and M. Ullrich. (978-1-63555-145-7)

**The Deep End** by Ellie Hart. When family ties become entangled in murder and deception, it's time to find a way out... (978-1-63555-288-1)

**A Country Girl's Heart** by Dena Blake. When Kat Jackson gets a second chance at love, following her heart will prove the hardest decision of all. (978-1-63555-134-1)

**Dangerous Waters** by Radclyffe. Life, death, and war on the home front. Two women join forces against a powerful opponent, nature itself. (978-1-63555-233-1)

**Fury's Death** by Brey Willows. When all we hold sacred fails, who will be there to save us? (978-1-63555-063-4)

**It's Not a Date** by Heather Blackmore. Kade's desire to keep things with Jen on a professional level is in Jen's best interest. Yet what's in Kade's best interest...is Jen. (978-1-63555-149-5)

**Killer Winter** by Kay Bigelow. Just when she thought things could get no worse, homicide Lieutenant Leah Samuels learns the woman she loves has betrayed her in devastating ways. (978-1-63555-177-8)

**Score** by MJ Williamz. Will an addiction to pain pills destroy Ronda's chance with the woman she loves or will she come out on top and score a happily ever after? (978-1-62639-807-8)

**Spring's Wake** by Aurora Rey. When wanderer Willa Lange falls for Provincetown B&B owner Nora Calhoun, will past hurts and a fifteen-year age gap keep them from finding love? (978-1-63555-035-1)

**The Northwoods** by Jane Hoppen. When Evelyn Bauer, disguised as her dead husband, George, travels to a Northwoods logging camp to work, she and the camp cook Sarah Bell forge a friendship fraught with both tenderness and turmoil. (978-1-63555-143-3)

**Truth or Dare** by C. Spencer. For a group of six lesbian friends, life changes course after one long snow-filled weekend. (978-1-63555-148-8)

**A Heart to Call Home** by Jeannie Levig. When Jessie Weldon returns to her hometown after thirty years, can she and her child-hood crush Dakota Scott heal the tragic past that links them? (978-1-63555-059-7)

**Children of the Healer** by Barbara Ann Wright. Life becomes desperate for ex-soldier Cordelia Ross when the indigenous aliens of her planet are drawn into a civil war and old enemies linger in the shadows. Book Three of the Godfall Series. (978-1-63555-031-3)

**Hearts Like Hers** by Melissa Brayden. Coffee shop owner Autumn Primm is ready to cut loose and live a little, but is the baggage that comes with out-of-towner Kate Carpenter too heavy for anything long term? (978-1-63555-014-6)

**Love at Cooper's Creek** by Missouri Vaun. Shaw Daily flees corporate life to find solace in the rural Blue Ridge Mountains, but escapism eludes her when her attentions are captured by small town beauty Kate Elkins. (978-1-62639-960-0)

**Somewhere Over Lorain Road** by Bud Gundy. Over forty years after murder allegations shattered the Esker family, can Don Esker find the true killer and clear his dying father's name? (978-1-63555-124-2)

**Twice in a Lifetime** by PJ Trebelhorn. Detective Callie Burke can't deny the growing attraction to her late friend's widow, Taylor

Fletcher, who also happens to own the bar where Callie's sister works. (978-1-63555-033-7)

**Undiscovered Affinity** by Jane Hardee. Will a no strings attached affair be enough to break Olivia's control and convince Cardic that love does exist? (978-1-63555-061-0)

**Between Sand and Stardust** by Tina Michele. Are the lifelong bonds of love strong enough to conquer time, distance, and heartache when Haven Thorne and Willa Bennette are given another chance at forever? (978-1-62639-940-2)

**Charming the Vicar** by Jenny Frame. When magician and atheist Finn Kane seeks refuge in an English village after a spiritual crisis, can local vicar Bridget Claremont restore her faith in life and love? (978-1-63555-029-0)

**Data Capture** by Jesse J. Thoma. Lola Walker is undercover on the hunt for cybercriminals while trying not to notice the woman who might be perfectly wrong for her for all the right reasons. (978-1-62639-985-3)

**Epicurean Delights** by Renee Roman. Ariana Marks had no idea a leisure swim would lead to being rescued, in more ways than one, by the charismatic Hudson Frost. (978-1-63555-100-6)

**Heart of the Devil** by Ali Vali. We know most of Cain and Emma Casey's story, but *Heart of the Devil* will take you back to where it began one fateful night with a tray loaded with beer. (978-1-63555-045-0)

**Known Threat** by Kara A. McLeod. When Special Agent Ryan O'Connor reluctantly questions who protects the Secret Service, she learns courage truly is found in unlikely places. Agent O'Connor Series #3. (978-1-63555-132-7)

**Seer and the Shield** by D. Jackson Leigh. Time is running out for the Dragon Horse Army while two unlikely heroines struggle to put aside their attraction and find a way to stop a deadly cult. Dragon Horse War, Book 3. (978-1-63555-170-9)

**Sinister Justice** by Steve Pickens. When a vigilante targets citizens of Jake Finnigan's hometown, Jake and his partner Sam fall under suspicion themselves as they investigate the murders. (978-1-63555-094-8)

**The Universe Between Us** by Jane C. Esther. Ana Mitchell must make the hardest choice of her life: the promise of new love Jolie Dann on Earth, or a humanity-saving mission to colonize Mars. (978-1-63555-106-8)

**Touch** by Kris Bryant. Can one touch heal a heart? (978-1-63555-084-9)

**Change in Time** by Robyn Nyx. Working in the past is hell on your future. The Extractor Series: Book Two. (978-1-62639-880-1)

**Love After Hours** by Radclyffe. When Gina Antonelli agrees to renovate Carrie Longmire's new house, she doesn't welcome Carrie's overtures at friendship or her own unexpected attraction. A Rivers Community Novel. (978-1-63555-090-0)

**Nantucket Rose** by CF Frizzell. Maggie Jordan can't wait to convert an historic Nantucket home into a B&B, but doesn't expect to fall for mariner Ellis Chilton, who has more claim to the house than Maggie realizes. (978-1-63555-056-6)

**Picture Perfect** by Lisa Moreau. Falling in love wasn't supposed to be part of the stakes for Olive and Gabby, rival photographers in the competition of a lifetime. (978-1-62639-975-4)

**Set the Stage** by Karis Walsh. Actress Emilie Danvers takes the stage again in Ashland, Oregon, little realizing that landscaper Arden Philips is about to offer her a very personal romantic lead role. (978-1-63555-087-0)

**Strike a Match** by Fiona Riley. When their attempts at matchmaking fizzle out, firefighter Sasha and reluctant millionairess Abby find themselves turning to each other to strike a perfect match. (978-1-62639-999-0)

**The Price of Cash** by Ashley Bartlett. Cash Braddock is doing her best to keep her business afloat, stay out of jail, and avoid Detective Kallen. It's not working. (978-1-62639-708-8)

**Under Her Wing** by Ronica Black. At Angel's Wings Rescue, dogs are usually the ones saved, but when quiet Kassandra Haden meets outspoken owner Jayden Beaumont, the two stubborn women just might end up saving each other. (978-1-63555-077-1)

**Underwater Vibes** by Mickey Brent. When Hélène, a translator in Brussels, Belgium, meets Sylvie, a young Greek photographer and swim coach, unsettling feelings hijack Hélène's mind and body—even her poems. (978-1-63555-002-3)